Strawberries
and Other Erotic Fruits

Strawberries
and Other Erotic Fruits

—⁓—

Jerry L. Wheeler

LETHE PRESS
MAPLE SHADE NJ

Book Design by Toby Johnson
Cover Photograph by Steve Berman
Model: Nick Rossano

Published as a trade paperback original
by Lethe Press, 118 Heritage Avenue, Maple Shade, NJ 08052.
March 1, 2012

ISBN-13 978-1-59021-212-7
ISBN-10 1-59021- 212-6

This book is lovingly dedicated to my late partner, Jamz Lackner—as much an inspiration to me now as then.

Contents

Introduction:
It All Started With
Edgar Allan Poe

The slim, dog-eared book I picked off the library shelf had been passed from child to child so often that its front cover was long gone and its back hung by a tenuous ribbon of tape at the spine—a collection of abridged Poe short stories and poems. I was about ten years old. I don't know why I picked it up instead of another book. I couldn't have been drawn in by the artwork because it had no cover. The only explanation is that we were meant for each other.

Poe's opium-induced fantasies and grotesqueries flowed from the intensity of his imagination straight into mine, creating images that still pop into my head forty-five years later—the pale blue eye in "The Tell-Tale Heart," the pallor of the victim tortured during the Spanish Inquisition in "The Pit and the Pendulum," and, of course, the King and his seven ministers from "Hop-Frog," dressed up as orangutans for a costume ball, their blazing corpses set afire by a demented dwarf of a court jester, hanging from a chandelier as they dripped hot tar and sparks of fake fur onto the guests below.

It was a match made in heaven. I carried Eddy around with me until well past the "Due Back" date, re-reading him in an endless loop until the back cover fell off too, a victim of a bus stop puddle and a loose strap. I even thought about stealing it, but I wasn't as afraid of my conscience as much as I was my mother finding out.

The fine was nearly out of my allowance's range when I returned the battered copy to the prune-skinned, indeterminately-sexed librarian, who sniffed and tossed it into a nearby cart, announcing and collecting the library's financial windfall. The next day in school, I ordered another book of Poe's from the Scholastic Book Club, waiting an interminable three weeks for the order to come in. I felt naked the whole time, jonesing for another late night re-read with the flashlight when I was supposed to be sleeping.

When the order arrived and the teacher distributed our books, I found to my surprise the tales I remembered had been transformed. I had ordered an *un*abridged copy. By the time I slogged through the first couple of stories, I made the connection. My stories were still there, but there were all these *words* on top of them. Big words. Big words I had to look up. Some of them in French. Or Latin.

The dictionary become my second best friend. I copied the foreign words and passages, giving them to my increasingly amused teachers who translated them, made sure I understood how they related to the story and sent me scurrying away with the eager curiosity of an obsessed ten-year-old trying to fit the next piece of the puzzle.

"The Cask of Amontillado" was where I nailed it—Montresor walling Fortunato up in the catacombs in revenge of some petty, drunken incident, rotting away in chains behind the brick as Montresor goes free. That's when the choir sang and the light shone in, illuminating the architecture behind the art. I had to master it. I had to learn how to tell stories. I had to make people feel something, believe something. The fever caught me, and I became convinced that somewhere or somehow, I'd be a writer. Which is what I told anyone who'd listen.

Several decades later, I've published numerous short stories and essays and have either edited or am in the process of editing, three anthologies of gay erotica—one of which was a Lambda Literary Award finalist. But have I hit the Poe moment? Am I truly what I wanted to be when I was that curiosity-driven ten-year-old? Sometimes. Other times I fall short of my own expectations. I'm still learning, as are we all. And the more I write, the more I know—which leads me to mention some of the people who have taught me lessons along the way.

Thanks go out to Steve Berman at Lethe Press and Radclyffe at Bold Strokes Books for giving my work such loving care, Greg Wharton and Ian

Phillips for publishing me for the very first time, and to all the marvelous friends and writers I've met throughout the years—Matt Kailey, William Holden, Dale Chase, Gavin Atlas, Jeff Mann, 'Nathan Burgoine, Hank Edwards, Jeffrey Ricker, Ron Suresha, David Pratt and Peter Dubé to name but a few. We all make each others' stories stronger. And, of course, I'd like to thank my dear friends Ryk Bowers, Keith Lucero and John Couture for their continued support on and off the field.

But the biggest thank you of all goes to those who are holding this book in their hands (or on their e-readers). If it weren't for the audience out there, I'd just be talking to myself—and I do far too much of that already. I hope you enjoy these pieces and can find a moment or two where your blood quickens or you smirk or you close the book and sigh, satisfied with where I've taken you.

It's only all I live for.

JW
Denver, CO
January, 2012

Strawberries

The young man bit into the flesh of the small end. Wrapping his lips around its firmness, he sucked slightly as a thin runner of red juice trickled into his scraggly blond beard. He lifted the hem of his grimy t-shirt and wiped his mouth, showing off a thick treasure trail that distracted the hell out of Kyle. He smiled while he chewed, seeds sticking to his teeth. "How much?" he asked.

Kyle shrugged with studied casualness and—for no reason other than effect—looked at the gold Rolex strapped to his wrist. He wasn't one of the company's top negotiators for nothing. He shaded his eyes against the sun as he surveyed a large, verdant space between two dusty construction sites bordered by high chain link fencing. "I dunno. Three fifty an acre. Maybe four hundred."

The farmer chuckled low and pitched the remainder of the strawberry over Kyle's head. It landed somewhere in the corn stalks on the other side of the road. He reached up and grabbed the bottom edge of the sign over the stand. It read *Farmer Howie's Produce*. "Man, I've been made lowball offers before," he said, "but that was the lowest and took the most balls to make."

He let go of the sign and hooked his long, spade shaped thumbs into the empty belt loops of his low-slung jeans. Kyle could see the sweat soaked waistband of his Joe Boxers. With the Chinese symbol tats on his biceps, his faint case of acne and a pierced tongue, he looked more like a sagger sk8tr dude than a farmer.

He ran a hand over his buzzed blonde hair. "No offense, man, but your offer's a fuckin' joke. You need my land to connect up these two malls, and it ain't gonna happen. It's not for sale."

"Everything's for sale. I just haven't found your price yet."

"*No* price, dude," Farmer Howie insisted. "Why would I wanna give this up? Land's blessed." He swept his arm around the field. "Look at those tomatoes, look at that corn." Reaching back to the produce stand, he plucked a strawberry from its box. "Check out these berries, man—sweetest you ever tasted." He held it out for Kyle.

"Can't. I'm allergic." He cast his eyes over the land again, with its tall rows of corn and flat expanses of strawberries as he drank in the earthy scent of tomatoes ripening under the watchful gaze of two scarecrows propped high among the corn silk tassels. Kyle stared purposefully into the farmer's nut-brown eyes, trying to discern any trace of guile, but all he saw was his own. "I'll double my offer, then," he said. "Eight hundred. Maybe I can even get my company to go for nine."

"Nope," Farmer Howie replied. "Not for sale." He reached his hand under his shirt and scratched his chest, exposing a swath of tan skin and a patch of downy blonde hair between his pecs. Kyle couldn't think of anything else to say. All he could do was stare at the farmer's half naked chest, wondering what he looked like with his shirt off. And wondering how to find out. When he raised his eyes, Farmer Howie was grinning at him.

Kyle's voice shook. "How many acres are we talking about, here?"

The front of his shirt dropped down again as Farmer Howie brought his hand to his eyes and gazed into the distance. "About two-fifty on both sides of the road."

"Five hundred acres. Look, if I can get my company to go a thousand an acre, you're lookin' at half a million in your pocket. Not a bad piece of change."

Farmer Howie grabbed three tomatoes from the farthest bin and began to juggle them. "Big money means big headaches. Don't need it. Got my little house up the road, produce stand makin' some money. I do all right. Sorry, dude. It's not for sale."

The juggling action dropped his sagging jeans even lower, dangerously close to his pubic line. Kyle thought he saw a few tufts of dark blonde hair peeking out of the Joe Boxers. Or was it his imagination? "Let me talk to my company and see what I can do. I'll be back tomorrow."

"Whenever," the farmer said. "It still ain't gonna be for sale." He stopped juggling and tossed one of the tomatoes to Kyle. "Here" he said, "on the house. Best damn tomato you ever ate. Land's blessed, I tell ya."

Kyle caught it with one hand. Even though it had been in the shade of the stand, it felt warm. Almost as if it had been alive.

—〜〜—

"Okay, Leo—okay, I *get* it already." He jabbed at his phone, flipped it shut and threw it across the seat. Fuckin' dickwad, he thought. Like I don't already know how important this deal is. Like I don't already know about the two guys who fucked it up and were so embarrassed they never even came back to work. Like I don't already know I'm out on my ass if I can't make this happen. Does he think the goddamn pressure *helps*?

Kyle pulled into the parking lot of the Sand and Surf, a rundown motel whose name was wishful prairie thinking, being five hundred miles from the nearest body of water. Despite its landlocked condition, ocean waves of blue neon washed over the "Vacancy" sign. This looks like as good a place to spend the night as any, Kyle thought. Fact is, it looks like the *only* place.

He opened the door and stepped down onto the dusty, weed-dotted pavement, reaching back into his Explorer for his New York Yankees baseball cap. He settled the cap on his head and trudged up a cracked sidewalk bordered by spindly yellow tea roses. A string of bells jangled against the door as he opened it, but no one appeared at the tiny counter in the lobby.

The moist breeze from a swamp cooler brushed Kyle's cheek and brought the scent of bacon frying. A sitcom laugh track brayed from a television somewhere in the room behind the counter. He hit the bell on the desk a few times. "Hello?" he ventured. "Anyone here?"

The query produced some shuffling from the inner room. A scruffy grey cat bounded out, followed by a large, tired-looking woman with orange hair and too much makeup. Her mottled red and white arms plumped out of her sleeveless daisy print housedress like summer sausages, and she gripped a greasy fork. Kyle heard her breathing from across the room.

"You lost?" she asked.

"Just passing through on business," he said. "Any rooms available?"

"Twenty-six rooms, twenty-six vacancies. 'Course the new shopping center they're buildin' up the road might change that." She scratched her nose and put the fork down on the counter, turning the guest register towards him. "That the business you're here on?"

"Yep." He fished a business card out of his wallet and handed it to her, letting her read it as he signed the register. The two most recent names had been whited out. After a momentary hesitation, he signed over one of them. "Kyle Arbogast, Armbruster Development. What can you tell me about the farmer who runs the produce stand up the road?"

"Howie? Not much to tell." She whirled the guest book back around and looked at it hastily before getting a key from the board behind her. "Used to be a ski bum in Colorado. He came back here a few years ago to run the farm after his granddaddy died. But if you're lookin' to buy that land of his, you can forget it."

"Why?"

"He won't never sell it. That's what I told those other two."

"What about the other two?"

"*Beatrice, where's my suppah?*" came a scream from the back room.

"S'cuse me." She, handed him the key. "I got to finish gettin' Daddy's supper. You're in room twelve—far end of the unit so's you won't hear our television or nothin'. Nearest cafe's in Taylorville about ten miles up the road, but they also got a pizza place that delivers out here. Just call if you need somethin'." Grabbing the fork off the counter, she licked at the congealing grease and disappeared into the back room followed by the cat.

Kyle picked up his suitcase and found his room at the end of the unit. The door stuck, so he put his shoulder to it and pushed. A wave of hot stale air greeted him. He threw the window open and turned on the swamp cooler. I'll just dump the bag and get something to eat in town, he thought.

He threw his suitcase on the bed, but it bounced off and landed on the other side of the bed near the bathroom. As he bent over to pick it up, he saw something shiny on the floor poking out from the bedspread fringe. A cell phone. A cell phone just like his, right down to the label that read "Property of Armbruster Development." He sat his laptop up on the desk and plugged the phone in.

Jack Dumont had five messages, but Kyle couldn't pick them up without his password. Probably from Leo anyway, he thought. No text messages, but there were seven pictures and one fifteen second video Dumont had recorded.

The pics were all of Farmer Howie's produce stand and the surrounding acreage except for one shot of two businessmen, one in a white shirt and red and blue striped tie and the other wearing tweedy tan sports jacket. Kyle knew the guy in the tie was Jack Dumont. He'd met him once. Phenomenal salesman with a real gift for connecting with people. The other guy was his closer, Mark something. They always tag-teamed their prospects. If Dumont and his closer couldn't pull it off, the deal couldn't be done. But, Kyle thought, how sweet would it be if I *could*?

The video was the real mystery—small red circles moving in a triangular motion over and over against the background of the produce stand. Kyle ran it again and again, zooming in as far as he could until he finally saw they were tomatoes.

Apparently juggling themselves.

—∿—

No shirt, Kyle thought as he drove up to the stand and saw Farmer Howie. *Oh my fucking God, no shirt. And baggy, sagging tan cargo shorts with—help me, sweet Jesus—no hint of the Joe Boxers he wore yesterday. Holy fuck, he's freeballin'.*

Farmer Howie bent over to pick up a crate, the shorts riding down to show considerably more than the top of his pale ass crack.

This is definitely going to make playing the tough guy a lot tougher, he thought.

Kyle pulled off to the side of the road and killed the engine. Farmer Howie straightened up and gave him a dopey, lopsided grin, waving as Kyle got out of the Explorer. The wave swayed his whole body, the baggy crotch of his shorts jiggling. Kyle could have sworn he saw the head of his cut dick swinging back and forth inside the fabric.

"What's the offer today?" he asked as Kyle approached.

Whatta goofball, Kyle thought. He's just a big puppy. "Well, I really don't have a better offer."

"No?"

"Nope. You won't sell it no matter how much I offer you, and I'm tired of looking like an idiot."

Farmer Howie grinned, pulling at a few hairs of his sparse beard before letting his fingers hook into the small gold chain he wore around his neck. "Soooo, you come to tell me you give up?"

"Not quite. Ever hear of eminent domain?"

He crossed his arms over his bare chest. "Sounds like one of them indie bands, but I don't get out to the clubs much since I moved here."

"Eminent domain is a legal concept that basically means I can take your land away from you and use it for my own purposes provided the community agrees that it would generate more tax revenue in my hands than in yours."

Farmer Howie uncrossed his arms without a word and walked back to the produce stand.

"Do you get that?" Kyle asked his tanned back.

"Yep," the farmer said, grabbing three tomatoes from the far bin and juggling them. Kyle flashed back to the video on Jack Dumont's cell phone, the hairs on his arm standing erect for a moment. Cheap goddamn company phones, he thought. Crap imaging technology. That's why the tomatoes looked like they were juggling themselves.

"And that doesn't worry you?"

Farmer Howie tracked the tomatoes with his eyes as he spoke. "Folks around here don't much like bein' told what's good for 'em. Especially by strangers."

"Beatrice at the Sand and Surf Motel will go for it. She's looking forward to the extra traffic the shopping center will bring in."

"M'kay, that's one. Who else you got lined up?"

"Nobody right now. But we haven't been to a town hall meeting to present our plans and profit projections yet. This land will be ours in six months, and you'll be back in Aspen schlepping snowboarders around the slopes. But it doesn't have to be that way. You can get a fair price and reopen your stand somewhere else. But you have to act quickly."

"Offer expires at midnight, huh?"

"Something like that."

He stopped juggling tomatoes, catching two in his right hand and one behind his back in his left. He put them back in the bin, propping one leg up on the wood.

"Hate to tell ya this, dude," he said, "but you'll never get that land. It ain't changin' hands on my watch. It'll be mine long after you're gone, doin' what it was meant to do—growing stuff. You go on and do what you have to. It'll be here next year givin' me tomatoes, corn, and strawberries. Land's blessed, dude. That's all I got to say." He turned his back on Kyle and squatted down, packing pint containers with strawberries from a big wicker basket.

I should have known that eminent domain shit wouldn't work, Kyle thought, *but it was worth a shot.* He craned his neck to peer down the gap between the farmer's cargo shorts and pale asscrack. *Fuck. What I wouldn't give to stick my finger down there and see what I come up with. Probably smells like strawberries.*

Plan B coming up.

—⟋⟍—

The night was perfect. A cool breeze ruffled the corn tassels, the sky was clear, the stars were bright, and the cicadas buzzed like a 10,000 megawatt lamp. A feeling of expectancy was in the air—as if the sky, the stars, the breeze and the bugs were all waiting for something to happen. And Kyle stood by the side of the road with a Bic lighter in his hand, making sure it would.

He had walked the three miles from the motel, lying low by the side of the road when a car came by so he wouldn't be seen. *It's got to look like an accident*, he thought. *People toss cigarette butts out their car windows all the time. A fire would be a shame—a tragedy even—but no great surprise. No more produce means no more produce stand, and Farmer*

Howie might think twice when sees the charred remains of his business smoking in the morning sun.

He stepped into the rows of corn, shook a Marlboro out of the pack and cupped his hands to light it. He crouched down and applied the lit end of the cigarette to a dried cornstalk, but it wouldn't catch. Kyle frowned. He held it close to the stalk again but nothing happened. *That's weird*, he thought. He thumbed the lighter and took the flame right to the dry stalk, but it still wouldn't ignite. *What the fuck?* Kyle wondered. Then he heard a noise behind him.

Farmer Howie stood there grinning, his hair a crown of blonde that seemed even brighter in the full moon. "You're not gonna get that to burn," he said. "I told you before, dude, the land's blessed."

Kyle dropped the lighter and stood up. "What are you doing here?" he asked.

"My job. Something's up with the land. It told me, so here I am."

"Okay," Kyle said. "So, you caught me. What happens next?"

The farmer's high laugh seemed to come from everywhere. "What happens next? Well, I'm gonna give you something you've been wanting. Then, I'm gonna give you something you need."

He unsnapped his shorts and let them fall to the ground, his hard dick bobbing as he put his hands on Kyle's shoulders and forced him to kneel. Not that Kyle needed much forcing. *How did he know?* Kyle thought as he sank to his knees. *Have I been that obvious?*

All thoughts of obviousness, all the questions Kyle would normally have asked, vanished in the face of Farmer Howie's cock—just as Kyle had pictured it. About seven inches cut, with a beautifully formed helmet head. The thick, veiny shaft curved slightly to the right, its heft hovering over a smallish but low hanging pair of nuts. Kyle nuzzled them, smelling his musky ball sweat as he wrapped his hand around the farmer's dick and began working a dollop of precum around the head.

Farmer Howie moaned low and moved his hands from Kyle's shoulders to either side of his head. Kyle felt him position his dick close to his lips, and he opened them to receive the hanging host. It tasted salty and earthy and the farmer slowly fed it to Kyle, who deep throated it, amazed he could take as much as he did. He'd always had a pretty shallow gag reflex, but this seven inches slid down his throat with no problem.

He cupped Farmer Howie's balls, stroking his taint as he tightened his throat around his cock. The farmer began to rock and buck his hips against Kyle's face, bracing his hands on the back of Kyle's head as he dug his bare toes into the dirt. One loud groan later, Farmer Howie pumped his load down Kyle's throat, his hand keeping Kyle's head impaled on his dick. "Swallow," he commanded breathlessly, "don't spit. Never waste the seed."

Kyle did as he was told, breathing through his nose as he gulped the farmer's cum. It tasted sweet—almost fruity—with a slight alcoholic aftertaste. With a final shudder, he leaned against Kyle's head and gave a satisfied sigh before he withdrew from his mouth. Kyle didn't want to let go, teasing and licking the head as Farmer Howie gently but firmly pulled up his shorts.

He bent over and grabbed Kyle by the shoulders, lifting him to his feet and embracing him roughly. Kyle melted into his bear hug like warm chocolate into a mold, letting the farmer kiss his neck. He opened his eyes and looked over the farmer's shoulder, noticing the scarecrows were closer. One of them had on a white shirt and a red and blue striped tie, and the other wore a ratty old tan tweed sports jacket with one long rip down the right sleeve. *Jesus Christ*, Kyle thought. Dumont and his closer. *They tag team their prospects.*

"Now comes what you need." Farmer Howie pulled Kyle's face close and kissed him with smooth, soft lips. They sank into each others mouths, their tongues exploring wet darkness. The cicadas buzzed so loudly, Kyle almost didn't hear Farmer Howie's voice.

"Bite my tongue. Bite it hard." *How could he speak?* Kyle wondered. Crickets joined the cicadas, adding their voices to the background chorale. Kyle felt dizzy, overcome by the sensuality of the kiss, so he did as he was told. He bit, amazed to feel his teeth breaking the flesh.

"Yeah. That's it. Bite it off."

Kyle couldn't stop himself. His teeth went through, and he sucked at the root until he felt it separate.

"Now chew it."

An explosion of strawberries filled his mouth as he began chewing. The flesh was tender and juicy, and the taste filled his head all the way down his throat and behind his eyes until he was dizzy and couldn't see. He couldn't feel the farmer or the kiss anymore. All he felt was strawberries and a vague sensation of falling.

He couldn't tell how long or far he'd fallen, but when he could see again, he found himself flat on his back in the cornfield. At least it looked like the same place—or did it? The stars seemed out of kilter, as if they'd been knocked them all out of the sky and rearranged. Cornstalks surrounded him, towering overhead like rustic skyscrapers.

Farmer Howie was gone, but the scarecrows were at his head and feet now, Magic Marker grins splitting their faces of straw. But those grins were moving. Their mouths were opening, but nothing came out. They nodded to each other, then they picked Kyle up and turned him over on his stomach. He tried to scramble to his feet, but Dumont pushed his shoulders down while his closer raised Kyle's rear until he was on all fours.

With a desiccated rustling, Dumont grabbed Kyle's head in his two strong straw hands and slammed it roughly into the crotch of his torn jeans. Kyle tried to back away, but the hands held him fast and crushed his nose up against the buttons of the scarecrow's fly. He felt something growing, lumping up beneath the fabric.

He brought his hand up and felt around, partly out of curiosity and partly to relieve the pressure on his head. As soon as he touched the scarecrow's crotch, its chest rose and fell in a sigh and the hands let go of his head. And something definitely got harder under the jeans. *Oh man, this is too fuckin' weird. But is it any weirder than anything else that's happened since I first saw this goddamn cornfield?*

Still dizzy, beyond curious and pretty horny after lusting after Farmer Howie for two days, Kyle couldn't believe he undid the buttons and reached inside. He didn't feel anything at first except the rasp of cornhusks abrading his palm, but on his second or third pass he felt a nub of something right between the scarecrow's legs. He applied pressure to it with his thumb and felt a moan coming from Dumont.

His hands caressed Kyle's head as he parted the fly and began rubbing the nub. It grew beneath his fingers, becoming longer and harder until Kyle finally bent his head down and licked at it. The scarecrow arched its back and pulled Kyle's head into the nub. His crotch smelled sweet yet fetid, like overripe fruit and rotting vegetable matter. The scent and the scene intoxicated Kyle. He really went to work then, teasing its smooth surface with his tongue, wetting it and blowing on it, lightly stroking the surrounding husks.

The nub had grown to a stalk about half the length of Kyle's index finger, more than enough to engulf with his lips. He sucked it and kissed it from tip to base and suddenly the tip split into a spray of fibers. Kyle nuzzled them, brushing them and pulling on them gently with his lips while the scarecrow ground his hips into Kyle's face.

Kyle took his hands and put them around Dumont's waist, pushing the jeans off his hips. As they fell to the ground, Kyle suddenly felt Dumont's closer reach around his own waist, unfasten his belt and pull his khakis down. The air felt cool and hot at the same time on his skin. He heard the clatter of his keys and cell phone as they slipped out of his pocket, but he made no move to pick them up.

Dumont's stalk kept growing, the tassels in a sensual tangle with Kyle's tongue like anemone fingers. Coarse straw hands slid Kyle's boxer briefs off his ass and parted his hairy cheeks. Kyle's dick stiffened in response. Dumont's closer reached around and began to milk it. A crackling rustle of leaves came from behind Kyle as he felt the scarecrow lower himself to his knees. Something bristly grazed Kyle's ass. He couldn't tell if it was a hand or a tongue. *Did they have tongues?*

Whatever it was, Kyle loved what it was doing. It was bristly, then it was rough, then it was slick, then it was all three—rimming him delicately then running up and down the length of his asscrack with long, broad strokes. He didn't want to cum yet, so he pushed the hand away and concentrated on the blowjob he was about to give.

Dumont's cock stalk was about six inches long, and the fibers had stopped dueling Kyle's tongue, making way for a warm, fleshy pillar that slid slickly out of the stalk. Kyle thought it looked like an ear of corn with its kernels flattened. It tasted sweet and sticky. As he sucked on it, the scarecrow's breath came quick and shallow. Kyle automatically raised a hand to cup his balls, but none hung there.

Kyle noticed an absence under his hand, he sensed a presence close to his ass. The hairs of his crack were being matted down by a stalk as slimy as the one slamming in and out of his mouth. With little prelude, Dumont's closer slipped inside Kyle and began fucking him with long, slow thrusts. The straw scratched Kyle's cheeks as the scarecrow buried himself deep inside.

They sandwiched Kyle, moving in a rhythm that threatened to squeeze the breath out of him. Silently pounding him from the front and back, they pumped faster and faster, their viscous syrup dripping down Kyle's chin and running down the backs of his thighs. His mouth and ass were numb. He couldn't even tell if his dick was still hard or not, and he didn't much care.

The motion became frantic, both scarecrows hammering away at him, puddles forming below his mouth and between his legs. Lost in a sea of sweet sweat, Kyle felt his own load building up. *I'm gonna shoot without even touching my cock.* But before he could, the two scarecrows issued the first sounds he actually heard from them.

They weren't the moans of passion he'd been expecting. They weren't moans at all but more like wails. And those wails carried a note of welcome, as if he now had something in common with them. When the last note had been borne away on the breeze, the scarecrows vanished and Kyle was left in a puddle of ooze.

He tried to get up, but he couldn't stand. He was dizzy, and their juices leaked from him. He felt full, plump with their seed even though he hadn't felt them cum. Sinking back down, his head fell into the slimy pool, too heavy to hold up. The stars began swirling again. Kyle grasped the surrounding vegetation, trying to stop the field from spinning out of control, but stability slipped through his fingers. He felt like he was falling again—past the rows of corn, past the rotting husks, past the slime and the stars, past the farmer and the scarecrows, past space and time, past his own body until it stripped itself away from his soul.

Which fell even further.

—⟋⟍—

The sun shone warm and strong on the cornfield. *It's gonna be hot today.* He watched the farmer as he waited on a couple of carloads of tourists parked at the produce stand across the road. Even farther away in the field, he saw the two scarecrows staring back at him at eye level. The sunlight glinted on the face of his gold Rolex, which was now strapped to a wrist of straw. He couldn't blink. He couldn't talk. He couldn't move, but it didn't matter. Along with Dumont and his closer, he had to keep watch over the fields and the farmer. That was his job now. Farmer Howie had been right all along. The land *was* blessed.

Spider Strands

The second he walked into the shop, I knew he'd want a spider.

He walked around a bit, looking at the pictures of my work on the walls—the hearts, the AIDS ribbons, the tribal arm-bands, the bears, the penguins, the linked rainbows—but they didn't capture his attention. He was looking for my specialty. What I did better than any other tattoo artist I knew.

Spiders.

When he found them, he didn't move from that spot. He put his skateboard down and shifted his weight from foot to foot, peering first at the picture of the huge black widow I'd put on the back of a leather daddy from Colorado Springs then getting closer to examine the hairy-legged detail of the brown tarantula I'd done on the arm of a bearded stockbroker. Then he saw the photo of the banana spider I'd put on Michael's shoulder: the body bright yellow dulled down with red and mottled with random splotches of black and long and sharp legs stretching up to Michael's neck and reaching underneath his arm—clutching his shoulder like a jealous lover, the way I did back when he was mine.

"Can you do one of these on me?" he asked.

I smiled. Just as Michael had asked. Not 'how much?' or 'will it hurt?' but 'can you do one on me?' As if canvas asked permission to host art. If he just wanted a tattoo, he would have stopped at the barbed-wire armbands. He was seeking commitment. That hadn't happened in a long, long time.

"Where would you like it?"

"On my shoulder, like in the picture."

"No. I've already done one on someone's shoulder."

"Oh." He crossed the room to where I sat behind the counter. "Where d'ya think it'd look good, then?"

It would have looked good anywhere on him. He was in his early twenties, with a short blonde *faux*-hawk and blue eyes that sparkled like face piercings. But he wasn't pierced or tattooed anywhere I could see. He was clean from his tight white-ribbed wifebeater to the baggy sagger shorts he was almost wearing. They rode obscenely low on his narrow hips, exposing a thin strip of faintly-haired midriff above his boxers.

"Give me your hand," I said.

He reached across the counter and extended a thin, masculine hand, bony-knuckled and skateboard-scarred, wisps of hair rising from his flesh like stands of ferns in the desert. He didn't recoil, even slightly, when I touched it gently. I couldn't tell if he was queer, but it wouldn't make a difference once I got him inked.

"Well?"

I put his hand on the counter, palm down. "Spread your fingers. Is this your first tattoo?"

"Yeah."

"You have any piercings?"

"Nope."

I knew it. An unspoiled canvas. I put my finger on his skin, lightly tracing where my spider would go. If he couldn't stand the touch, he couldn't stand the ink. "The body will cover the back of your hand. One leg reaching down each of your fingers and the last three wrapping around your wrist."

He began to withdraw his hand, but I held it by the wrist. "Think about the image—*see* it. Imagine what it'll look like when you flex your hand or reach for a cigarette or caress your lover's face. Visualize what it looks like as a fist. And if you're really *seeing* it, you'll understand that as you get older, its power will remain even though its colors may fade."

To be honest, some people leave when I start describing my work, hinting how important it is to me and should be to them. Let them leave. Let them walk out the door and get their stenciled-on tats done by a cartoonist at a strip mall somewhere. I give them art. I give them something to appreciate for the rest of their lives and, frankly, some people aren't worthy.

Not this boy. He stared at his hand, doing what I asked. Even though I didn't know exactly what was going through his mind, I knew he was seeing whatever vision he needed to convince himself. The proof was the excitement in his eyes and the slight curve of a grin that appeared on his face like the morning sun breaking a dark horizon. He raised his head and nodded to me.

"When do we start?" he asked. "Now?"

I shook my head. "Tomorrow morning." I took the digital camera from where I kept it beneath the counter. "Keep your hand still. I'm going to take a few pictures so I can keep its shape fresh in my mind."

"How much is this gonna cost?"

I smiled as the camera clicked. A price would have to be paid, but not now. "I can't say. There are so many factors involved. Is it important?"

He shrugged. That meant it was. Boys his age can't afford half of what they want, but this meant more than money. To both of us. "It won't be out of your reach," I said. "Nothing is free but everything is negotiable. Just show up tomorrow morning at nine."

"Cool." A wide grin split his face. The muscles rippled on his hairy calfs as he turned to leave, tendons tensing all the way down to his sock-less sneakers. I wanted him to stay, to start right now, but I had to prepare. He'd be back soon enough. Again and again.

"What's your name?" I asked.

"Kurt," he said, pausing a second at the door.

"Your *full* name." I'd need that.

"Kurtis Richard Hollander."

"Got it. See you tomorrow."

He turned around and smiled over his shoulder before heading out into the morning sunshine that had brought him, flashing me a peace sign as he left. Was that back in fashion now? Did kids even know what it used to mean? Everything old is new again. That phrase ran through my head, making me think of Michael. I rearranged the spider pictures on the wall, clearing a space for Kurt's hand. I'll never be able to bring Michael back, I thought, but I've learned from that experience. This time the tat will be in a much better location and on someone much younger, more malleable. Yes, I thought. This will work out fine.

Just fine.

—⟋⟍—

I put the *Closed* sign on the door right after he left. There was much to do, and I wanted as few interruptions as possible. I downloaded the pictures of Kurt's hand to my laptop, printed them on high-gloss photo paper and spread them all out in front of me on the counter—top view, left and right side views, front view, back view—trying to create a three-dimensional composite in my head.

I brought out my markers and sketched on the pictures, trying various color combinations before finally settling on a deep red for the body, muddied with a bit of brown, and a bluish-black for the legs. Nothing too bright or bold. This would be a sleek, dark creature brought to scuttling life with every movement of his fingers. Ink to be reckoned with.

By the time I settled on the length of spider legs extending down his fingers and figured out how the odd three would wrap around his wrist, it was nearly dark outside. Michael and I had already made love by this time. When he had stripped to the waist so I could take pictures of his shoulder, his pale flesh drove me crazy. I had to touch it. When he responded by caressing my arm, I grabbed a handful of his long, dark hair and yanked his head back, biting his lip as I sealed his mouth with my own, the coppery taste of blood—the first I'd draw but not the last—sweet and hot on my tongue.

We fucked on the tattoo chair in the back room minutes later, both panting and grunting as I buried my cock in his ass and bit his lip again when we came. I savored the wound with my tongue until the shop bell announced the arrival of customers and I let him off my lap with instructions to come back the next day. It had been a mistake to fuck him so soon, I thought, but I was younger and vastly more stupid then. That won't happen with this one.

I packed up the laptop, gathered the pictures and turned out the lights in the shop, leaving the computer in the back room but keeping the pictures to study as I walked upstairs. I filled the teakettle, put it on the stove and threw the pictures on the kitchen table. Walking through to the living room, I lit a cigarette and took up my perch on the open windowsill, looking out over the intersection of Colfax and Josephine, where Michael had been killed.

The possibilities Kurt presented brought the memory of that night to the front of my mind. The images had been colliding in my head all day long, caroming off each other like a game of mental eight-ball. I had to remember them, like it or not. That was the only way to clear my head for the task before me. Fine.

Let them come.

It wouldn't have happened if Michael hadn't had such a strong will. If he'd only let me take control, he'd be alive today. I think. But he couldn't...no, he *wouldn't* submit to me for long. That's what made the whole damn thing such a failure. Maybe I had called him to me too many times, but I couldn't help myself. I became enthralled by the power I had over him. That won't happen this time either. Thanks to my Michael, I've learned restraint.

My grandmother was known in three counties for trafficking in the supernatural. The very churchgoing biddies that shunned her during the day pleaded for her help after sundown. I found many charms in the marked-up Bible she left me. Also a warning never to use them on people. That's why I charmed the ink instead of Michael.

The spider on his shoulder brought him back to me again and again. He thought it was love, that it was obsession, that it was unhealthy. We fucked, we argued, we fucked again—then I began to relish controlling him. I would meditate on the spider, seeing it crawling to me as I called him back time after time, just to prove I could. When he got to my door, I'd turn him away.

I should have known he'd want to escape. Who wouldn't?

I had been sitting on the windowsill watching him lurch down the sidewalk on the opposite side of the street, forced forward by the charm but made hesitant by his will. He looked drunk as he staggered across Colfax, his consciousness receding long enough for me to drag him halfway. Then it returned with a vengeance. I felt it tug at the spell as he turned and started running back to the curb.

That's when the bus hit him.

Something slammed into me, nearly knocking me off the windowsill. It could have been the return snap of a spell whose subject had been obliterated, or it could have been Michael's energy slapping me back for once as it left his body. I righted myself and held my position, watching like a carrion bird circling above as the crowd gathered, the ambulance scraped up what was left of him and the police arrived to officiate, authorize and disperse. Then I went to bed and vowed never to do it again.

But never is a long time to keep a vow made in haste. Magic has a powerful allure; use it once, you *will* use it again.

So I will meditate and fast and sharpen myself, get up tomorrow morning and charm the inks after I mix them. When Kurt arrives, we will begin the work. Line by line, with shading and color, my spider will appear, dark and dangerous on his skin. When it has healed, I will call him. The strands will pull taut, and he will come to me.

I will use him whenever I wish. However I please. Because I *can.*

"How fuckin' cool is *this*?" Kurt said, leaning forward in the chair. He beamed as he flexed his hand. The spider curled and uncurled, its body a blood-red menace with long, spindly needle-legs stretching down his fingers, just brushing his cuticles. I had been worried about his pale skin but the contrast was startling. It would settle just right after it healed. It was, indeed, pretty fuckin' cool.

Even cooler were the conversations we'd had during the long inking sessions. I discovered he was newly out; just moved from a small town in Indiana to try life in a bigger city like Denver before making the leap to New York. He was doing the clubs, eating in all-night joints, going to art galleries, doing Craigslist hookups and taking a class or two at UCD so he could justify asking his parents for money every month. He wasn't dating anyone but was sleeping around a lot, finding out what his type was. His life stretched luxuriously before him, a long, lush carpet he was walking down barefoot.

"How much?" he asked with some hesitation. "I mean, you *said* not to worry about the money, but this looks too cool to be cheap."

I snapped a few photos, put the camera away and shrugged. "Fifty bucks."

"You're shittin' me, dude," he said. "Fifty bucks for *this*? That's, like, the first payment, right?"

You haven't even begun to make the first payment, I thought. "No. Fifty bucks period."

He nodded. "Lemme pay you before you change your mind." He, stood up to reach for his wallet, attached to a thick chain that led to his back pocket. He counted out fifty dollars and handed them to me, the spider fluttering with ominous motion. We both noticed it.

"This is so fuckin' *cool*." A broad grin rose on his stubbly face. "Are you *sure* all you want is fifty bucks?" He moved closer to me, almost nose to nose. "I mean, I'm not usually into older dudes..." He took another step. "But you're kinda hot." He took my head in both his hands and guided our mouths together. This would be a preview, I decided. No more than that. I would not let what happened with Michael happen again.

I could still taste the Starbucks he'd come in with, as sweet and bitter to me as his youth. He kissed softly, with too much romance. Did he prefer that or was he assuming I did? I wanted to jam our faces together hungrily and eat him like a ripe melon, but this was *his* kiss—what he wanted to give me. I would take what I wanted later. I allowed him to kiss me until his hand slipped down to cup my crotch.

"That's not how I want this to end," I said gently as I broke contact and moved away. "Besides, you'll be back."

"I will?" That grin returned.

I began cleaning up the tools on the bench. "Of course. Tattoos are addictive, you know. You won't be able to stop with just one."

He flexed the spider once again, looking at it proudly. "Maybe you're right. Where should I get the next one?"

"You've got three or four weeks to think about it," I said as I handed him his post-tattoo care package. "Read the brochure, use the skin-care

products and call me if you have any questions or problems." I stepped
past him and drew the curtain aside. He seemed puzzled but not angry at
my dismissal.

"Thanks again, bud." The fuzz on his arms and legs gleamed in the
fading afternoon sun from the shop window as he tossed his skateboard
down and wheeled away. "I'll be seein' ya."

Oh yes, I thought. *You will indeed.*

—m—

I couldn't resist tugging the strands a few times before I called Kurt
back to me in earnest. I concentrated offhandedly, pulling a little until I
felt him thinking about me, then I stopped. I didn't want to bring him cold.
It would have made no sense to call him out of nowhere. There had to be
a context. Not like that was a problem with Michael. We were fucking all
through his healing process, so it was no trick to get him to come to me
once it was over.

It rarely rains in the dry climate of Denver, but it was pouring the
night I called him to me for the first time. I took that for a sign. I spread
all the photos I'd taken of the tattoo and his hand in front of me and
meditated on them, seeing the spider come alive and scuttle towards its
maker. I don't think I've concentrated that hard on anything in my life.

I was getting a headache, just about to take a break when the
connection finally clicked into place like the hum of a dial tone. I smiled
and took my usual place in the windowsill, feeling the warm rain beat on
my shoulder as I visualized my spider returning.

I saw it scrabbling over rocks and under yellowed, soaked newspapers.
It skirted puddles and surmounted twigs, leaves and tree detritus brought
down from high boughs by the rain. It crawled stealthily through deserted
parking lots and paused in the streets, waiting for the cars to whizz past
before striding safely into the fringe of a suburban lawn, never stopping
or slowing, creeping inexorably towards me.

How long did it take? I had no idea. It was dark and rainy when
I started and it was still dark and rainy when Kurt appeared at the
intersection below my window. He wore baggy jeans and a dark green

Princeton hoodie with the hood down, his blonde hair matted with rain. He held his spider hand outstretched for a moment, as if he were consulting a compass, then jammed it back in his pocket. He crossed Colfax and stopped in front of the shop, standing on the sidewalk with a puzzled expression, like he'd reached his destination but was unsure about what was to happen next.

I wasn't.

The rain turned to little daggers plunging earthward in the glare of the streetlight, and I whispered his name softly in my head so that we alone could hear. That's when he looked up, drops of moisture glistening in the scraggly beard he'd grown since I'd last seen him—a queer punk Romeo about to perform the balcony scene. But I wasn't Juliet.

He would *not* be invited up, not when the rain was falling rare and warm like bathwater from the sky. I dismounted from the windowsill and shut the window, mentally commanding him to meet me in the alley to the left. I pissed as best I could through my already stiffening dick and thought about taking off my half-soaked t-shirt, but I liked the way the wet cotton felt against my skin.

I went downstairs through the back room and paused at the alley door, masochistically delaying the moment I'd been waiting for. He was young and beautiful, a punk wannabe with all of the attitude and none of the experience, but I'd cure that. I'd turn him into what he wanted to be. Feeling my hard cock through the pockets of my worn jeans, I took a deep breath and stepped out into the alley.

He stood there at my door, wet and wondering, his face full of questions. When he opened his mouth to speak, I held my hand up to silence him. I beckoned him forward and stripped the sodden hoodie off him, letting it fall in its own puddle. Then I took his head in both my hands and slammed our faces together so hard I felt the skin of his lip split and heard the clack of our teeth over the rain pelting the dumpster next to the door.

He resisted a second, but the spell was too powerful and his youthful strength was no match for the intensity of my passion. He yielded to me, wrapping his strong, hairy arms around me, the spider finally completing its journey. Our mouths welded together, I let go of his head and ran my hands up and down his back, chewing on his split lip as if I could gobble him up in one bloody mouthful.

My lust for his coppery taste satisfied for the moment, my kiss grew softer as my hands reached under his t-shirt and worked their way up his warm skin to his nipples, jutting erect from their faintly furry base. I rolled them between my fingers and thumbs until they were hard as ball bearings. Kurt arched his back and craned his neck into the rain, moaning like a wild thing in heat.

I twisted and chewed and bit and licked and sucked his nipples until it seemed they might break loose from their hairy moorings and pop right into my mouth. The spider clutched at my hands and neck as Kurt begged me to stop so he could catch his breath, but I had no intention of doing so. His breathlessness inflamed me even further.

Grabbing the waistband of his loose jeans with both hands, I yanked them down revealing the hard cock tenting his thin boxers. They weren't tented far, mind you—but that didn't matter. A small dick was fine with me. I inserted my hands into the fly of his shorts, Kurt moaning as I brushed his dick. I grabbed the fabric and ripped it off his body. All that remained was the waistband and some stray threads clinging to his skin. Then I bent him over the side of the dumpster to claim my prize.

His ass was everything I'd fantasized about for the last month—taut, muscular, and hairy. Two fuzzy globes of undeniable pleasure. I ran my hands over his cheeks, scarcely able to believe they belonged to me now. I slapped the right one then the left, watching his flesh tighten as the satisfying smacks reverberated in the alley.

But he wasn't bent over far enough. I pulled him back roughly by his t-shirt with one hand, threw the dumpster lid aside with the other and forced his head inside until the crack of his ass opened wide for me. I ignored his grunts and feeble protests. Next time I would consider his feelings, his comfort—maybe even allow him to participate as an equal. This time, however, was for me. After all, boundaries *must* be established.

I sank to my knees in the wet alley, spreading his cheeks apart with my hands and running an exploratory tongue down his crack. I won't lie with a lover's overstatement and say his ass was sweet. Boys' asses are never sweet—they're musky, they're pungent, they're redolent with the scent of shit and sweat and the essence of maleness, but they're never sweet. I wouldn't like them if they were.

Hungry, I lapped at his hole. My nose tracking through the wet hair as rain funneled down his crack. I licked his most intimate creases while I reached around to caress his balls and milk his hard cock with my hands. Sucking and nipping at his pucker, I pushed my tongue deep inside where the taste was bitter as he squirmed and backed up for more.

I didn't dare touch my own cock. I wanted to fuck him as long as I could, and I could already feel how close I was. I just kept working his rain-soaked and spit-slick ass until I lost track of time and my tongue got tired. Then I opened him up with my fingers. I gave him one last long lick, stood up and unbuckled my sopping jeans, keeping my middle finger in his ass. They dropped heavily to the concrete, my aching cock standing out stiff and hot in the warm rain. I rubbed the precum I'd been leaking up and down the wet shaft, moaning softly with anticipation.

I butted the head of my cock up against his tight, hot hole and pushed him against the dumpster, drawing a gasp from him when I entered. I sank myself into him slowly, feeling his warmth engulf me. The rain fell harder, fat drops beading up on the small of his back in a puddle that trembled with every long, slow stroke.

The cold metal edge of the dumpster felt gritty and slimy on my fingers as I grabbed it for better leverage and crushed Kurt into it, my thrusts becoming harder and faster. But his moans were annoying me. I usually don't mind noises of passion, but they seemed wrong and out of place, echoing in the wet alley.

My fingers scrabbled around the dumpster, landing on something yellow and papery—a used hamburger wrapper from some fast food joint, filthy with mayo and limp shredded lettuce. I wadded it up and stuffed it in his mouth. His hands were trapped, and his muffled disgust made him buck furiously. I leaned into him with all my weight, pounding his ass as hard as I could, his struggle and the sound of our skin slapping together sending me over the top.

I came harder than I can ever remember coming before, even with Michael. My hot seed filled him, spurt after spurt, until my knees almost buckled. I leaned forward to steady my chest on his back, both of us shivering with post-coital trembles. My dick shrank out of his ass as I reached around to pluck the wadded up burger wrapper out of his mouth. The rain seemed colder than it did before and the wind was starting to whip up a bit more.

Expecting colorful sk8tr invective flecked with "fuck" and "dude," I got silence in return. I dismounted and pulled up my pants. He straightened up, a smear of mayo on his scruffy cheek, as he looked around for his boxers. Seeing them in a puddle, he shrugged and pulled his jeans up too. He started to say something then stopped, more questions in his eyes than he could ask in a lifetime.

Before he started posing them, however, I turned around and went back inside, closing the alley door quietly but firmly. I leaned my back against it and sighed with satisfaction, feeling rainwater and sweat drip down my face. After a few moments, a soft knock came from the other side, but I wasn't about to open the door.

He'd have his answers soon enough.

—⚇—

Four months later he told me he hated me. "But I *can't* stay away from you. Is that love?" We were lying in my narrow bed, him staring at the ceiling and me looking at the bruises I'd inflicted around his nipples.

Common sense says if you have to ask whether or not something is love, it probably isn't. But he didn't know why he kept coming back to me. Like primitive man inventing gods to explain natural phenomena, he needed a frame of reference for what was happening to him. Love was the only logical choice.

"I don't think it is," Kurt said, answering his own question. My spider lay in repose on his slightly furred stomach, twitching whenever he moved a finger. "We never even go out anywhere. I just show up here, we fuck and then I go home. I mean, that's not love, right? Half the time I don't even remember how I got here. One minute I'm hangin' at home or out with my crew and the next minute I'm here and you're chewin' on me. What's up with that?"

Did he expect a response or were these rhetorical questions? I decided to wait it out. After a few seconds silence, he swung his legs around to the side of the bed and stood up. He walked to the chair where his clothes hung, his low-hanging balls swinging from thigh to thigh. My spider clutched and clenched as he put on his cargo shorts.

"I mean, don't get me wrong dude—the ink's cool and all, but this whole biting and hurting thing doesn't do much for me." He pulled his t-shirt on and stepped into the flip-flops he'd kicked into the corner. "I don't know how I let it get this far, but it's over man. No more."

"I see," I replied, getting out of bed and getting dressed too. "And you think you have a choice in the matter."

"Well, *duh*—if it's not my choice, then whose is it?"

"Mine," I said. "You come back because of me." He wasn't as smart as Michael. Michael had been able to figure it out for himself, but this one will have to be told.

Kurt laughed, mocking me with his eyes. "Yeah, right," he said. "I come back because of the charming way you draw blood when we kiss or the way you pinch my tits until they ache or screw me with my head in a fuckin' dumpster. Uh-huh. That's why."

"Okay, if you don't come back for that, smart ass, why *do* you come back, then?" I asked.

He stopped laughing and looked out the window a moment. "I don't know."

"Let me enlighten you." I grabbed his arm. He flinched and struggled but I held on tight, raising the spider to his eyes. "You come back to me whenever I call you, and I call you with *this*." I let him go and he scurried away from the window, still looking at his hand.

"You're fuckin' *nuts*, dude."

"Am I? Let's say you're sitting at home or work, just minding your own business. My spider starts to throb, doesn't it? It pulses. You can feel the blood beating and rushing through the veins in your hand. You try to ignore it, but you can't. It distracts you. It draws your attention from whatever you're doing. The only way you can stop it is to start your journey to me. It feels better once you get on your way, doesn't it? But you can't stop at 7-11 for a Slurpee or linger in one place too long or it begins to throb again. Shall I continue?"

He just stared at me.

"Your silence is permission. When you get here, the throbbing ceases but you feel out of your own body somehow—participating yet watching from outside as well. You feel powerless to stop me because my spider sucks the defensive energy from you, allowing me to do whatever I wish to you. And I do. So you see, the only choice in the matter belongs to me. *Dude.*"

His eyes darted back and forth from me to the door. The disbelieving snarl of his mouth hardened into anger then melted into the impotent knowledge that I was right. He was marked. "How?" His voice was hoarse, unsure of itself.

"Charmed ink. You could have the tattoo obscured and scarred with lasers, but as long as a molecule of ink remains—no matter how deep in your flesh--you're mine. And there will be serious consequences if you fuck with that tattoo."

He glared silently at me.

"Tell me you understand."

"I understand."

"Good. You can go now. I'll call you when I want you."

I read so much on his face as he turned to leave. Hatred, loathing, disgust—all the glittering black facets of his blue eyes. It was beautiful. The stony set of his stubbled jaw said he would kill me if only I didn't control his hand. In the end, he just walked away.

The door downstairs slammed, and I took my place in the window, waiting for him to appear on the street. I let him get to the south corner of the intersection before I started to call him again. He took his hand out of his pocket and looked at it a second before finding me watching him in the window. When he saw me, I jerked back hard on the spell, putting enough into it to stagger him backwards a step.

Then I smiled at him.

—m—

I waited a few days before calling him again. I wanted to give him time to understand the situation; to reflect on being marked and to dread when I would bring him to me again, knowing he was powerless to control it. Maybe, just maybe, he would arrive as angry as he was when he left. That would be sweet, indeed. I'd make him fuck me then. There's no hotter fuck than an angry fuck.

Of course I anticipated more resistance than I'd felt recently. After all, he now knew what was happening and would use all his willpower to prevent it. That's why I fasted and meditated and did concentration exercises. And on the appointed night, I spread all the pictures out on the floor in front of me, cleared my mind and set to work bringing him to me.

The connection was easy to establish now and the strands pulled taut. I felt a tug back but didn't overreact. I applied gentle, steady pressure until I sensed the spider coming towards me. I visualized it on its slow, unrelenting way—its journey safe and its progress smooth until suddenly it stopped.

I could still feel the spider, but it wouldn't budge. I tugged harder, encountering a sensation of unyielding, as if I was trying to drag something large through a very small hole. I concentrated harder, imagining my spider forcing itself through—first two legs for traction, then the body filling the hole, legs pushing on one side and pulling on the other, squeaking through hair by hair until finally it popped through so fiercely my head snapped back. Then it continued as before.

The pulling became easier and easier, and I could feel my spider within range of sight. I sat in my window, peering down Colfax and before long I saw Kurt lurching his way down the sidewalk. There was no resistance as with Michael, but he was walking the same way—staggering as if exhausted from effort or worn down by another's will. His hands were stuffed in the pockets of his jeans but he carried a brown plastic bag in the crook of his right arm.

It looked like a gun.

I would have been a fool not to have anticipated violence, so his carrying a gun didn't particularly surprise me. Nor did it worry me. My spider would never let him shoot me with his right hand and unless he had acquired some skillful aim with his left, he'd most likely miss. Still, weapons were to be taken seriously.

It had been my habit to leave the alley door unlocked so that I could bring Kurt right up to my apartment, but that would be unwise. I saw him crossing Colfax and slipped downstairs to lock the heavy door. Standing beside it, I waited for his knock for a few minutes. Then a few more. And more minutes after that. Was he waiting for me to open the door? Why didn't he knock?

Overcome by curiosity, I reached for the lock and the doorknob but stopped myself in time. *That's what he's waiting for*, I thought. When I open the door, he'll be standing there pointing a gun at me, and he could hardly miss at point blank range even with his left hand. I'd continue waiting.

But his knock never came. Instead, I heard a soft thump, as if someone slumping against the door. Again I went for the lock and again I stopped myself. I still felt the spider nearby, so I knew he had to be around somewhere. I ran upstairs and went to the window in time to see Kurt running down Josephine towards the bus stop.

Confusion clouding my head, I raced downstairs, nearly falling down the steps in my haste. When I reached the bottom of the stairs, I stopped to breathe a few times, calming myself. I approached the door cautiously and put my ear to it, straining to hear something from the alley.

Nothing.

I unlocked the door and twisted the knob, opening it wide. The alley was empty, but the connection was still there. The spider strands were taut. I jerked at the spell, and that's when I saw movement in my lower peripheral vision. I focused on the doorstep and saw the brown plastic bag lying there. The fingers of Kurt's severed right hand poked out of its confines, curled up and looking for all the world like a dead spider.

Waafrneeaasuu!!

"OOOHHHH YEAH! THAT'S IT, *PAPI*!! FUCK ME HARDER!! *HARDER*!!! FUCK MY *MANGINA*!!!!

Harvey's dick wilted faster than microwaved lettuce.

He pulled out of Eduardo's ass, concentrating on getting his erection back so he could at least cum. It only half worked, but at last he coaxed out a gooey stream that shot halfway up to Eduardo's chin. Panting, Harvey flopped forward on the bed, landing beside Eduardo, who grabbed a warm, wet towel from the bedside table and mopped his smooth chest.

"Mmmm, nice," Eduardo said as he snaked one muscled arm around Harvey's back. Harvey turned over and stared up at the ceiling, tracing a crack in the plaster until Eduardo started snoring softly and snuggled into his armpit.

Dammit, Harvey thought. This a great guy. He's a good kisser, he's really nice and he's not an alcoholic like the last two. He even has a job, for Chrissakes, and that's better than the last *four*. He's handsome, he's smart and he makes me feel good about myself. And then there are those brown eyes, warm and eager. They turn me into a puddle every time I look into them. If it's not love, it's the closest I've been in a long time. It's the mangina thing that kills it.

Okay, he could be a little hairier, too, but *mangina*?

Harvey had been able to ignore it the first time. Caught up in the passion of the moment, the word had rolled right out of his ears when Eduardo screamed it. It barely registered. The second and third times, he heard it but it didn't matter. Somewhere around the fifth or sixth time, though, it became irritating. Now, hearing it was like rubbing his dick on a cheese grater.

Eduardo was a gentle soul, easily hurt. Harvey knew that from the second date, when he'd happened to mention in passing that the *paella* Eduardo made for dinner was a touch too spicy for his ulcer. Harvey had to eat three helpings to quell his tears. No, a direct confrontation was definitely out of the question.

He looked down at Eduardo as he slept, his steady, rhythmic breaths tickling the small hairs on his side, and he smiled. How could I be so petty? he wondered. It's only a word, right? He closed his eyes and tried to sleep, but the word seemed to be imprinted on his eyelids in flowing, femmy script.

Mangina.

His balls recoiled, drawing up into his body as if he'd just been plunged into a cold swimming pool. He didn't know what he was going to do, but he'd have to do something. Soon.

—∞—

He managed to avoid sex the next morning by letting Eduardo sleep late, then rushing him to get ready for the day ahead, but Eduardo was staying the weekend, so he wasn't going to be able to put him off that night. Once they got home and took a nap, Eduardo's mangina would be primed and ready to go. As it was, Harvey barely held him off through breakfast.

"It's a long drive to the Renaissance Faire," Harvey told him through a long, hard kiss at the front door.

Eduardo reached down and squeezed Harvey's hard dick. "Let's stay here for a while, and you drive me."

Harvey finally got them on the road, reaching the *faux* castle gates as trumpets blared and the King and Queen began the morning processional. Eduardo waved away the busty wenches who greeted every entrant to the realm with a sloppy, smeary kiss.

"No girls." He turned to Harvey and giving him a full-on kiss with tongue as several nearby mothers shielded their children's eyes from the depravity while their husbands looked on with shock and disbelief that this was happening at a family venue.

Harvey chuckled and hugged him as they kissed. He loved Eduardo's fierce insistence on being who he was, and Eduardo was big enough to intimidate anyone who dared question him. He was about six two, with well-defined arms, massive legs and a solid, gym-built chest. He had a bit of a gut, but Harvey found that hot.

They walked around the Faire, enjoying turkey legs and cold beer, stopping to watch sword-swallowers, jugglers and magicians. Eduardo especially liked the falconer's show, never taking his eyes off the birds. "They are so beautiful," he whispered to Harvey. He bought Harvey a set of Pan's pipes, and Harvey bought him a short, black leather vest with two crossed swords stitched in white on the back.

"Thank you, *papi*." He, stripped off his wife-beater on the spot and donning it. The sight of that bronze body in the short vest got Harvey hard instantly. The lady who ran the stand murmured an appreciative comment that turned to a mild curse of disappointment when Eduardo took Harvey in his arms for a long, wet thank-you kiss. Had it not been for their little problem, Harvey would have put an 'out of order' sign on the nearest privy and fucked him senseless then and there.

Taking a break from shopping, they sat down on a sun-dappled log and sipped their beers. Eduardo unfolded the map of the grounds.

"What do you want to do next?" he asked.

Harvey looked around to get his bearings, and that's when he saw it right in front of them. It was just another fortune-teller's tent—the placard outside said Gypsy Davey's—but under palmistry, tarot reading and crystal tunings was a menu item that caught his eye.

Magick words a specialty!

Harvey couldn't believe what he was thinking, but the thought wouldn't leave him alone. Not that he believed in crap like that. All his life he'd been skeptical about magic, but this mangina problem called for creative solutions. And he was desperate. Eduardo must have seen him looking at the tent.

"You go in for that stuff?" Eduardo asked, pointing towards Gypsy Davey's.

Harvey smiled, challenging him playfully. "And what if I did?"

Eduardo chuckled. "It's your money," he replied. "Go ahead. Do it if you want. I'll look at the map while you get your fortune told. And when they tell you you are going to meet a tall, dark, handsome stranger, tell them you already have a boyfriend." He laughed and sipped his beer.

"I'll be right back."

Surprised he was actually going through with it, Harvey stood up, walked across the trail to the tent, pushed aside the flap and entered. The place smelled like feet, sweaty silk and Egg McMuffin.

"Sorry, bud. Haven't finished breakfast yet," explained the young man sitting barefoot behind a low makeshift counter that held a Mickey D's bag. He wore a purple scarf wrapped around his head, harem pants and a brocade vest with no shirt, revealing a mat of dark hair on his chest. Harvey saw McMuffin crumbs sticking to the wax of his handlebar moustache.

"You look kinda young for this," Harvey said.

"Do you think the Fates speak only to old crones?" His accent was lousy. "What do you seek?"

"A magic word." He felt like a moron saying it out loud.

"For what purpose? To charm a young lady? To make an enemy feel your power? To make money, perhaps?"

Harvey lifted the tent flap. "See that guy sitting on the log over there?"

Gypsy Davey nodded.

"He's my boyfriend, and I want to butch him up some."

"He looks pretty butch already."

"Okay, maybe not butch. How about...more *bearish*?" That would have to do. He wasn't about to explain manginas to a fake gypsy who couldn't even do a decent Slavic accent.

Gypsy Davey fiddled with the end of his moustache. "Ah yes," he said after a few moments. "I believe I have what you need. It is a word of transformation—very ancient and quite potent, indeed. It must be spoken in the throes of passion only. The word is... *waafrneeaasuu*."

"Um—could you write that down?"

"Writing down a magick word robs it of its powers. Ten dollars, please."

Harvey pulled out his wallet and handed the ten over. "Okay, if you can't write it down, could you at least *say* it again? Or will that cost me another ten bucks?"

"*Waafrneeaasuu.*"

"*Waafrneeaasuu,*" Harvey repeated. "Got it. What if I just walk up to him and say it now?"

Gypsy Davey rolled his eyes. "You're the kind of guy they put directions on shampoo bottles for, aren't you? Just whisper it in his ear the next time you make love, and all shall be as you wish."

"Right. Thanks."

"Whatta *schmuck,*" he heard Gypsy Davey mutter as the tent flap dropped behind him.

—〰—

Gentle kisses tickled the back of Harvey's neck, waking him up from his nap. He thought about jamming his face further into the pillow and waving Eduardo away. No, that would cause more problems than it would solve. *I can't do that to him,* he thought. He didn't want to deal with the situation but couldn't see a way not to have sex. Maybe Eduardo wouldn't say it this time.

The sheets scratched Harvey's sunburned legs as he rolled over, drew Eduardo close and kissed him. He tasted like the mead they'd had at the fair, sweet and addictive, and Harvey's dick hardened as he ran his hands over Eduardo's smooth, hard back muscles. Eduardo's fingertips traced Harvey's nipples and skated down the hair of his chest to his cock. Eduardo broke the kiss, his tongue trailing across Harvey's neck.

"Mmmm, nice," Eduardo breathed in his ear, gripping his dick. "Such a hard *pinga.* You should have let me take care of that this morning."

Harvey felt Eduardo's cock stiffening against the outside of his thigh and knew he'd be getting his *pinga* sucked in a few seconds. *That's key*, he thought. *If I can just keep something in his mouth at all times, I've got it made.* True to form, Eduardo slid down the sheets and began to work Harvey's balls with his tongue.

The silence was heaven, and so was Eduardo's warm mouth on his cock. Harvey was hornier than he thought, and he began to buck against Eduardo's head, fucking his mouth until he started to feel a load building up. He grabbed his head and pulled Eduardo up for a long kiss as he rolled over onto him and got into position.

"Yesssss," Eduardo hissed. *"Papi* wants my mmmm..." Harvey sealed his mouth tight with a vacuum kiss, as if he could suck the word right out of Eduardo's brain, but Eduardo managed a smothered moan. Harvey knew it was a lost cause. He'd get that word out somehow. Harvey felt his dick start to shrink, but then he remembered Gypsy Davey's ten-dollar word. Feeling desperate and ridiculous at the same time, Harvey unsealed Eduardo's mouth and whispered in his ear.

"Waafrneeaasuu..."

Nothing.

Maybe I said it wrong, Harvey thought, but he felt too stupid to say it again. *There's ten bucks shot to shit.*

Eduardo's moaning continued unabated, though its timbre suddenly changed; it became lower and more gruff than before. And Harvey had the weird sensation of grass growing beneath him, like the time-lapse photography in a lawn fertilizer commercial. He looked down and saw a covering of hair on Eduardo's chest where there had been none, lengthening and darkening before his eyes.

"What th—" Harvey looked into Eduardo's warm, curious eyes for an answer. They were as warm and curious as ever, but they were now set into a face unlike the one Harvey had laid down for a nap with. This one was covered with hair and had a snout instead of a mouth, its breath reeking of something Harvey couldn't identify but sure as hell wasn't mead.

"Mrrrppphhh!!" Eduardo growled into Harvey's ear.

Eduardo's strong arms, now shaggy with hair, closed around Harvey's back. He heard the clack of claws and felt their sharp hardness pressing into his skin, but that wasn't all. Eduardo's erection was pressing into his thigh too. But it was now considerably larger than before. Harvey didn't have time to look, however. Before he realized what was happening, Eduardo shifted his weight to the right, neatly flipped Harvey over and...

...well...

...*bearbacked* him.

—〰—

Harvey took Eduardo back to the fair before the morning trumpets blew, waiting in line for the gates to open. People stared and pointed at Eduardo, but he didn't seem to mind. He sat patiently leashed at Harvey's side, scratching every now and then at the studded collar around his hairy neck, smartly outfitted in tan cargo shorts and the leather vest Harvey had bought for him the day before.

Gypsy Davey sat outside his tent eating an apple. "Good lookin' bear," he said as they approached.

"That's not a bear, it's my boyfriend."

"Mrrrppphhh," Eduardo added.

"I thought I recognized the vest." He threw the apple core over the fence behind the tent and held the flap open for them. "C'mon in." He sat down behind the low counter and crossed his legs in a tight lotus positon. "So, what is it you seek today?"

"What is it..." Harvey's temper rose, but he controlled himself. Flying off the handle wasn't going to get Eduardo changed back. "Ummmm, let me see," he said, "how about something to kinda tone down your magic word? Maybe an adjective or an adverb or something."

"Does this look like grammar class? You wanted a bear, you got a bear. And you're not gettin' your ten bucks back, either. Gypsy profit margin sucks this season." The accent was gone.

"I don't give a *shit* about your profit margin," Harvey said through clenched teeth. "Have you ever been cornholed by a fuckin' *bear*? It ain't pretty—I mean, I'm versatile, but Jesus *Christ*... You gotta change him back."

"No can do."

"Whaddya mean by that?"

"Mrrrppphh?" Eduardo looked confused, his eyes meeting Harvey's.

"Once done, magic's kinda tough to undo."

"Yeah?" Harvey slid his hand down the leash to Eduardo's collar and put his finger on the release button. "Well, you better *find* a way, or there's gonna be one pissed off bear loose in your tent."

Eduardo shifted his eyes to Gypsy Davey and began to rumble, flexing his clawed paws. *"MRRRRRRRRRRRRRPPPHHHH!!"*

"Okay, *okay*," the gypsy said. Harvey noticed his hands shook as he grabbed a cell phone and started dialing. "Hang on a minute."

"Who are you calling?"

"My grandmother in Craiova."

"Craiova? Where the hell's *that*?"

"Romania. Just keep the fuckin' bear cool, all right?"

Harvey took his hand away from Eduardo's collar and started petting him. "Sssshhh, it's gonna be okay…"

"Bunica?" he said, *"Buna dimeneata, bunica—ca s 'schimbare s 'urs?"*

Harvey tuned out the conversation since he couldn't understand it anyway. Eduardo never took his eyes off the gypsy, but at least he stopped growling.

Then Gypsy Davey turned pale. *"Voi sigur?"* he said. *"Multumesc, bunica. La revedere."* He flipped the cell phone shut.

"What'd she say?"

"You're not gonna like this, bud."

"What?"

"She said the bear will tell you what to say."

"The *bear*? What the fuck is *that* supposed to mean?"

"Look, she's a hundred and two years old. She's forgotten more about magic words and gypsy curses than I'll ever know. If she says the bear will tell you what to say, the bear will tell you what to say. Trust me."

"Like we have a choice," Harvey said with a snort. "C'mon, Eduardo."

Eduardo sniffed and scratched his armpit with his hind leg. *"Mmrrpphh,"* he said, following Harvey out of the tent.

"Losers," Gypsy Davey muttered, putting up his *Out To Lunch* sign.

—m—

Sloppy bear-licks coated the back of Harvey's neck, waking him up from his nap. He buried his face in his spit-soaked pillow, but it was like burrowing into a sponge. He waved the bear away, but Eduardo was insistent. Harvey felt his hairy warmth beside him and heard his claws ripping through the comforter. And the mattress. And the box springs.

"Not now, Eduardo," he said, wrinkling his nose at the feral stench that filled the bedroom. He was getting used to it, though. There was something *primeval* about it. Elemental. Savage. Musky but spicy at the same time; a piquant odor that had an undeniable, animalistic urge to it. In fact, as unbelievable as it was, the smell was making him horny.

Harvey snuggled his back into Eduardo's underside, feeling the bear's belly hairs tickling his back and ass. His dick rose. Harvey found himself uneasy about this at first, but he got used to the idea. It's not like this is a strange bear, he said to himself. It's not a one-night stand. It's *Eduardo*. As if to reassure himself of that, he turned over and looked the bear square in the eyes.

And he saw what he'd seen the first time they met. Warm, soft brown eyes, curious and eager to please. Eager to love. Eyes that had always been able to melt his heart. He reached his arms around the bear and squeezed him as hard as he could. He would have tongue-kissed him if he could have figured out how, but he settled for a peck on the end of his big, black nose.

"*Mmmrrppphh,*" Eduardo bear-sighed in response. Apparently, he'd noticed Harvey's erection too. One hairy paw came up between Harvey's legs, tickling his balls softly with his claws as the rough pads scraped the shaft of Harvey's dick with delicious friction. Harvey ground his cock harder into Eduardo's paw as the bear began licking Harvey's neck.

Harvey knew that, on some level, other people might find this whole thing odd, but he couldn't help what was happening. Eduardo's tongue felt smooth and slick as it slobbered a wide swath of pleasure down his chest. Harvey's dick was at full mast as he anticipated what it would feel like on his cock and balls. A bear blow-job. Harvey couldn't help but smile as he tugged on Eduardo's ear to get his attention.

"Watch the teeth," he said with a grin. He could have sworn Eduardo grinned back.

Harvey felt like a postage stamp as Eduardo's tongue ran over every crevice of his crotch then worked its way underneath for the rim job. His ecstasy was only slightly hampered by the thought of Eduardo's huge bear-cock, which was plainly on the rise. It had hurt like hell last night, but he hadn't really been prepared. He wasn't sure he was prepared now, but Eduardo had turned into a total top.

Among other things, he said to himself with a chuckle.

Eduardo centered himself between Harvey's legs, threw his ankles into the air and leaned forward. *"Mmrrrppphhh,"* he growled.

"Mmrrrpphhh," Harvey responded, trying to match Eduardo's breathy grumble.

Eduardo suddenly got a little smaller.

The bear will tell you what to say.

"Mmrrppphhh," Harvey said again.

Eduardo's claws began retracting and his fur got shorter.

"Mrrrppphhh!! Mrrrppphhh!! Mmrrrppphhh!"

Eduardo's snout flattened out and his breath returned to normal. Harvey kept repeating it until Eduardo was at last back to himself, except for a thick coating of fur on his chest and legs.

"Papi..." he said, but Harvey didn't give him a chance to say anything else. He turned him over and fucked him hard, gluing their mouths together with so much lust, love and relief they could barely grunt and gasp for air. Harvey pumped away frantically as Eduardo groaned and squirmed beneath him until finally they both shot in geysers of cum, Eduardo not even touching his own cock.

Harvey collapsed beside Eduardo, soaked with sweat, cum and bear-spit. The bed was a tangled, sticky puddle of ripped sheets and blankets that clutched at Harvey's skin as he put his arm over Eduardo's now hairy chest.

Eduardo settled into his usual position beneath Harvey's armpit. "Mmmmmaaaaannngiiiiiinnnnnahh ... " he said.

Harvey sighed, then smiled. He was just going to have to get used to it.

The Fireside Bright

He'd be called a bear these days, but in 1969 when this happened, the only bears on the landscape were named Yogi or Smokey. He was tall and stocky, with blue eyes that gleamed when he laughed, which was a lot. Dan Brankowski (not his real name) was perpetually amused—unlike my unceasingly dour father—and his laugh was both deep and deeply infectious. It always started as a dry chuckle in his throat, gaining momentum until it rocked his hairy barrel chest.

And I got a chance to see a lot of that chest while he was washing his wife's Delta 88 and cutting his lawn, sweat trickling down through the matted hair into the densely forested territory around the waistband of his faded denim cutoffs. His legs were even hairier—lean, tan and muscular beneath the fur. I used to jack off while watching him from my bedroom window. I wanted to see him naked more than anything else in the world.

I was thirteen.

He was thirty-six.

I had no plan, just a fervent hope. In my barely adolescent optimism, I figured the more I hung out with him, the better my chances would be, but I had no idea how to make that happen. No matter. They had just moved in and were in the "getting acquainted" stage with my folks. It was only June, and I had all summer to achieve my goal. I just had to be patient and watch for my opening.

I'd figured out I was attracted to men a few years before that, but I'd known from almost the beginning that I was somehow different from other boys. I just didn't see things the way they did. I didn't like playing with them, either. I preferred to spend time by myself—an easy feat for an only child—reading books or playing with my Tonka trucks.

When puberty kicked my hormones into overdrive, the difference became apparent. So I did what I always did when I couldn't figure something out by myself—I went to the library. And that's where I found out what I was, as well as what popular culture told me what would happen to me should I continue down that path. I didn't believe a word of it.

It made no sense to me that I should be considered "less than" just because I liked boys instead of girls. My parents did not raise me with any particular religious beliefs, so I didn't have that hurdle to overcome. Still, I thought it prudent not to advertise my preference. I'd wait until I was older and could live as I chose. Until then, I'd put it on the back burner and out of my mind.

Until Dan, that is. Ever since the spring day he and his wife and little girl moved in next door, I'd been able to think of nothing else. He not only brought my libido to the front burner, he turned it up to full boil. But it wasn't just his (I thought) smoldering good looks and fascinatingly furry body that attracted me—it was also his jovial, imperturbable nature. Nothing seemed to bother him very much.

No matter how often the lawnmower or the car would break down, he'd smile and shrug, rubbing his stubbly chin once or twice before shuffling off to the shed for his toolbox. And I never heard him raise his voice to his wife Marjorie, a shrill, hovering confluence of dissatisfactions and "female troubles" she'd relate to my mother in occasional hushed conversation over the fence.

Mid-June brought the first bad wind and rainstorm of the season, knocking down several big branches of the Brankowski's elm tree. The next morning, Dan got out there with his chainsaw and axe and began making firewood. Only too happy to volunteer me, my mother semaphored to him over the fence.

"He can help you with that," she said, pointing at me once he'd stopped the saw.

He smiled widely at me. "You sure, buddy?"

"Yeah," I replied. "No problem."

Great. C'mon over, then."

I hopped the fence and took the work gloves he handed me. These days, I'd be tricked out with all manner of ear and eye protection, but that wasn't backyard protocol then. Satisfied I'd be out of her hair for a good part of the day, my mother turned to go back into the house. She had one more thing to add before she left.

"You know, Dan," she said over her shoulder, "you're always welcome to use the pool. Maybe you'd like to take a dip after you're finished."

He grinned again and my knees went weak. "I just might do that, thanks much." She waved without looking back as she walked towards the house.

"You ready to work, buddy?" he asked, the heady smell of his sweat mingling with the spearmint from the gum he chewed.

"Sure."

"Well, all right. Let's get to it." He cut the branches with the chainsaw while I stacked them up against one wall of the huge toolshed at the very back edge of his property. The sun came out, turning the humid morning hot and sticky. Dan unbuttoned his denim shirt, letting it hang free as the chips and sawdust flew. I had stacked almost all the wood when he stopped the chainsaw and motioned me over.

"You wanna give 'er a try?" he asked, thrusting the chainsaw at me.

Power tools had always scared the bejusus out of me. My dad wouldn't let me near his. "Mr. Brankowski, I never--"

"Dan. Just Dan."

The chainsaw hung between us; a challenge I'd have to accept whether I liked it or not. I tried to smile as I took hold of its grips. Dan let go and I nearly dropped it, the blade clunking on the branch.

"It's a little heavy." Dan chuckled. "But you'll get used to it. You start it with this cord here, just like a lawnmower. Hold it with both hands and cut straight through the wood real slow so the chain doesn't jam. Let's do one together."

He positioned himself in back of me, taking my scrawny hands in his massive ones. He put my hand on the cord and we jerked it back. The chainsaw roared, but the noise was no sensation at all compared to the scent of him and the rough feel of his chest hair on the back of my neck. I immediately got a boner, but my cock wasn't all that was reacting.

I felt an incredible sense of security and inclusion nestled between his chest and the chainsaw. I was not being turned away for once. I was not being cautioned. I was not being made fun of for not knowing what I was doing. Before we had even sawed through one branch, I knew I was in love with Dan. Well, maybe not love—more like infatuation. But to a thirteen-year-old boy starved for male attention, the two weren't all that different.

I sawed off four or five logs, Dan encouraging me and correcting my technique until he figured I had it. Then he started stacking. We worked like that until most of the big branches were chopped up, then he took over again and raced through the little ones while I stacked. In a couple of hours, the job was finished.

"Nice work, buddy," he said while clapping me on the shoulder. "How about some lunch? All this yard work gives you an appetite."

I followed him through the back door into the kitchen. He washed up at the sink and bade me do the same while he poked around the fridge and began taking sandwich stuff out. As I soaped up, rinsed off and dried my hands on a dishtowel, he said, "Marge took Cindy to her sister's for the afternoon, so we're on our own."

Soon he had two plates of bologna sandwiches with mayo on white bread with krinkly cut potato chips and a jar of pickles. He grabbed two Cokes and two bottles of Schlitz and handed them to me. "Let's eat out in the shed," he said with a grin. "The kitchen's too clean."

"That's some mighty fine chainsawin'." He nodded towards the pile of wood stacked against the shed. "You sure you never done that before?"

"No sir."

"Stop that 'sir,' stuff," he replied, pushing the shed door open with his backside. "I told you, it's Dan."

"Dan." I repeated, following him in. I hoped I didn't sound as moon-eyed as I felt.

The shed was even bigger than it looked on the outside, which was considerable. Two huge, bare windows on the back wall let in air and light with one smaller, curtained one at the front. The inside was roomy, with space enough for a sofa, an easy chair and a card table on the right and yard equipment and tools hanging on the left. The whole place smelled like sweat, motor oil, and earth-clotted metal. And right next to the sofa was a record player and a cabinet of records.

"Go on, grab yourself a seat."

I put the bottles down on the card table as Dan unloaded the plates and the jar of pickles. "Coke or beer?" he asked, grinning.

"Coke, thanks," I said distractedly as I went over to the cabinet of records and started looking at the album spines. I had no idea who most of the artists were—Ramblin' Jack Elliott, Dave Van Ronk, Pete Seeger, Leadbelly, Camp and Gibson, Muddy Waters, Ian and Sylvia, Howlin' Wolf, The Weavers—the only one I had even a passing familiarity with was Woody Guthrie and that was by way of Bob Dylan.

"Good man. Don't start drinkin' until you're married and you got a reason." I heard him open the bottles and put them on the table. "I don't think you're gonna find anything you like over there. It's folk and blues music, mostly."

"I like Bob Dylan." I went back to the table and sat down.

Dan interrupted a long, healthy swig of beer. "Bob Dylan is a goddamn *thief.*" He gestured towards the cabinet with his Schlitz. "And *these* are the people he stole from." Scooting me aside, he bent down, made a selection and removed the album from its paper sleeve, blowing on it before he put it on the record player. He dropped the tone arm down and opened up a whole new world for me.

"Listen and learn, son." He wore a wry smile as he handed me the album jacket. It was Howlin' Wolf's *Moanin' in the Moonlight*, with a simple line drawing of a wolf baying at the moon, and the song was "How Many More Years." The barrelhouse piano and sax intro was cool enough, but when I heard Howlin' Wolf's voice, the hair on my arms stood up. It was beautifully coarse, a sandpaper rasp that had a music and a meaning all its own.

And I fell in love for the *second* time that day.

We went back to the table and had lunch, Wolf's mournful wail filling the room and punctuating Dan's lecture about blues and folk music, delivered between huge, manly bites of sandwich, the crunching of chips and loud gulps of Schlitz. Dan's appetite was huge—he went back to the kitchen for two more sandwiches and ate them both—and he was prone to loud, assured overstatements that sounded convincing enough to be truths even if they weren't.

But I bought them.

I turned my back on Bob Dylan that very day (though we've since made up) and eagerly accepted the five albums Dan loaned me for further study: the aforementioned Wolf album along with his first, simply titled *Howlin' Wolf,* with a picture of a rocking chair on the cover, a two-record Folkway set of Woody Guthrie tunes, Dave Van Ronk's *Gambler's Blues* and *The Weavers at Carnegie Hall.*

I must have played each on my little tinny-speakered kids record player at least five times by the next morning when I showed up at the shed eager for more. I loved them all, but particularly Van Ronk's quirky voice and the magnificent blend of harmony and politics that was The Weavers. I was a more than apt pupil for Dan's teaching.

And he had a lot of time to teach me. He was on disability leave from his job because of the blinding headaches he was sometimes prone to—so we spent a good part of that summer together working around his yard or mine, playing ball in the park, splashing around in our swimming pool, going on errands in his beat-up Ford pickup (which he also taught me to drive) and, of course, listening to those amazing records in his shed.

We were together so much that my father actually got a bit jealous. Not jealous enough to spend any kind of time with me but enough to make snide comments during dinner. He and my mom fought about it. "He needs to be with *some* kind of father," she said, hitting at her favorite spot below the belt.

Dan never got frustrated with me. He never got mad at me or called me names or lashed out at me or made me feel inferior for not knowing about things he liked. He answered my questions as we worked on his wife's car or his pickup or the eternally broken lawnmower, listening to the Detroit Tigers games on the radio. He let me hold the wrenches and talked me through the process and didn't snatch it all away and do it himself, swearing and grumbling when I screwed up.

But my original goal had permutated. Just seeing him naked wasn't enough—I longed for some sort of sexual contact. Maybe my thirteen year old naivete confused sex with intimacy, maybe I wanted to give him some kind of pleasure in return for all he had given me, or maybe I was just horny.

In spite of the amount of time we spent together, no opportunity or opening had appeared. Whenever we used the pool, he came over in his trunks and went home to change. But in between, we laughed and splashed as I stole glances at him and we talked about everything. Except sex. Never girls or anything to do with sex. I wondered if he was interested in the subject at all.

At the end of August, with Labor Day and a return to school just around the corner, that question was finally answered. I had been downtown shopping with my mother and had scored a copy of *Muddy Waters at Newport*, which Dan didn't even have. Excited about my find, I hopped the fence and ran to the shed as soon as we got home. I burst through the door to find Dan sitting on the sofa with his pants around his ankles, one hand holding a *Penthouse* and the other holding his cock.

Startled, he dropped the magazine and stood up, his unbuttoned denim shirt falling off one shoulder. "Shit!" he said as he pulled up his pants and tried to stuff himself back into them—no mean feat considering the size of his tool.

"I'm sorry," I said. "You told me not to bother knocking." And he had.

"I know. It's okay—you just..." He sat down again without finishing his sentence.

"You want me to leave?" Okay, I should have just left. You would have, right? But I was praying he'd say no. I had no idea what would happen from here, but this was the closest I'd come to my goal, and I wasn't backing away from it—not with the hottest guy I'd ever seen in my life sitting beside me all horned up, the top clasp on his jeans still undone.

"No, it's okay." His voice trembled. He pointed at the album I still clutched "Whatcha got there?"

"*Muddy Waters at Newport*." The *Penthouse* lay between us, open to the very picture he'd been masturbating to.

"Great. I'll put it on the stack." He opened it up and took it over to the stereo, and I saw my chance evaporating. Determined to keep hope alive, I picked up the magazine and began to feel myself through my shorts. I was already half hard from seeing Dan, so it was no time before I sprang fully to life. While his back was turned, I eased my cock out of its confines.

What was that look he had on his face when he looked over and saw me? I don't remember. But he didn't tell me to stop. In fact, he sat back down on the sofa beside me and began rubbing himself again. Before long, we were both jacking, looking and touching ourselves and each other. Just two guys having a wank.

When we were both spent, I drew my knees up on the sofa and curled up in his lap, resting my beardless cheek on his forested chest as he stroked my hair. Neither of us said a word. We listened to the Weavers finishing up their Carnegie Hall concert. The last song was Leadbelly's "Goodnight Irene," one my mother used to sing to me when I was a little boy.

The chorus echoed through the shed, and then Pete Seeger reached the line where the narrator exhorts the gambler to stop rambling and staying out late at night; suggesting he go home to his wife and family and stay there by "the fireside bright." Dan's huge chest began to quake. But it wasn't mirth that caused the motion. He was crying. His sobs increased in volume and intensity so that I could barely make out the words he was uttering. But I heard them all the same.

"Not again. I can't let it happen *again*." His chest was heaving so wildly I could no longer rest there. I sat up and begged him to tell me what was wrong, but he only repeated what he'd said. I knew I was in over my head. I'd opened up something I had no idea how to deal with; something deep within Dan that had been better left closed. I pulled up my pants, frightened and afraid not for myself, but of what I had done to a man I considered my friend. And how I had irrevocably broken that friendship. Things would never be the same between us.

I ran out of the shed out into the field in back of our house where I sat amidst the tall wild grass and cried. And when I thought I'd cried myself out, I picked myself up and went back home. But I cried all the way there as well. I ignored my mother, ran to my room and shut the door, taking my pillow from the bed and sitting in my closet. I buried my face in it and cried even harder.

I didn't come out for dinner. I told my mom I didn't feel well. She knew something was wrong, but she also knew, with that uncanny prescience mothers have, that she could do nothing for me. I had to work it out for myself. Even my dad –evidently sent by her to ferret out the reason for my anguish—paused outside my door. He did not, however, come in. He watched me in silence then walked away.

That was the end of my friendship with Dan. There were no more errands in town, no more fixing cars, no more splashing in the pool, no more amazing music in the shed. His headaches began to worsen and he was diagnosed with a brain tumor. The doctors operated and botched the job. Dan's headaches were replaced by a bland, blank stare and a struggle to respond to the simplest questions. They moved away by Thanksgiving.

I can't really say I learned about sex that day. What I learned about was the *power* of sex—the way it can obsess, the way it can control and the way it can destroy. I learned about consequences. I learned about regret. I learned that not all goals are worth achieving.

And I learned how quickly innocence can dissipate in the humid air of a hot summer day.

Snapshots

Benny demanded they get his husband up.

The nurse behind the desk smiled a bureaucrat's tight grin as she patted her hair into place. "That's not a very good idea, Mr. Hoffman. Mr. Santini has had a difficult night. His breathing was--"

"I don't care how his breathing was. I want him up."

"That's not in the best interests of the patient, Mr. Hoffman. Besides, it's morning shift change."

He put the scrapbook he was carrying on the counter and folded his hands over it slowly and deliberately. He did not smile as he leaned in closer. "I am your patient's husband, and I pay top dollar for his care here at Morningside Heights. I did not build that wing off to your left because I had no idea what to do with my money," he continued. "I did it so I could walk in here whenever I want and see my husband – cleaned, dressed and in his wheelchair. I suggest you find an aide to accomplish that."

The nurse sighed and picked up the phone as Benny paced, scraping his fingernails over the textured surface of his scrapbook as if brushing a snare drum. She spoke curtly into the phone and placed it back with exaggerated care in its cradle, throwing an annoyed glance at him. "I just sent Odessa down there."

"Isn't Carlos around?"

"No, he won't be in for fifteen minutes or so."

"We don't really like Odessa," Benny said with a frown as he turned and strode toward his wing. Tucking the scrapbook beneath his arm, he spoke to the nurse over his shoulder, getting louder as he went down the hall. "I'll get him up myself. Mr. Santini and I will be having breakfast

together, so tell Carlos to bring two trays when he gets in." The nurse
saluted Benny behind his back.

He stole sidelong glances into half-opened doors, glimpsing withered
figures slumped in wheelchairs or sunk in the stiff linens of mechanical
beds that suggested decline rather than repose. Pumps wheezed and
monitors beeped, playing an antiseptic counterpoint to the rhythm of
Benny's hard-soled steps on the tile floor while old man Benino bleated
out his usual melody in a smoky, hysterical baritone.

"Ohmi*god*! Ohmi*god*! Ohmi*god*!" he sang—softly for now, but it
was early and his Ativan was still working.

"Dunno why he want you up this early, but we gotta get you in this
chair," Odessa was saying as Benny approached. He paused outside the
room, standing and listening to her grunts of exertion. "C'mon now,
Mister Doug—grab hold on my neck and push off'n the bed when I get to
three. One. Two. *Three*." Benny heard the zip-slide of fabric and the rattle
of the wheelchair as she settled him in it.

He waited a few more seconds to see if Odessa was going to say
anything he could report to the charge nurse, but all he heard was the
splash of water in the basin and the snap of a dry towel. "We got to get you
cleaned up," she said as he pushed the door open wide.

"I'll take it from here, Odessa. Thank you."

The tall black woman stood up to her full height, washcloth in hand,
narrowing her dark eyes at Benny for a moment before regaining a more
dispassionate look. "You stayin' to feed Mister Doug breakfast?" she
asked as she dropped the cloth back in the basin.

"I am. Carlos will be in with the trays in a bit."

"Mmm-hmmm," Odessa said, picking up the basin and dumping it in
the sink. Her back to Benny, she wrung out the washcloth and spread it on
the side of the basin to dry. "I'll be back to check on you before I leave,
Mister Doug."

"You don't like me much, do you Odessa?" he asked as she turned
to leave.

"Ohmi*GOD*! Ohmi*GOD*! Ohmi*GOD*!"

She stood in the doorway and looked at him for a long time before
replying. "What I like ain't got nothin' to do with it. Mister Doug

is sufferin'—sugar diabetes took his legs, he can't talk, he can hardly breathe. His heart stopped three, four times, but they take him off to the hospital and get him goin' again cause you signed some papers sayin' they got to. Be best off if things happen like they's supposed to. Sometimes you just got to let go." She took a breath as if there were more she had to say on the subject, but she didn't elaborate. "You want this door closed?"

"If you wouldn't mind." His face flushed with anger, he crossed the room to open the drapes.

The pinkish yellow light of dawn fell strong on the figure in the wheelchair, but he didn't even blink. Doug's dull blue eyes sank so far into his skull, they were shaded by their sockets. Long, greying hair fell dankly around his sallow face, his patchy beard growing in uneven and unkempt on parchment yellow skin.

His leg stumps stuck out in front of him, balancing him awkwardly on the seat of the chair. Too short to reach the armrest, the stump of his left arm hung useless at his side. His right arm—his only intact appendage—was crossed over his thin chest in a permanent crook, the hand twisted into a discolored claw with an ulcerated back.

Benny tossed the scrapbook on the bed and pulled up the threadbarely upholstered chair from under the window. "Sorry to hear you had a rough night," he said, sitting down beside him. "I slept very well, myself. I rented the most superb boy from Gino. Oh, I know you don't care for Gino, but he gets the most magnificent boys. This one was blonde and gorgeous. Just the way you like them."

Doug stared ahead.

"You *are* listening to me, aren't you?"

Doug's head turned, a low grating squeak coming from his throat like a rusty gate hinge swiveling towards Benny. Then an almost imperceptible nod. The only real motion seemed to be the hate emanating from his small eyes. His claw hand began to tremble.

Benny smiled. "There's no reason you can't speak. You're just being stubborn. I often wonder what you'd say if you'd bring yourself to talk to me. Would you tell me how much you want to die?"

Doug turned his head again, continuing to stare impassively ahead.

"No? You wouldn't give me the satisfaction, would you? You just sit there, silently enduring. And you have them all fooled. Odessa, the doctors, the nurses—they all hand you their sympathy as if you were worth it, but they don't know, do they? They don't know the man in those pictures."

He nodded toward a series of framed photos sitting on top of the TV set, still-lifes of smiling times in sunnier places. Benny got up and brought over the hinged triptych in the middle of the grouping, studio-taken color portraits of Benny, Doug and a blonde, blue-eyed little boy in the middle panel.

"These were taken right after we got Michael, remember? What a sweet boy, despite being your late sister's. Too bad you never took time to get to know him. You left it to me to raise him, wipe his nose, teach him right from wrong. He's never come to see you here, has he? I didn't think so."

A soft knock came from the door. "Well-timed," Benny snorted, "but I doubt it's Michael. It's probably Carlos. Come in."

"Two breakfast trays," said Carlos, wheeling in a small cart. He was short and thin. Even though he looked young enough to be a teenager, Benny knew he was already married with three kids. His brown skin was soft and lustrous against the tan of his uniform, and he smiled at Benny.

"Well, hello there." Benny rose, rolled the cart away from Carlos and wrapped him in a big bear hug, covering his neck with kisses. Carlos pulled away, seriousness clouding his brown eyes as he frowned and gestured at Doug in his wheelchair.

Benny waved his concern away and pulled a white envelope stuffed with bills out of his back pocket. "Oh, don't mind about Doug. He doesn't care. It wouldn't do him much good anyway." He handed the envelope to Carlos. "This is for the stuff you did around the house the other day. I told you I'd make it worth your while."

"OHMIGOD! OHMIGOD! OHMIGOD!" Benino sang.

Carlos blushed and started to stammer something, but Benny cut him off. "Now, I don't want you to think it's *just* for…well, the yard looks spectacular and that back wall of the garage looks brand new. It might need a second coat, though," he said, moving closer. "Maybe you can come again tomorrow."

"Maybe," Carlos replied hesitantly, watching Doug. "We'll see."

Doug continued staring at them silently, his claw hand now resting on his chest. His eyes tracked between Benny and Carlos like he was watching a slow tennis match.

"Oh," Benny said with slight surprise, as if he'd been expecting a different response. "Well, you have my number. Just give me a call." Carlos just nodded, not taking his eyes off Doug until he turned and walked out, closing the door behind him.

He took one of the trays off the cart and put it on a rollaway table that he positioned near the wheelchair. Sitting on the bed, he took the cover off Doug's breakfast plate—fried eggs, hash browns, three strips of bacon and toast—and removed the plastic lid from the coffee.

"That looks good," Benny said, ripping two packets of sugar open and pouring them into Doug's coffee. "I just hope the eggs aren't too hard for you. I know you like them runny." He cut into them with a fork, but no yolk oozed. "Uh-oh." He speared a piece of egg and stabbed some potatoes on the end of the fork. "Open wide."

Doug opened his mouth, showing yellowed teeth and a pasty, grey tongue as Benny fed him. "These eggs remind me of the first time I made you breakfast, remember? It was at your old apartment on Polk Street. We'd been out drinking Saturday night at the Gaslight. We closed the bar and went back to your place to fuck the night away and then Sunday morning I got up and made you eggs, but they were too hard. That was the first time you ever hit me. Bacon?"

He nodded, chewing slowly for a moment then opening his mouth again. Benny broke a piece of bacon in half and laid it on the half-chewed egg on Doug's tongue.

"I should have walked out right then," Benny said. "Walked out and never looked back, but I knew I could change you. Then your sister died and Michael needed a father. You couldn't have done it alone."

Doug motioned for the coffee with his claw hand, but Benny reached over him and got the scrapbook from the bed. "I don't think I have any shots of that place," he said, turning pages filled with Instamatic snaps of body parts—close-ups of Benny's bruised arms, bloodied foreheads and blackened eyes. Most of the pictures showed multiple injuries, like a rogue's gallery of car accidents. Except these hadn't happened in cars, and they hadn't been accidents.

A whimper escaped Doug's throat and he tried to turn away, but Benny moved the scrapbook closer, knocking over the coffee. A steaming puddle of brown spread across the tray and leaked down into Doug's lap.

"What's the matter?" Benny asked. "You shouldn't be so squeamish. It's not like you haven't seen these pictures before. I rather like having them all gathered in one place. It's more organized than that damn shoebox. I can flip right to something if you have a question. I have a question for you, though. Do you remember *giving* these to me as vividly as I remember *getting* them? Or were you too fucking drunk?"

His whimper continued unabated, and he shut his eyes. Benny grabbed the back of his neck and gave it a hard shake as he leaned down and whispered into Doug's ear. "Open your eyes." The noise from Doug's throat choked to a stop, and he followed Benny's orders with a hateful glare.

"That's better," Benny cooed. "That's the man I know and love." He flipped a few pages in the scrapbook. "I just want to show you one more, and then we'll finish breakfast. You haven't seen this one for a while." He stopped at a series of innocuous pictures of smiling men posing with Benny, holding drinks and cigarettes, their faces harsh in the glare of the flash.

"You remember this, don't you? My book release party. The one we had to celebrate *Smith's Retreat*. You know, I *still* get royalty checks from it every now and then." He pointed to a picture in the upper left hand corner that looked much like the others, but Benny was not in it. It was just Doug and an older man with a walrus moustache. The older man was smiling but Doug faced the camera with a dour expression.

"That's you and my publisher, Martin," Benny said, "and right after I took this, you told him, 'Benny couldn't write captions for coloring books.' And you repeated that to anyone who'd listen all night long. One of the reasons I wrote that book was to make you proud of me, but how could you have been proud of me when you weren't even proud of yourself? Toast?"

Doug opened his mouth, not even nodding this time. The hate was gone from his eyes, as was everything else. He bit off the end of the toast triangle Benny offered him and chewed.

"I haven't written another word since," Benny said, wiping his fingers on the cushion of the chair. "I can't. Every time I try, I think about what you said. Those seven little words hurt me more than anything else you ever did to me. There's one book left in me, though. And I swear I'll write it. I just don't have an ending yet. But I will. Coffee? Oh, you spilled yours. Take mine."

Benny held the cup to Doug's lips. He drank slowly at first, then with more assurance as he watched Benny with wary eyes.

—⟋⟍—

"How long was he in the…ah…"

"Nursing home," Benny supplied for the tall grey-haired woman in the black dress and veil. He couldn't remember her name, but he and Doug had met her at a fundraiser. In fact, most of the people in attendance were 'fundraiser friends.' "Just under four years."

"My," she said, shaking her head as the waiter passed by with a tray of drinks. She snatched one deftly. "Has it been *that* long since you two were out of circulation? Well, you must come to the Cheshire Ball next month. You should feel up to going out by then. It's for the GLBT Center, you know."

"Yes, I know." *We were on the committee that started it fifteen years ago*, he thought. He ached to hit her. He wanted to slap that martini out of her hand, break the glass and grind the shards in her face. But the glass was really plastic. And he was a coward. Always had been. "Excuse me," he said instead as he turned away from her. "I just saw someone I need to talk to."

But he did not talk to anyone. He walked over to the big floor to ceiling window and stared out at Denver's skyline, watching the lights blink on and off in different parts of the office building across the street.

They reminded him of the display lights on the monitors in Doug's room at Morningside. Only now those were all dark.

Maybe I need to get away. Move someplace else and start all over again. But where? I hate moving. It will just interrupt my routine, and I really need *that right now. That's the only way I'm ever going to start this book. Or finish it. I should stay right here and do what needs to be done.* Firmly resolved for the moment, he turned away from the window to get a drink. That's when he saw them.

They were at the funeral, of course. Michael and that woman. They'd come late, getting out of their rented car halfway through the service and lingering on the fringes of the crowd like strangers. *Michael shouldn't be hanging back like that. He has more right to be here than the idiots from the nursing home who cried and grieved as if they had a fucking clue.*

Michael was every bit the handsome man Benny knew he'd grow up to be. His hair had changed from blonde to reddish-brown, but his eyes still blazed so blue he could see them from across the room. She was definitely older than Michael, with little makeup and lifeless frizzed-out brown hair that fell around her face in no discernable arrangement.

He finally locked eyes with Michael, who leaned over and touched the woman's shoulder, whispering into her ear. She then searched the room until she saw Benny as well. Her dress floated behind them like a dark blue contrail as they weaved through the crowd of mourners and servers.

"Hello Michael," Benny said on their approach.

"Hello Benny." His voice was deep and rich. An announcer's voice. Benny had always hoped he go into TV news or something like that. He was good-looking enough, even with that scar on his forehead and the accompanying one on his cheek. Benny wondered if Michael even remembered how he got those.

"Is that all?" the woman said, "'Hello?' Not even a hug or a handshake?"

Michael did not take his eyes off Benny. "We don't exactly have a hug or a handshake kind of relationship."

"No. We don't." They stared at each other silently for a few seconds as if reloading, waiting to fire once the right trigger was pulled. "Is this your wife?" Benny asked, breaking away to signal the waiter for a drink.

"Yes. Alice, this is Benny Hoffman. Benny, this is my wife, Alice."

"Very glad to meet you," Benny said. "How long have you been married, Michael?"

"Three months."

"It's an absolute honor to meet you, Mr. Hoffman," Alice said, her smile wide enough for Benny to see the braces on her rear molars. "*Smith's Retreat* was a very important book to me."

It was Benny's turn to smile widely. "Well," he said, accepting a martini from the waiter, "it's nice to meet a fan."

"I've always wondered why you never did another book. Have you ever thought about writing something else?"

Benny tried his self-deprecating chuckle. He used to be pretty good at it. "My dear, I *think* about it every day. The problem is *doing* it. But you'll be pleased to hear I have something on the drawing board right now."

"You do?" Michael said.

"That's right. Doug's passing freed me up, so to speak."

"Is it along the lines of *Smith's Retreat*?"

"Yes and no."

"Oh." She sounded disappointed. "You know, that book was just so true to life, and the characters were wonderful—especially some of the women in the shelter. Did you have any experience with domestic abuse before you wrote it?"

Benny and Michael exchanged quick glances as Benny tried to formulate a response. *He wouldn't have told her anything,* Benny thought. *He'd always been too ashamed. And she wouldn't have asked if she'd known.* He shrugged. "Writers make things up. That's our job."

"Well, you did it beautifully. Michael, would you get me a Coke from the bar? I don't feel like alcohol tonight."

"Um...yeah, sure," he said after a moment's hesitation. He looked like he was going to say something to Benny, but he stopped. "Be right back."

As Michael left, Alice nervously brushed her hair back behind her ear. "Mr. Hoffman ..."

"Benny."

"Benny. I don't know how to start. When the nursing home called and said Mr. Santini had passed away, I practically had to *force* Michael to come out here. He never talks about his childhood. He doesn't even want children of his own. I'm...well...I'm hoping to change that, but I don't know. He's a sweet, wonderful, warm man but there's something hidden inside that I can't touch. Something dark. I was hoping you could tell me something."

What to say, what to say... "Michael came to us when he was very young. His mother, Doug's sister Naomi, and his father were killed in a car accident. As provided in their will, Doug became his guardian. But Doug didn't know much about raising kids. He was all about working and providing and leaving the details to me. There weren't many gay couples with children back then, so I was presented with some rather unique challenges I had no idea how to meet. And I'm sure you know yourself how willful Michael can be. He was worse as a child. I know I made mistakes. They were hard to prevent, but I did the best I could. Has he said something to you?"

They both glanced over at the bar. Michael was watching them, not paying attention to the bartender. "No," Alice replied. "That's just the point. He never talks about you or Mr. Santini. I thought coming out here would spark something, but he's even quieter than usual. Unreachable."

Benny shrugged. "I don't know what to say about that. He's always been distant. Very self-contained. I figured he'd grow out of it, but apparently not. I'm sorry. I wish I could be more help."

"It is what it is," Alice said with an unconvincing smile. Benny winced. He hated that phrase. Looking towards the bar again, he saw that Michael was gone. He whipped his head around and suddenly felt Michael's presence at his shoulder.

"What's the big discussion?" Michael asked, handing Alice her drink.

"Nothing dear. We were just talking about *Smith's Retreat*, but I'm sure he must be tired of the praise by now."

"Whatever gave you *that* impression?" Benny said, grinning.

Michael wasn't grinning. Benny couldn't remember the last time he saw Michael grin. "Look, Benny," he said, "I just want to say I'm sorry about Doug. I know you two...well, no. Actually, I don't know anything about you two when it comes right down to it. Maybe I'm not even sorry he's gone. I don't know. It's just what you say, right? Maybe I shouldn't even have come here, but I thought…well, I should pay my respects, even though respect is the last thing that comes to mind when I think about you."

"*Michael*," Alice breathed, "what a terrible thing to say."

The look Michael turned on her froze Benny solid. He'd seen it so many times before Doug's explosions, coming up from some deep, black crater. He thought he'd beaten Michael's anger out of him, but he should have known better. That kind of madness never really goes away. It rests, coiled inside, waiting for the right moment.

"We should go now," Michael said to Alice. She didn't seem to notice the look on his face or the warning in his voice. Benny then realized Michael hadn't hit her yet. But tonight…

It was nice to meet you, Mr. Hoffman," she said with a smile of blissful unawareness.

Get the fuck out, he wanted to tell her. *It's going to happen to you just like it happened to me. It's a trap, it's a cheat, and it will steal your life away. Find your own retreat and guard its entrance with all the strength you have. Learn from your mistake and for Chrissakes don't repeat it with someone else.* "The pleasure was mine, Alice," he said instead. Because he was a coward.

"Goodbye, Benny," Michael said.

"Goodbye, Michael." He and Alice walked off, not looking back. Michael had hold of her arm, rushing her through the crowd so fast she barely had time to put her Coke on an empty table.

He sipped his martini and turned back towards the window. A car far below was speeding down the street, weaving in and out around the other traffic in a hellbent rush to get somewhere. Benny thought it might be Michael and Alice racing away from him except they hadn't had time to make it downstairs yet. *How could things have gone so wrong with Michael?* he wondered.

How could things have gone so wrong with me?

—⁂—

Benny stared at the lamp on his desk, forcing himself to look at the brightness of the bulb until his eyes hurt. When he turned away, the ghost image obscured the words on the screen of his laptop. *They look better that way*, he thought. Breaking his own rule about not smoking in the apartment, he lit a cigarette and balanced it on the rim of an empty shot glass nearby. He put his fingers on the keyboard again.

He wrote: *I thought his dying would fix everything, but the months since the service have shown me how terribly wrong that was. It fixed nothing. The serenity I thought was in sight has eluded me again. The chemistry that once alchemized my thoughts into words seems to have vanished as well, rendering the story I anticipated telling lifeless and impotent on the page.*

"Are you coming back to bed?" he heard from across the apartment.

Benny didn't respond. He took a drag from the Marlboro, tapped some ash into the shot glass and blew smoke at the screen as he reviewed his paragraph. By the time he decided it was crap but he needed to have something written, the boy had padded into the room and was standing beside the chair. He stood so close that Benny could feel his coarse pubic hair and the head of his semi-erect dick on his shoulder. "I said are you coming back to bed?"

"No."

"Oh." He didn't leave. "What are you writing?"

"It's either a first chapter or a suicide note. I won't know which until I've finished it—a process your presence is delaying."

"Whatever," the boy said. "If you're not comin' back to bed, I might as well get outta here, but don't think it's gonna be cheaper. It's the same as always."

Benny reached into the center drawer of the desk and stuck his hand into the pile of money inside, coming up with two hundred dollar bills that he threw over his shoulder. "As you said—whatever.'"

The money made the boy a bit more agreeable. He smiled as he bent over and picked it up. "You want a bump?" he asked. "I got some left."

"Not for me. I'd like a clear head for once. Feel free to do as much as you like, however. As you're getting ready to leave."

He shrugged and walked away as Benny took another drag, exhaled and put his fingers on the keyboard once again.

I try to distract myself, hoping the life I want to have will magically appear if I stop looking so hard for it, but nothing helps—not the alcohol, not the drugs, not the sex. None of them holds any relief or diversion for me anymore. How could it? How could I lose myself in any of it when I was never able to find myself in the first place?

Benny heard the boy pissing in the bathroom and the sound of running water after, and he thought about joining him for more coke and another fuck session. But the boy had already been paid and Benny didn't want to encourage him to stay any longer. He needed to be alone. He had to get his thoughts down while he could. Stubbing the cigarette out in the shot glass, he went back to work.

I miss him. Even worse, I miss the anger—both his and mine. Anger has such a delicious, vital edge. But it's demanding. Its energy consumes your own, requiring more and more fuel from your reason until it becomes your life. Once it burns itself out, you're left spent and exhausted. Empty. Nothing matters except the well you cannot fill.

Benny heard shattering glass followed by a thud. He raced into the bathroom and found the naked boy face up on the floor next to the sink. His upper lip, still dusted with cocaine, twitched a few times before falling still. His brown eyes were open but lifeless as a thin trickle of blood seeped from the back of his head along the grout lines of the tile.

He bent over and put his ear to the boy's chest but had no idea what he should be hearing or what he should be doing. He had some vague idea of mouth-to-mouth resuscitation but would not have known if he was even doing it right. In the end, Benny settled for a few useless thumps on his chest and one last look at his death-shrunken cock before going back to his desk.

Picking up his cell phone to call 911, a thought struck him. He put the phone down again and went back to the keyboard. *And now I have a dead rent boy in my bathroom,* he typed. He read everything over again but didn't change anything. He opened the center drawer of the desk, reached underneath the pile of money and withdrew a key.

He unlocked the bottom right drawer of the desk and took out the .38 he'd bought to protect himself, feeling its heft in his hand. He opened the chamber to make sure it was loaded, then he snapped it back in place and stuck the barrel in his mouth. It felt cool, slick and oily between his lips.

Is this the only option you have? he asked himself. *Is this really the best response to the situation at hand?*

No, the answer came back, *but when has that ever made a difference?* And he pulled the trigger.

—⚏—

"Is Mr. Hoffman up yet?" Michael asked the nurse at the desk.

"Yes," she answered with an officious smile. "Odessa just finished feeding him breakfast. You must be Michael Donovan."

"That's right."

"How long has it been since you've seen Mr. Hoffman?"

"Not since the hospital," he said.

"So you pretty much know the situation. Your uncle is a very lucky man."

Michael couldn't help but grimace. "I guess that all depends on how you define luck, doesn't it?"

"His paralysis could have been much worse," she said. "Most of his motor skills are gone and speech is beyond him, but he can think and see and hear. That's quite a marvel considering the extent of his injuries."

"Yes," Michael said. "In that respect, he's very lucky to be here. Say, you wouldn't happen to know of a place for rent around here, would you? I'm looking for somewhere to stay until I find something permanent."

"Oh, are you and your wife moving here to take care of your uncle?"

"My wife?"

The nurse gave him a confused look. "Your paperwork says you're married," she replied, shuffling files on the desk, trying to find the right one.

"Recently divorced."

"Oh, I'm sorry."

"Don't be." He looked down at his wedding ring. "I guess I should stop wearing this, for starters." He didn't take it off.

The nurse smiled and shrugged. "Well, in any case I really don't know of any places to stay in the area. You can always post something on the bulletin board if you want." She handed him a slip of paper. "Feel free to come and see Mr. Hoffman any time you like. He's down the hall to the left all the way at the end."

"OHMIGOD! OHMIGOD! OHMIGOD!" Boroni directed.

"Thanks," he said. "I'll just pop in and say hello for right now. Could I make sure we get some alone time for about fifteen minutes?"

"Of course. I'll tell Odessa."

"I appreciate it." He smiled and strode off down the hall, adjusting a scrapbook of his own he carried under his arm.

Changing Planes

I stood up. "Watch the bags. I'll be right back."

But there was nothing to protect the bags from except frayed blue carpet, empty leatherette benches with worn, tufted corners, and a bank of monitors displaying arrivals and departures to no one. Two girls slept sitting up by the window, leaning against each other with a blanket over their laps. Beyond them, jets stood silent as the rising sun gilded the vast backdrop of the Colorado plains.

Donnie shook his head. "Can't do that, Mr. Parker." He started to pick up the carry-on bags. "I'll come with you."

"Jesus, Donnie, I just want to pee."

"The Foundation pays me to watch you, Mr. Parker," he said wearily. We'd had this conversation before.

"Well, they don't pay you to watch me *piss*—and I should know because I sign the damn checks."

Cataracts of frustration clouded his eyes as he stood there clutching the bags and looking around again. It wasn't his fault. He was trying to do his job, no matter how much shit I gave him.

"I'm sorry," I said. "I hate redeye flights, and I hate going to these fundraisers. I just want to go pee, that's all. By myself. It's four in the morning. There's no one around. Nothing's gonna happen."

Donnie took a long time to do it, but he nodded and sat back down. "Don't be too long," he cautioned.

I bit back a mean reply and headed across the corridor for the men's room, feeling his eyes on me. Something was wrong with my life when I got a sense of freedom from being allowed to go to the bathroom by myself, but I'd known something was wrong for a long time. This was only the most recent illustration. But caution had become my default setting, and I suddenly wanted Donnie by my side as I entered the cool tiled room.

Because it had happened in a room just like this.

Even after ten years, the acrid smell of urinal deodorizer brought it back as if it happened ten minutes ago. I tried not to look towards the stall closest to the wall, tried not to see Jim's outstretched legs with his toes pointing down, his arms hanging on either side of the toilet bowl, bloody water pooling on the floor around his knuckles. But, of course, I did.

I remembered lifting his head out of the water, trying not to panic when I saw what was left of his face; cutting my lips on his broken teeth as I tried to breathe life back into him. And I remembered realizing he was dead. I didn't remember screaming, and I didn't remember the faces of the four men who knocked me down as I went into the bathroom. Not right away. But they came back to me in time for the trial.

Now my own face stared back at me from the mirror. Fifty-three years' worth of creases, lines and wrinkles framed by greying brown hair and green eyes that looked so damn serious these days. Would Jim even recognize me now? He used to say he fell in love with the laugh in my eyes, but that had been erased by the solemnity of a thousand fundraisers. Funny. The Parker Foundation had started out as a tribute to Jim, funding anti-hate agencies so no one else would be killed. But little by little, it was killing the survivor too. How many more times was I supposed to I relive it?

"Are you okay, Mr. Parker?" Donnie poked his head in the men's room, then stepped inside, his shoulders criss-crossed by the straps of our carry-on bags. Poor, patient Donnie. Doggedly watching me for the last five years, ever since two of those bastards got out of jail. My bodyguard-slash-valet—vigilant, protective, and loyal to a goddamn fault.

How I hated him.

"Fine, fine," I said, trying to keep it out of my voice. "I just want a few minutes to myself, okay?"

His face took on a pinched look of annoyance that I knew meant business. He bent over and peered underneath the stall walls, then swiveled his head for a quick check of the room. "Ten minutes," he said.

"Then I'm dragging you out." The bags bumped softly against each other as he turned and walked away.

Great, I thought. Ten minutes. I'd better make the most of it. I really *did* have to pee, so I stepped up to the urinals, choosing the middle one of three. As I unzipped my khakis, a service door opened up on the other side of the room and a young man stepped through, leaving it ajar. He looked surprised to see me.

Small and skinny with short brown hair, he was lost inside his baggy olive green uniform. A black lanyard with a picture ID dangled from his tanned neck, which was spotted with a few pimples. He couldn't have been more than nineteen or twenty, judging from the sparse goatee sprouting from his chin. His eyes were brown and friendly, without any affected sullenness. Even more remarkable, he wasn't wearing ear buds.

"What up, dude?" he asked as he stepped up to the urinal on my right.

"Not much." There weren't any privacy shields between the urinals, so I tried to keep my eyes to myself. He didn't seem to have the same reservations.

"You look familiar," he said as we pissed. "You famous?"

"Nah. I just have one of those faces."

He grinned. "You got a pretty nice dick, too."

I grinned back. Jesus, it had been a long time since this had happened. My cock thought so too. It started stiffening, cutting off the piss flow. He was stroking a nice average-sized dick with a dark circumcision scar and a perfectly shaped head. When he eased his nuts out of his fly, I couldn't help but start stroking too. They were huge in comparison to his cock. And hairy too. I hated guys who shaved their pubes. Manscaping, they called it. Stupidest thing I ever heard.

He reached his hand out, his long, cool fingers closing over my hard dick, and I sighed. It had been so long, and this felt so good. But no matter how good it felt or how horny I was, I couldn't get that day out of my head. I had to back away.

"I can't." My voice shook a little. "Not here."

He grinned wider and motioned towards the door he'd just come out of. His dick swung from side to side as he strode across the room and opened it wide. "Step into my office, man."

I had never been as forward as Jim had been. That's what got him killed. But there was something innocent about this boy. He didn't have the kind of eyes you'd expect to see staring back at you from a mug shot or beneath a headline. They were sweet and a little vacant, like a smiling stuffed animal sitting on someone's bed, but it didn't make any difference. My dick was doing the driving now. "C'mon, dude," he said with a laugh. "I won't bite ya—well, maybe a little on the neck."

I wrestled my stiff cock back into my pants and zipped up for the ten foot trek across the floor, pausing at the threshold to take a quick look inside. Utility rooms always smelled stale to me, and this one was no exception. Maybe it was the bucket of dirty mop water I bumped, splashing some on my shoe as I stumbled inside. He closed the door after me.

The small room had one wall of shelves with rows of green disinfectant and yellow cleanser cans and another with a sink and a horizontal rack of mops and brooms. He maneuvered me between the handles, pressing his skinny bones into my soft middle as he took my head in his hands and kissed me hard. His mouth tasted like Cherry Coke and chewing tobacco. I felt the Skoal can in his back pocket when I grabbed his ass and ground him further into me.

He broke the kiss and whispered hoarsely in my ear. "You can fuck your boy right after he sucks your dick." He knelt down slowly in front of me, nuzzling the crotch of my khakis as he undid my belt. With one motion, he slid my pants and my boxers down to my knees and nodded his head as my hard cock sprang free. "Damn." The word come out in one long breath.

If he noticed the grey hairs among the brown, he didn't mention it. He brought his hand up and stroked my nuts as he took the head of my dick in his mouth and worked his way down the shaft. I could feel the hot air from his nostrils parting my pubes as he deep-throated me, my cock hitting the back of his throat.

But he didn't gag. He backed off and grinned again. "Fuckin' *hot.*" He, spit and pre-cum trailing from his tongue. He went back to working my dick with his mouth and fondling my balls with his rough hands, sometimes reaching underneath to grab my ass cheeks and push me forward. I wanted to stand him up and suck his dick too, but it felt too good for him quit.

Instead, I closed my hands around his head and held it while I fucked his mouth. He moaned, his breath getting quick, and I knew that was what he wanted. I grabbed a handful of hair and rammed my dick harder and harder into his hot mouth, feeling the load building up in my balls. His neck muscles loosened. He let go of my ass and let me drive it home.

"Mr. Parker—*Mr. Parker*?" Donnie yelled from the room beyond. "Where are you? Where the hell did you *go*?"

It was the panic in Donnie's voice that made me cum, I know it was. I don't know how I stopped myself from crying out, but I managed to keep it to a quiet grunt as I shot a huge load down the boy's throat. He didn't pull away, though. He swallowed every bit, sucking the last drop out of my dick before he settled back on his haunches and smiled widely, wiping his mouth. "Hottest skull fuck *ever*, dude. I'm *serious*."

"Mr. Parker!"

The boy looked at me closer, squinting his eyes in the dim light, then they grew wide and round. I motioned for him to be quiet, pointing to the door. Donnie's footfalls sounded heavy and hurried, with no discernable pattern until they came closer to the door. The knob rattled briefly then stopped.

"Shit!" Donnie said. "What the fuck am I gonna *do*?" I heard him drop the bags, then his footsteps retreated until the room was quiet and I knew he was gone—probably to get security, if he could find any this time of morning. I didn't know what I was gonna do either, but I didn't have much time to do it in.

"Is there another way out of here?"

"Hey," the boy said. "I know who you are."

"Good for you." I pulled up my pants. "Is there another way out of here?"

He nodded and pointed to a door opposite the one we'd come in. "This goes into the service hall."

"Let's go."

He led the way without question. I felt like a captive whose kidnapper had unexpectedly been rendered helpless—giddy with the possibility of escape even though I had no idea what I was escaping to. But when a way out presents itself, you have to move.

The corridor we entered was large, with concrete walls decorated by various vents and grilles and recessed lighting in the ceiling. The boy turned to the left, and we walked for a few feet until I saw a camera perched in the corner. "Where's the monitor for that?" I asked, stopping.

"Airport security office, fourth level, but don't worry. It's dead. No red light, see? They quit workin' all down this hall about six months ago and nobody ever came to fix 'em. So, you're Benjamin Parker, huh?" He stuck his hand out. "I'm Kenny Racine."

Gay manners, I thought. First you suck dick, then you shake hands. His grip was firm and confident. "How does a young guy like you know who I am?"

"Long story, man. I'll tell ya when we get to the break room."

"Break room?" I said. "Look, I really don't want to run into anybody."

"Yeah, I kinda figured that. Chill, man. Nobody's here except me for a couple hours yet. Whoever's lookin' for you is gonna have a helluva time till then. Why are you running away?"

"Long story . I'll tell you when we get to the break room."

He grinned again. "You're pretty cool—a famous dude with a sense of humor *and* a hot dick. You're gonna fuck your boy, right?" He leaned in close and cupped my crotch with his hand as he parted his lips for another kiss. I grabbed his goateed chin and kissed him as hard as I could, my dick stiffening again. He pulled away and opened his eyes. "I *knew* there was another load down there. C'mon, let's go."

No red lights flashed and no alarms sounded as I had always feared. My escape was quick quiet steps on concrete. It had been unexpectedly easy for me to slip away, but it wasn't going to be easy on Donnie. He was going to get a ration of shit from the Foundation, but I didn't want to think about them at the moment. I'd already spent way too much time at their dinners and luncheons and benefits and speaking engagements. If one more person told me how brave I was, I'd punch him in the goddamn mouth.

We walked a bit further, Kenny in the lead as I followed him, trying to discern what his ass looked like. It was tough to tell from those baggy uniform pants. I got hard again just thinking about it. I hadn't been laid for a long, long time. "A man in your position shouldn't be trolling Manhunt," Donnie had told me. "It only makes trouble."

What I desired most, however, was a little trouble.

"Watchin' your boy's ass, huh?" Kenny asked as if he was reading my mind. "That's cool." He stopped in front of an unmarked entrance that looked like any of the others we'd passed. "Okay, everyone, clear out," he yelled inside. "Got a celebrity comin' through." I froze, and he gave me that lopsided grin again. "Just messin' with ya, man. Nobody's here, trust me."

I was still a little tense when we entered, but we were the only two in sight. A row of vending machines stood against one wall. Round tables were scattered around the room, decorated by open soda cans and candy bar wrappers, the chairs in disarray. The smell of microwaved burritos hung in the air like floating heartburn.

Kenny looked around and clucked his tongue. "Fuckin' pigs." We wound our way through the mess to another doorway. "Believe it or not, it's cleaner back here in the locker room."

A bank of lockers stood in the middle of the room with a bench on either side. An even smaller room with two shower heads was off to the left. Kenny opened a locker in the middle, reached into an orange backpack and took out two Power Bars. He offered them both to me. "Chocolate or apple cinnamon?"

"Apple cinnamon sounds healthier."

"You got it." He handed one to me and unwrapped the other one as we sat down on the bench. "You wore me out, dude. Need some quick energy."

"I wore *me* out too. So, how come you know about an old fart like me?"

A few crumbs dropped from his mouth. "If I answer your question, you gotta answer mine."

"Not a problem."

He nodded. "I musta been about twelve when your man got killed. My mom made a big deal out of it. Every time it came on the news she'd tell me, 'That's what those people get.' Course, she wouldn't have said shit about it if she hadn't caught me suckin' my best friend's dick in the basement a couple weeks before that. Guess you could say she was tryin' to teach me a lesson."

"Obviously, it didn't stick."

"Nope." He shucked the foil off the last half of his breakfast and stood up, holding his hand out for the wrapper on mine. I took it off and handed it to him. "I mean, y'are what y'are, right?" he said, shrugging as he tossed them both in the trash can. "Anyhoo, about a month later she caught me jackin' my stepdad while he was watchin' a porno. Tossed me out on my ass and told me not to come back. I didn't even get a chance to pack."

"She threw a twelve-year-old boy out?"

He shrugged again. "Twelve, thirteen—somethin' like that."

"Where did you go?"

"Vegas for a couple years, then I came back to Denver. Slept in a lotta doorways, turned a lotta tricks. Old story, man. Then a dude gave me a hundred and fifty bucks to blow him. Went back to his place and he beat the holy shit outta me. Broke my fuckin' arm. I figured maybe that wasn't the healthiest way for me to earn my nachos. And that's where *you* come in."

"Me?"

"Yup." He sat down beside me on the bench, reached behind him into his backpack and came out with a Cherry Coke. "Last one," he said, popping the top and holding it out to me. I took a quick swig and gave it back. Nasty stuff. "Well, the Parker Foundation anyway. They fund the GLBT youth center. Met up with a counselor, and she got me a place to live. Went back to school, got a job and before y'know it, I'm a responsible adult."

"Got a boyfriend?"

"Nah. Too much drama with dudes my own age. Wouldn't mind a daddy, though—not a *sugar* daddy, y'understand. I like payin' my own way." He shut up suddenly, as if he thought he might have crossed a line with me. We sat in silence for a couple of minutes until he belched and grinned again. "Okay, that's my sad-ass story. Why are you runnin' away?"

"I'm tired."

"Of?"

"My life. What it's become, what's been built around it. Tired of being the poster boy for tragedy." I reached out for his Cherry Coke and took another sip so I could keep my voice from shaking. I'd never said any of this before. "Most people get to bury their dead. Mine's on a Power Point presentation the Foundation trots out when donations are low. I spend half my time feeling good about helping people and the other half wondering how I get off this fucking train."

"Why don'tcha just quit?"

"I can't. It's too big. It's not just me anymore."

He nodded. "Who's the dude lookin' for you?"

"Donnie. My bodyguard."

"You need a bodyguard?"

"The Foundation thinks I do. I have to beg to take a piss by myself anymore."

"That's fucked up." He shook his head and looked me in the eyes. "What are ya gonna do?"

"I don't know." I didn't, either. But that life seemed very far away at the moment, and Kenny was right by my side. His eyes didn't look vacant anymore. They looked sweet and perceptive and wise, and before I even realized what I was doing, I'd leaned over to kiss him.

He'd sensed what I was going to do, because he met me halfway, reaching up and closing his arms around me. I returned the hug, feeling his sinewy arms and strong shoulders as we crushed each other awkwardly. I broke the kiss and bit his lip. "Lie back on the bench," I whispered into his ear.

"Yeah, your boy needs to be fucked."

We both straddled the bench and Kenny reclined, starting to unbutton his shirt. I took his hands away. "I'll do it." The buttons were small, and I tried to stop my hands from shaking. Daddies' hands weren't supposed to shake, but if Kenny noticed, he didn't say anything.

His chest was smooth, his dark nipples the size of half-dollars. I kissed and nuzzled each of them, drawing sighs from his thin ribcage. My hands worked their way down to his crotch. His dick was already hard. I grabbed it roughly with one hand while I undid his belt with the other. I unsnapped his uniform pants and reached inside, feeling the warmth as I jacked his cock through the thin fabric of his boxers.

He moaned softly, indecipherably, and I bent over to kiss his navel. His hips rose slightly as I traced my tongue down a surprisingly thick treasure trail and eased his pants down. His blue and white checked boxers tented tightly, the head of his cock straining against the worn cotton. I rubbed my cheek against it, feeling its heat for a few seconds before I pulled his shorts down to his ankles.

"Yeah," he breathed. "*Please* suck it."

I hovered over his dick, studying the hard shaft lying on his furry belly, watching the precum seep out of his piss slit as I ran my hands over his hairy thighs. For not having any hair on his chest, his lower half was dense with it. I buried my nose in his soft, oddly fragrant pubes, wondering if he used conditioner on them. Then I stood his dick up with my fingers and slid my mouth over it.

He sighed and reached for my head with his hands, but I pushed them away. I swallowed as much of his cock as I could, opening up my throat to take more until I got to my gag point. Then I backed off. I stroked his slick shaft with my hand and nuzzled his nuts until his hips started to rise off the bench.

"Unh…oh, *fuck*, dude."

His balls tensed. I knew it wouldn't be long before he shot, so I stopped jacking him and cupped my palms under his ass, lifting him up. My hands weren't shaking anymore; they were sure and in control. I rubbed my nose in the crack of his ass – less fragrance and more musk down there, but the smell only got me harder. His hands went to his dick, and I pushed them away again.

"Not until I say you can." I liked taking control more than I thought I would.

"Yes, sir."

I pushed his legs behind his head, his pink hole spreading for me as his hairy cheeks parted. I ate it eagerly, hungrily—teasing his pucker with my tongue before I plunged it in dead center. I'd never gotten into anyone's ass this way before. In fact, I'd never cared all that much for anal sex. Too much prep work, too much performance anxiety for me, but I was beginning to think I could fuck this kid all day long.

My cock was so hard it hurt, and when I looked down I saw a huge wet spot on the front of my khakis. I undid my belt. "I'm gonna ride your ass like it's never been rode before, boy."

"Yeah, daddy," he whispered, "make…" That's when the buzzer sounded out in the corridor—loud, blatting blasts joined by the sound of voices and feet running down the hall. We both sat up.

"*Shit!*" Kenny struggled with his pants. "Your Donnie musta made some phone calls, dude. I *never* heard those go off before."

"Goddammit, is there another way out of here?"

"Yeah, but not without goin' out into the hall." The steps and voices were getting closer. "Don't worry. I got your back. Get behind the lockers and don't say anything." I did what he told me just in time. I didn't even get a chance to catch my breath before I heard voices in the doorway.

"*Racine!* You see any civilians back here?"

"No sir, Mr. Moore. I was just havin' my break."

"Here, take this radio. If you see anybody you don't recognize on the premises, you call me on the emergency frequency. You copy?"

"Yes, sir. My shift's almost over, though. You want me to come with you?"

"No, you have no experience in these kind of ops. You'd just be in the way. Stay where you are until it's time for you to go home, but look sharp. He might duck in here or something."

"Right. Gotcha, Mr. Moore." The feet stomped out of the room, and Kenny came around to my side of the lockers holding a walkie-talkie. "Lame-ass prick," he said. "I knew he'd say that. I wouldn't sweat it, man. Anything he's in charge of's *bound* to be a clusterfuck."

"You said there's another way out of here?"

"Sure," he said, "but where do you wanna go? I mean, is this *it*? You're not gonna go back?"

Good question. Escaping had always seemed so romantic, but I never figured on what to do after that. I'd have to go back, eventually. I knew that. Maybe I just wanted to cause a fuss—show them I was more than just an opportunity to make money, no matter how much good was done with it. "Do you have a place?"

"Yeah, a shitty little apartment out in bumfuck Aurora. You wanna go there?"

"Why not?" I reached around and grabbed his ass. "Besides, we have some unfinished business."

That lopsided grin was back. "We *do*, don't we? Okay, dude. It's cool."

Consequences suddenly started coming to me. "You know, this is going to make the papers."

"No shit." He laughed. "They're probably gonna fire my skinny ass, too."

"Don't worry about it. I'll see that you have a job—a better one than cleaning up airport bathrooms, too."

"Hey, you meet some pretty interestin' people that way," he said. "Okay, dude, you're on." He led the way through the break room to the door, stepping out in the corridor. "It's clear. We're gonna go two doors to the left, down a short hallway, then out to the parking lot. Head for the monkey-shit brown Celica with the busted tail light. Dunno if the camera on the door is workin' or not, so we gotta hustle. Ready?"

"Yep."

"Let's *do* it!"

His sneakers squeaked as he took off, and I almost fell on my ass trying to keep up with him. We darted into the doorway and down the short hall, coming to a door with an exit sign and a camera over it. The red light was definitely on.

He slammed through and doubled his speed once he was out of the building, looking back a couple of times to wave me in the right direction. By the time I reached the car, he already had the passenger door open. I climbed inside, he started it and we took off, tires squealing.

"This is so fuckin' *cool*." He began to laugh over the loud music coming from speakers somewhere in the back. The car smelled like pot and the pine-tree deodorizer hanging from the rearview mirror. I was laughing too, excitement and freedom buzzing in my head as I nodded to the guitar riffs ringing in the car.

"It *is* pretty fuckin' cool."

He turned down the stereo. "Hey, you hungry? There's this Greek place not far from me that makes the best buttermilk pancakes you ever had."

"Sounds good," I said. "I'll buy."

"Uh-uh, dude, it's on me. I told ya, I like payin' my own way."

"In that case, I'm having a double order."

He chuckled as we barreled out onto I-70, the sun behind us. There would be time enough for recriminations later—apologies to be made, flights to re-book, sponsors and administrators to placate. Right now all I could think about was breakfast and the hot boy beside me.

And the feeling that there might be something left for *me* after all.

Love, Sex & Death on the Daily Commute

I'm the worst driver you'll ever see. I speed, I tailgate, I don't signal and I don't brake for shit. Yield signs mean nothing to me and pedestrians mean even less. I run red lights as often as I run yellow ones because I can't stand the thought of mechanical, synchronized signals telling me what to do. If you get in my way, you're headed for a serious scare. And don't think I won't do it, either. I've frightened everyone from suburban soccer moms in SUV's to Lexus-driving executives with cell phones all ready to call my license plate number in. And in twenty odd years of near accidents, I've never gotten a ticket. Never.

I didn't start out this way, though. I used to follow all the rules, from always watching for cars before pulling out into traffic to keeping my hands at ten and two on my steering wheel. I learned my current behavior from my fellow drivers. They showed this formerly law abiding teenager the short cuts to the fast lane—the ability to weave in and out around slower vehicles, the art of cutting off buses and trucks, and how to lightly kiss the bumper of the victim ahead and grin coldly at him while he shakes his fist.

Since they taught me everything they know, you'd think my fellow commuters would be more forgiving of my trespasses, but they aren't. They flip me off instead. They're all angry, squinched faces and rude middle fingers extended from clenched fists. In the summer, they holler their obscenities out their windows at me and in the winter, their mouths move silently, curling around curses I can't hear. But I see them all the same.

However, that's only in the afternoons. My morning commute is as peaceful as a loft full of doves. I work the early shift, so I leave my house at three-fifteen in the morning. I can count the cars I see going downtown on the fingers of one hand. It gives me time to think. Maybe morning isn't the best time to reflect on your station in life, but self-improvement seems like such a big chore in the afternoon, and who knows? One day I might carry through with one of the resolutions I make during my morning trip, before the events of the day negate all my good intentions.

Even though the mornings are dark enough for my headlights, sometimes I'll drive with them off anyway. I know it's risky, but there aren't many cops out at three-fifteen, and I like to imagine myself gliding down the road like an eagle flying headfirst into the first salmon shades of sunrise. I can almost touch the white reflective stripes with my talons as I swoop low to the pavement, following the gentle sloping curve of the highway skirting the city.

When I turn my lights on again, the dashboard gauges flicker harshly in my eyes, and I realize how earthbound I really am. I look at my reflection in the rear view mirror, but no eagle stares back. Just another forty-something commuter with graying brown hair and the beginning of sag in his jowls. Another disembodied, gym-tightened torso tethered to the upholstery of his not-yet-paid-for steel and safety glass canister. As the bumper sticker says, I'd rather be gliding. I don't glide when I'm late, though.

I'd rather not come in at all than be late, but my boss doesn't consider tardiness a valid excuse for taking the whole day off, so I have to drive extra fast to make up for a few whacks of the snooze alarm. I was late the first morning I saw him.

I noticed him from the time he merged onto the freeway at the University Avenue entrance. You don't see many bright orange Ford pickup trucks on I-25 at three thirty in the morning. Most of the vehicles out then are older, rust-spotted cars and trucks, usually driven by tired looking Mexican laborers, with other men sleeping in the passenger and back seats, the bills of their baseball caps crushed up against the windows.

The finish on this pickup was shiny and new, the chrome of the bumpers, mag wheels and row of fog lights on the roof of the cab twinkling under the cool blue streetlights lining the freeway. And it wasn't driven by any wetback melon picker, either. He was gorgeous. Okay, he wasn't gorgeous by conventional standards, but he had that trailer trash insouciance that gives me a hard-on every time I cruise the male guests on the Jerry Springer Show.

He wore his black Caterpillar cap backwards, a shock of short blonde hair poking through the space above the sizing band. Cavernous dimples creased his clean-shaven cheeks as he smiled and sang along with the radio, the bass line and tinkling piano leaking out the driver's side window. I was speeding in the fast lane to keep even with him, watching the streetlights strobe his tanned, muscled arm as he reached up to readjust his cap.

He sped away from me in a puff of exhaust like a GQ roadrunner while I drooled in mute helplessness. His rear license plates read JOEBOB, framed in moving blue neon. Being late, I had a perfect excuse to floor it. I revved my puke-green '65 Dodge Dart up to eighty and flew by the next six exits before I drew even with him again. He signaled and got off at the next exit, the one before mine, his brake lights flashing, enveloping his name in a soft red glow.

I would have gotten off and pursued him if I hadn't been late…no, that's a lie. I wouldn't have. I'm not that impulsive. I like routines and schedules and hate any deviations. That's what's kept me in the same dead-end job for ten years. Routines and schedules. Even if I had all the time in the world, I wouldn't have followed him. Not then, anyway. I just drove on by, got off at the usual exit and pulled into the covered parking spot I won in an employee raffle. I stuck to schedule.

That's how it started. It *always* starts with something small; some insignificant thought that finds a crack in your psyche and roots itself there, gathering strength from the groundwaters of your imagination. Now that I've gotten some distance, some perspective on it, it's all clear to me. But I'm getting ahead of myself. I looked for him on the way home, surprised at my disappointment in not finding him. That should have been my first clue. As I pulled into my driveway at home, I wondered if I'd see him again tomorrow morning. That should have been my second.

—ᴍ—

I stop for coffee and a doughnut to go every morning at the same 7-11 near the freeway. The owner is a short, swarthy man named Rafi. He has olive drab skin and tightly kinked black hair graying at the temples. His handlebar moustache is perfectly twisted, the end points as sharp as scimitars. He's Lebanese and feels the need, below his name tag, to wear a large red button that says *I'm Not From Iraq!*

He's usually buffing the floor when I come in but as soon as he sees me pouring coffee, he turns off the machine and hops in back of the counter, straightening the novelty lighters and rearranging the Tic-Tacs. "Good morning, Mister Dave." His English has never improved. "How are you today?" His eyes are dark, eager friendliness and his breath is garlicky halitosis. After six years of mornings together, he still asks for my driver's license and work phone number every time I write a check for gas.

I used to take it personally. I'd start my day miffed that someone considered me untrustworthy, but now I can see he was as caught up in his routine as I in mine. Asking for a license is an automatic response in learned in management trainee school, part of the clerk routine. We all get them from different places, I guess. Sometimes I wonder if Rafi ever thought about jumping out of his routine.

"To *hell* with the driving license. You have nice eyes, Mister Dave. I trust you. Have a good day." He'd go back to buffing the floor. Or maybe he wouldn't. Maybe he'd just leave the buffer standing in the middle of the half-polished aisle and wander away to re-stock the cooler or step outside and smoke a cigarette in the parking lot, twisting the ends of his perfect moustache as he watched the tiny points of headlights moving along I-25.

Routines are insidious because we don't know we're mired in them until it's too late. A few are necessary to keep you from combusting with spontaneity, but when your routines develop their routines, you're in trouble. You're following life rather than living it.

Of course, there's a danger to breaking routines. You can break too many. Or go too far.

The fresh breath of an early March breeze was sweeping away the stagnant winter road dust on the shoulder of the highway, creating little dust devils that capered briefly before dashing themselves to death against the guardrails. A torn white paper bag buzzed my windshield like an albino bat.

I don't mind driving in rain or snow, but I hate wind. It pulls and tugs at the Dart, making me think I have a flat even though I know I don't. I'm afraid a sudden gust of wind will send a trucker swerving into my lane or blow something out of the back of a pickup and blind me, but I can envision death scenarios while driving in dry, sunny weather if I try hard enough. That's one of the reasons I try to distract myself with the radio.

Unfortunately, I couldn't find anything good on that morning. The more buttons I pushed, the more commercials I heard. I tried looking into the few cars on the road, but their heavily tinted windows prevented me from doing much peeking. I love watching people pick their noses while they drive, but no such entertainment that day. I was anxious and nervous. I pretended not to realize why, but when I came within a mile of University, the conclusion was inescapable. Would I see JOEBOB again? The wind whipped the car, sliding the steering wheel through my sweating palms, and I had to squeeze harder against its pull.

Having only seen him once, I was surprised by my reaction. True, he was an amazing looking man, but what could possibly happen even if I caught his eye? What were we going to do on the *freeway*, for Chrissakes? I didn't even know if he was gay or not. Still, a little voice told me, even straight boys can be had. That dim possibility was what kept hope, however irrational, alive. I hate myself when I'm not rational, but that doesn't mean I can stop it from happening. I had to make eye contact with him. Whatever happened after that would just have to happen.

My anticipation sharpened, intensifying to the point of nausea as I approached the University Avenue on-ramp. Not a car in sight. Just the lonely blue glow of the streetlamps shining down on the pavement. I passed it with keen disappointment, my hopes falling through the Dart's rusting floorboard. Unwilling to concede defeat, I stared in the rear view mirror at the green and white exit signs growing smaller and smaller.

My persistence was rewarded with the sight of two faint dots of light shooting down the freeway ramp at a good seventy mile an hour clip. I slowed down a little, squinting into the rear view until I saw a bright orange blob coming up behind me. I accelerated, my veins flooding with delicious tension. He wasn't going to leave me choking on his exhaust again, I thought. I intended to pace his car and think of a way to establish some communication.

He was in my lane, his headlights growing larger in my mirror as I wound the Dart up to seventy. It sputtered in protest but obeyed. Suddenly, JOEBOB's turn signal blinked and he switched to the left lane. Perfect, I thought. Just where I want him. He was only a few yards behind me when I looked up and saw the slow Safeway truck doing forty right in front of me.

Swearing and screaming with the same breath, I locked my brakes in screeching panic as the horribly huge circled *S* on his back door raced to meet my face. I must have left an inch of tread on the road, stopping close enough to kiss his bumper. He laid on his airhorn in obvious disgust. JOEBOB whizzed by, no more than a streak of orange I saw out of the corner of my eye. I'd missed him again, but maybe I could catch him before our respective exits.

Fearless now that I'd cheated death by semi, I stuck my nose out in the left lane and gunned around the obstacle, my old Dart rattling in shock as I floored the accelerator. I was up to seventy-five before I got close enough to see his name plate again. Checking for slower traffic this time, I moved back to the right and began gaining on him, but only because he was slowing down for his exit. As I drew even with him, he reeled away and left me doing eighty-solitaire.

I was going so fast I almost missed my own turn off. My left rear tire spun dangerously in the fast flying gravel of the shoulder, but I forced the Dart back onto the pavement and stopped for the light at the termination of the exit. My feet and hands trembled as I waited to make my turn into the parking lot, adrenaline and sweat soaking my thin cotton dress shirt.

My cock was so hard I had to wait a few minutes before I went inside the building.

Before the light turned green, I knew there was no turning back.

Thirty seconds a day for thirty days is a grand total of fifteen minutes, hardly enough time to learn anything substantial about anyone—especially without benefit of conversation, the give and take of face-to-face communication. JOEBOB and I didn't have that. What we had, or rather what I had, were stolen glances. Tidbits of information gathered from scrutinizing his bumper stickers and blown up to assume whole aspects of his personality.

The MENSA logo affixed to the right corner of his rear cab window and the KYGO-FM sticker on the left bespoke the contradiction of a brainy country music fan, an image that made the possibility of actual conversation with him incredibly tantalizing. If I hadn't already noticed the similarity between our driving styles by the way he speeded down I-25, the legend *As a matter of fact, I DO own the road* just below the big white Ford letters on his tailgate would have clued me in. And, although I saw no rainbow sticker anywhere on the big orange truck, there was a line of dancing Grateful Dead bears in rainbow colors decorating his chrome bumper. He could have been either a friend of Dorothy or a fan of Jerry Garcia.

My mind no longer confined him to the freeway. JOEBOB and the big orange truck drove around the flying toasters on my screen saver at work like an obstacle course. He accompanied me to lunch, his shiny mag wheels bogging down in my mashed potatoes and gravy. Just before going to sleep at nights, I even dreamed of him outside my building, his halogen headlights probing the dark, bare walls of my one-bedroom apartment as he pulled into the driveway.

Until JOEBOB, I'd always lived my life by one overriding rule: Don't Get Involved. It had served me pretty well, sparing me a lot of pain and grief. I had been able to survive both parents' funerals, being the strong shoulder each of my four sisters had cried on, simply because I had never really gotten involved in the family. Oh sure, I loved my mother and father. I even love my sisters, but I've never been as close to them as they were to each other. I guess I've always been the outsider—no, if I'm telling the truth here, I've got to say I've always made myself an outsider.

That's not an easy place to be. You don't get hurt, but you don't feel much joy or happiness, either. Of course, if you've done without it long enough, you don't miss it much. Except on cold nights when the wind whistles lonely through the cracks in your casement windows and the snow brings an urge to snuggle. Or on holidays. Or at the movies. That's why I rent a lot of videos. Don't get me wrong, I'm not bitching about it. I chose it, and I'd been satisfied with it up to that point.

For the first time in my life, I *wanted,* no *needed* involvement. With JOEBOB. I knew he was only a means to an end, a catalyst. If only I could meet him—accomplish that one goal—somehow I'd be free. The very act itself, no matter where it led, would force me off my treadmill and catapult me into another life. A different life. Another chance. The thought thrilled me and terrified me at the same time. I knew nothing about that other life. I didn't know the social structure or the rules or how to meet new people or talk to them about anything other than work or the weather, but I wanted to learn.

Oh God, how I wanted to learn. Maybe JOEBOB could teach me.

I'm not out at work. I'm not out to my family or friends, even though I've known since junior high school that I'm gay. I'm not overly concerned with what they'll think, but I just don't believe it's necessary. I'm not tortured about it. I don't agonize over it. I'm not ashamed of it, but I don't go around with rainbow flags on my clothes or march in the Pride parades. I guess I should, but that Don't Get Involved rule applies. I'm not much of a joiner, and it doesn't look like the movement needs my help with the agenda anyway.

I work for a large, multinational corporation; a mid-level manager of a mid-sized department somewhere in the middle of the building. The breaks and lunches I don't spend working in my corner office with a view of the parking lot I take with a fellow mid-level manager named Gina. She's a bitter stump of a woman, short and round with aged brown skin rough as bark and eyes deeper and blacker than the most twisted knotholes. She always reminded me of the talking apple trees in *The Wizard of Oz,* only with more attitude.

And you can't really say we were good friends, either. Given a choice, she wasn't the kind of person I'd hang around with. As I've said before, I'm pretty much of a loner. It was one of those friendships borne out of workplace necessity more than an actual need for companionship; a lunch partner to keep you from looking like a total loser who brings Robert Heinlein or Danielle Steele books to read while shoveling in that Tupperware-encased microwaveable tuna casserole. I did not cherish her. Nor did she me.

"Looks like Tammy's gonna get that marketing job," she said one day as she sat down opposite me in our usual booth in the back of the cafeteria overlooking the blue and white sign with our corporate logo on it. She wore another of the big flower print blouses that, for all I know, had kept her from getting anywhere in the company. This one was pink hibiscuses on a field of scarlet.

"Like you didn't already know that." I was peeling a mostly black banana.

She waved a hand covered with rings, their blue and white stones as gigantically fake as anything worthy of the after-midnight slot on the Home Shopping Network. "Oh sure, she's been sniffing around the VP like a bitch in heat, but I thought they'd at least give me an interview. I mean, I have a degree in Marketing. You know that."

Everyone in the whole damn building knew about her degree, especially me. I heard about it every fucking day for three years, from the bastard professors who weren't perceptive enough to grace every one of her papers and projects with A's to the utter futility of finding a job commensurate with her newly acquired skills. She even sent me a graduation invitation. "Maybe they're not done interviewing yet."

"Oh, they're done all right. The posting came down last week. Anything opening up in your department?" She grinned, showing uneven, coffee-stained teeth. "It'd be fun being your boss. I'll bet we'd work great together."

The thought left me nauseous enough to throw away the whole banana. "I don't know, Gina. I doubt there's anything coming up, but they keep me pretty well out of the loop. I'm probably not the best person to ask." I sipped my coffee and listened to my next sentence as if I were standing outside my own body. "There's something I have to tell you."

"What?" All job-related inquiries fleeing her eyes. The only thing she liked more than complaining was gossiping.

I couldn't hold it back. I was unable to dam the confessional tide. "I-I'm gay."

I'm not sure what reaction I expected or if I had even thought that far ahead. Her eyes, however, registered complete surprise, especially disconcerting from someone who took great pride in knowing everything about everybody. Her spoon dropped back into her vanilla yogurt with a wet plop, spattering her upper lip with yellowish goo. She didn't even bother to lick it off. "Oh. My. God."

Her tone wounded me. "It's not *that* big a deal. People come out every day. Does it bother you?"

She frowned, her bushy eyebrows a big black hedge above her eyes. "I don't know--I guess not. Have I ever said anything offensive to you?"

Gina, Gina, Gina. It's all about Gina. "Not that I can remember."

She picked up her spoon and began to eat again. "Good. I'd hate to think I've been pissing you off all these years and not even knowing it." Rolling a spoonful of yogurt around in her mouth, she seemed to be looking at me as if she'd never really seen me before. I was new to her now and deserved a different, closer scrutiny. I felt myself reddening under it. "So, what changed you?" she asked.

"Nothing. I've been this way since I was thirteen."

"Hmmm. Maybe I'm asking the wrong question. Why did you decide to tell me just now?"

That confessional tide began to surge again, only this time the substance was more speculative fiction than actual fact, which made it no less easy to stop. "I've got a boyfriend."

Her spoon paused on its way to her mouth, yogurt dripping back into the cup, which tipped dangerously towards her lap. She affected more nonchalance this time. "My, you're full of surprises today. What's his name?" She looked over her glasses at me as the spoon completed its journey.

"Joe..." I trailed off, not wanting to say Joebob for fear it would sound too country hick. I didn't have any recollection of ever censoring my own fantasies before, but my brain was charting new territory here. I could hardly wait to hear what I was going to say next.

"Where'd you meet him?"

My mind, now apparently operating under its own will, ran through a short list of possible meeting places I didn't even know it had compiled. "The library." I immediately disliking my choice.

"The library?" Confused disbelief loomed obvious in her eyes. "Since when did you start hanging around the library?"

"Since I found out there were a lot of cute guys there." I was hating this conversation almost as much as I was regretting it. "Forget it. Forget I ever mentioned it."

"No, I'm glad you told me." She concentrated on scraping the sides of her yogurt cup, making sure she got every last bit. That was Gina. Never let anything go to waste. "I'm just a little surprised, that's all. I mean, one minute we're talking about Tammy and the marketing job and the next minute, you're telling me you're gay. Haven't you ever heard of segues?"

"I guess it was a little sudden, but I just wanted you to know because..." Because why? Not because I cared for her in any way but because I was using her for a sounding board. After all, I'd never made it official by saying it out loud before. But I couldn't tell her that. "...you're important to me."

I could tell from the warm glow which came into her eyes that the lie had been received as enthusiastically as I feared it would have. Great, I thought. I now have a relationship I didn't want with a woman I don't really like.

"Thanks." Her cheeks reddened as she reached across the table and took my hand. Hers felt warm and moist, and she looked as uncomfortable as I felt. "I think you're pretty important too." Something in her shaking voice told me I might be the only person she ever said that to, and I felt smug for a half second until I realized I had just fictionalized a boyfriend out of thin air and a few sightings on the freeway. Given that, it was hard to tell which of us was more desperate and lonely, but I was sure I had the edge.

"Can I ask you a question?"

Christ no, I thought. No telling what the hell I'll say. "Sure."

"Well, when you guys…uh…you know…*do* it, who decides who gets to be the man and who gets to be the woman?"

I knew this question, as moronic as it was, would be genius compared to the ones I'd be getting once my predilections became known around the building. "We flip a coin. C'mon, break's over with. Back to the salt mines."

In the days to come, I was subjected to numerous liberal sympathies ("I just want you to know it doesn't make any difference to me, as long as you're not demanding any special treatment"), various confessions ("My brother is gay, and we love him the same as the normal members of the family") and questionable permissions ("Live and let live, that's what I say, as long as you don't try to grab *my* ass"), not to mention the out and out hatred of "AIDS KILLS FAGGOTS DEAD" written in Liquid Paper on my computer screen. Somehow, the security camera tapes for that incident came up missing.

Despite all this, however, I went to work on a daily basis, cashing my checks at Rafi's 7-11 and timing my commute so that I hit the University Avenue exit the same time JOEBOB merged onto the freeway every morning. The timing was so precise that you'd think he would have noticed me sometime in two months, but he didn't. Or if he did, he never acknowledged me with a honk or a wave as he so often did in my hallucinations.

I had long ago exhausted the fantasy possibilities of his bumper stickers and was, at this point, basing my daydreams on sheer speculation—

the sound of his voice (soft and deep, with barely a trace of a Georgian accent), the timbre of his laugh (husky and masculine, like Bea Arthur with a cold) and the size of his cock (long and thin, with a slight curve) were all products of my fearfully warped imagination with no basis in fact or any way of finding out for sure. Until the morning we actually met.

I was running late, both for work and for my usual JOEBOB sighting, so I only got coffee at Rafi's, figuring I had at least enough gas to get to work. I hit sixty on the entrance ramp to the freeway and never slowed down, blazing through the northern suburbs past downtown in record time. As I approached the University Avenue entrance, I looked around but I-25 was clear of traffic in all directions. A quick consultation with my watch told me I was a few minutes earlier than usual.

As I was wondering how to handle the situation, a more worrisome problem presented itself. The Dart's engine sputtered, lost power and then died. I didn't even have to look at the gas gauge. I did anyway. I should have gotten a couple of bucks of regular instead of the coffee, but there was no sense lamenting what I didn't do. I took the commuter's gamble and lost, washing up on the shoulder of I-25 with no cell phone and a long walk to anywhere.

I coasted to a dead stop just past University, pulling off into the space where the entrance lane meets the freeway proper. I felt the weight of the door as I pushed it open and got out of the car, suddenly overwhelmed with an urge to slam it hard. I swung the door further open to get the best possible leverage, then let it fly with all my strength. The resulting bang was startling, but not as startling as the sound of the driver's side window shattering. Shards of safety glass flew everywhere, littering the front seat and pavement.

The early spring breeze felt chilly. I snuggled further into my battered brown windbreaker and looked off towards the dark horizon. The moon was still up and half full, and the sunrise seemed a cold eternity away. I contemplated which direction the nearest gas station would be, psyching myself up for the walk when I saw headlights following the curve of the entrance lane behind me.

I knew it was him even before he hit the first pool of light thrown by the streetlamps lining the ramp. It had to be. It was too perfect, too once-in-a-lifetime, too fucking B-movie to be anyone else. And, of course, it was. I saw pinpricks of light before my eyes, and my stomach flipped back and forth as if trying to throw me off balance, propelling me irrevocably into an event bound to change my life. I knew, as he slowed down and pulled over to the side of the road behind me, that neither one of us would ever be the same again.

"Hey buddy, need a hand?" he asked in a voice more or less matching the one I'd been hearing in my dreams the last few months. Blinded by his headlights, I couldn't really see his face until I approached his driver's side window, but what I *could* see was the hand he offered. It was big and broad, the fingers spade-like with a layer of grime lining the cuticle of his poorly trimmed nails. The back of his hand was hairy, the fur easy to spot in the semi-dark even though he was a blonde. The skin itself was chapped and red, and as I pictured rubbing my dick against that rough palm, I began to get hard.

"Yeah," I managed to say. "Ran out of gas. I forgot to get some this morning—in too much of a hurry I guess."

He chuckled. "And now you're *really* gonna be late. Funny how shit works out, ain't it?" Sitting there, half lit by the sunrise and half by the harsh yellow glare of the streetlamp, he was the most handsome man I'd ever seen. His face was beautifully proportioned, his jawline straight and noble, and his nose was endearingly bent—broken, I fantasized, in a bar room brawl or a baseball game. He wore his black Caterpillar cap backwards as usual, but no shock of hair stuck out above the sizing band. He must have gotten a haircut. His deep brown eyes were as warm and friendly as a cup of coffee on a cold morning, and the faint shadow on his upper lip told me he was growing a moustache. When he chuckled, his lips parted in a crooked smile that almost left me faint.

"Yeah." I leaned against his door. "Real funny."

"I'm runnin' kinda late myself, but I guess I got time enough to run you down to that 7-11 on University. You got somethin' to put gas in?"

The question startled me. He had so captured my attention that I had forgotten I was out of gas, had broken my window and was late for work. What was in my trunk? Not much, I thought. A flat spare, a jack, a pair of dusty jumper cables, and a couple of road flares I'd intended for emergencies, not that they were doing me much good in this one. I hated to admit I was so ill-equipped, but that was the situation. "Not really. Maybe they'll have a gas can or something for sale."

He barked out a gruff laugh. "Yeah, for four times what it's worth. I got a spare you can have somewhere in the back."

"Thanks," I said, catching myself smiling far too broadly for someone who had run out of gas and was going to be late for work. I tried to tone my smirk down a little but only succeeded in looking even more idiotic. To myself, at least. He didn't seem to notice.

"Well, c'mon. Get in and we'll get 'er done." He leaned over and unlocked the passenger door as I jogged around the front and grabbed the handle. The cool smoothness of the chrome plated fixture brought the reality of the situation home. This was no fantasy. I had a momentary vision of refusing the ride. It wasn't too late to stop the inevitable course of events but then again, it was. I couldn't go back to the way things were before. I wouldn't. I opened the door and climbed into the cab of the truck.

The inside smelled of motor oil, Marlboro Reds and sweaty leather that threatened to overpower the puny pine tree-shaped deodorizer dangling from the rear view mirror. Hanging under the dome light was a necklace made of bullets and a bunch of polished, irregular stones. "Them's elk teeth. A buddy of mine made that for me a while back."

"It's..." Well, pretty isn't the right word, I thought. Cute is definitely out of the question, and unique implies an insult. "...I've never seen anything like it before."

"Me neither." He thrust his hairy paw out at me, the wrist at least an inch longer than the cuff of the tan, long-sleeved workshirt he wore under his leather jacket. "Name's Billy," he said.

Billy? "Nice to meet you, Billy. I'm Dave." I gave him my firmest handshake. I was out of practice. I don't shake a lot of hands. "From the license plates, I thought your name was Joebob."

He grinned, showing that crooked smile that made my heart stop. "Joebob's my cousin," he said. "He's lettin' me drive his truck to work and back 'til I get on my feet again. I'm goin' through a pretty wicked divorce right now." He wiped his nose on the back of his hand. "You married?"

"Nope. Not me."

"Smart man." He threw the truck in gear as he glanced in the mirror and sped off around my car. "We'll just take the next exit and double back. Tell you what, the only good thing that came outta that marriage was my daughter Leigha." He shifted around on one buttcheek and dug his wallet out of his back pocket, whipping it open and handing it to me.

I struggled to see in the half light, painfully distracted by the warmth of his body still pervading the smooth calfskin. My dick, already semi-erect, hardened fully, and I had to cross my legs as I twisted towards the light of the sunrise to see the picture of a smiling little towheaded girl with soft blue eyes. She was riding a battered coin-operated hobby horse like the ones you see by the grocery store carts, a grey steed with a cartoon expression and a chunk of its plastic mane missing. "She's cute," I said, handing the wallet back.

"Sure is. I only get to see her a couple of weekends a month, though. I can't even pick her up from day care anymore." When he twisted around to put his wallet back, I saw the bulge of his flaccid cock and watched his thigh muscles tighten through his faded Levis.

Strong legs, I thought, envisioning him with his naked legs around my waist, squeezing me as I bent forward and put my mouth on the pouch of his white briefs. I re-crossed my legs away from him, rubbing the head of my cock through my khakis. "That's a shame," I replied as we slowed and took the next exit. The thought of those thighs tightening around me wouldn't go away. "Maybe your lawyer could get you more time with her."

"Lawyer." He snorted the word as he stopped for the light. "Don't even talk to me about fuckin' lawyers. All they care about is the goddamn money."

We sped off down University, and I watched his legs working the clutch and the gas. I didn't even hear the rest of what he said. All my senses could process was the smell of the cab, the heat of my crotch and the look of his slim, strong legs. The Seven-Eleven sign was only a few blocks away, the end of the journey and the end of my one and only chance. I could never arrange this again, I thought. I've got to make my move.

I boldly reached over and put my hand on his upper thigh, feeling the warm denim as I brushed my fingers over the fabric. His thigh muscles tensed, but his legs did not part in further invitation. I couldn't look at his face. I tried to think of something clever to say, something that would make him mine, but nothing came to me. Had I come up with a good line, maybe things would have turned out differently. My eyes closed in ecstatic fear...

...I'm glad they did. That way, I didn't see the first punch coming. He hit me square in the nose. Silent despite the excruciating pain, I could feel the cartilage giving way and was dimly aware of the blood dripping down my burgundy tie.

The pickup squealed to a stop and the sound of horns honking behind us melded with the screamed words bouncing off the interior of the cab. None of the noises was distinct enough to separate, an angry cacophony punctuated by blows that seemed to come out of nowhere—my right ear, my left cheek, the side of my head hitting the passenger window—then suddenly the door I had cowered against was open and a hand shoved me roughly out of the truck. Something whizzed by my head and clattered against the pavement.

I hadn't even realized I'd hit the ground, but the pain in the back of my head told me I must have landed against something hard. I groaned and rolled over on my stomach, my forehead resting against the cold metal of a sewer grate. Sweat blinded me, and as I reached up to wipe it away, I saw it was blood. Flattened cigarette butts and bits of grimy paper clung to my shirt when I tried to sit up. Once the dizziness had passed, I tried standing but fell back into the gutter, catching a glimpse of myself in the window of the Burger King I'd landed in front of. I was a mess. I won't be going to work today, I thought.

Out of the corner of my eye I saw the orange and yellow gas can resting against a nearby Denver Post kiosk. I staggered to my feet and grabbed it, ignoring the dizziness this time. Now that was downright Christian of him, I thought. The Seven Eleven was still three blocks away, and I started laughing as I headed for it, a trail of blood following me down the sidewalk. I'd been right. The inevitable had happened, and I'd never be the same again.

We'd never be the same again.

—⟋⟋—

Rafi smiled widely, Twinkie crumbs salting his black moustache. His rough, horny fingers played the pads of the cash register like a computerized Steinway as he rang up my coffee and doughnuts. "Good morning, Mister Dave. Are you feeling better today?"

"Not bad, Rafi." After a week and a half, my nose was still bandaged, but the rest of the cuts and abrasions on my face were scabbing over. Although they looked awful, they didn't hurt too much anymore. The pain pills the doctor gave me helped some. "That's my ten dollars on gas."

The register blooped and bleeped. "Eleven seventy-nine, sir. You are working this holiday?"

"Holiday?"

"Memorial Day. I was so busy yesterday I could hardly catch my breath."

I opened my checkbook and began to fill in the amount. "I'm doing some overtime."

"Did they catch the boys who did this to you, Mister Dave?"

It was the first time since I'd been back to work that he addressed my injuries directly, but he was making the wrong assumption. I hadn't turned the incident over to "them," which I figured meant the police. I knew who did it, and I guess I could have pressed charges, but I never seriously considered it. Some might call it internalized homophobia or some subconscious feeling I had that maybe I deserved a beating for being gay, but they'd both be off base. I simply didn't think of the police as an option. My insurance paid for the emergency room and medical bills, and I even kept the source of my injuries vague when I talked to them or filled out forms, usually telling them I was assaulted by unknown persons while I was getting gas to take back to my car.

"Not yet, Rafi." I ripped out the check and handed it to Rafi, not bothering to go for my wallet.

He stood behind the counter, drumming his fingers on the glass top enclosing the lottery tickets as he waited for the next step in the transaction. "Your driving license, sir?"

"Why? I've been coming here for five years. Surely you trust me by now."

His eyes clouded over and his smile drooped. "I trust you, Mister Dave, but I have to have your numbers."

"Why?"

He shrugged his slightly humped shoulders. "It's the rules, sir."

"Not *my* rules. What if I don't give it to you?"

Rafi's agitation manifested in the trembling of his hands and the twitch of his moustache. He rubbed it clear of crumbs. The check lay between us like an unwanted orphan. He wasn't picking it up, and I wasn't taking it back. "Please, Mister Dave, why do you give me trouble this morning? Give me your numbers."

"No."

He tried to look stern. "Then give me cash money."

"I don't carry that much cash on me since I got attacked. What are you going to do? Make me suck the gas back out of the tank? Call the cops for eleven dollars and seventy-nine cents? Face it, Rafi, you have to trust me. Is it that hard? You know the check's good."

His eyebrows ran together in a hairy line of confusion. "But the numbers, Mister Dave," he mumbled, "the numbers..."

"Make some up. Nobody will know the difference. No one ever checks them anyway.

He scowled. "You sure?"

"Positive."

He grumbled what I assumed were Lebanese obscenities as he scribbled a string of near-numbers across the back of the check and initialed it with a flourish. "I see you in the morning, right?"

"As usual." I smiled, picked up my coffee and doughnuts and headed for the door before he could change his mind. "Have a nice day, Rafi."

All traces of annoyance gone, he shook his head wearily, came out from behind the counter and went back to buffing the floor. "You too, Mister Dave," he yelled over the noise. "I hope you are better tomorrow."

Tomorrow? Who the hell needed tomorrow? I felt great *today*. Success and confidence flowed through my veins like twin hits of crystal meth, stoking a fine, white buzz that echoed in my ears, telling me how good I was, how on top of my game I was, how I could break any routine I wanted to.

Snap.

That easy.

—⁓—

It would have been far too easy to be angry with Billy, both for masquerading as JOEBOB and for beating the crap out of me. Both situations were matters of circumstance. He was borrowing JOEBOB's truck, and the assumption that its driver was the same person as its owner was mine. And the beating? Let's just say that it goes with the territory. I'm not attracted to the prep-school intellectual type of guy who would have smiled sweetly and told me how flattered he was, but he wasn't gay and wasn't interested in that kind of experience. My taste runs towards the type who'd kick your ass if you stepped out of line. And I stepped *way* out of line.

So, it really wasn't Billy's fault. I couldn't blame him any more than I could blame a dog for biting when it's cornered. I had put him in the situation, so I really wasn't surprised when I got what I did. That's one of the reasons why I didn't call the police. I should have known he was one of those guys who needed to be loosened up with six-pack of Bud first. What I should do was apologize, and that's exactly what I had intended to do when I got on the freeway that morning—flag him down and apologize to him. That's all.

Easing into the middle lane as usual, I hit sixty and flipped on the cruise control. When the few cars around me had disappeared, either flying ahead or dropping back out of sight, I switched off my headlights and took to the air.

Great feathered wings seemed to sprout from either door, suspending my radials an inch or two above the pitted, pocked highway. I reached out the window, my hot fingers dipping into a cool, smooth pool of force not unlike what my fellow raptors must feel when they dip their wings and swirl in the morning sky.

I picked out downtown traffic patterns with keen eyes, as if searching for small mammalian prey among the slower moving cars. Shooting around the Mexican construction workers, I barely felt my hands as they twisted the wheel with a powder-dry assurance they had never before possessed. When I looked at them in amazement, however, they began to shake. The spell was broken. I was in a speeding car with no headlights on, one of those keen eyes now peeled for a cop sitting by the side of the road.

The few cars on the road thinned out even more as I headed towards the University exit, not really knowing what I'd do when I got there. I knew I wanted to see JOEBOB, or rather Billy, and try to apologize to him somehow; make him understand that I knew what happened wasn't his fault, that he was really a good person and a great father, and that I wanted to get to know him better. I hadn't meant to put the moves on him—well, not so *soon* anyway—and I needed for him to know...no, that's not right. *I* needed to know that he forgave me.

I slowed for the entrance ramp, no headlights in sight. I considered pulling over to the side of the freeway and waiting, but that seemed too stalker-ish, so I slowed even further as an eloquent apology began to form in my mind. But how would I deliver it? I doubted he'd stop if he saw me standing by the side of the road like last time. Nope, that was a one-time shot I'd already fucked up. *What if I never get another chance?* I refused to even consider the possibility. I'd come this far. I'd make him stop somehow.

If he even showed up. I mean, who works Memorial Day? But I saw his headlights coming down the entrance ramp before the thought had finished forming. Fathers who have child support to pay, I thought. That's who works Memorial Day. I slowed even more, moving over into the left lane as I waited for him to hit the freeway. When he roared off the ramp, I gunned the Dart, eased into the lane behind him and was soon on his tail.

He must not have noticed me at first because he was doing his usual sixty-five, and it was easy for me to tail him for a few exits. When I finally got up the nerve, I sped up and got back in the left lane, drawing even with him in no time. I looked over and saw him singing along with the radio, totally unaware of me. I waved at him, but the movement didn't seem to attract his attention. I honked my horn, and the blare in the early morning stillness seemed to startle us both. He looked in his rear view mirror then, finally, over at me.

I had my dome light on and my face was pretty heavily bandaged, but if he didn't recognize me, he certainly remembered my car. I smiled and waved, expecting...well, I'm not sure what I expected. I know I wasn't surprised when he sped up. I paced him, doing a good seventy, and honked the horn again. When I caught his eye this time, however, there was something else there. Fear.

Up until that time, I hadn't considered the possibility he'd think I was out for some kind of vengeance. Such a thought couldn't have been further from my mind. However, considering the fact that he'd beat the holy hell out of me, I could see how he'd be wary of contact. Maybe he thought I had a gun or something. I was never good at charades, and I couldn't think of how to convey my benign intention of apologizing to him. I tried smiling, but he probably couldn't tell for the bandages.

He cranked the orange Ford up to seventy-five and I followed suit, ducking back behind him to avoid a slow-moving yellow Ryder truck in the passing lane. By the time we'd passed him, Billy was doing eighty and I had to try to catch him. Thanks to the ministrations of a lesbian auto mechanic I know, however, the Dart was more than up to the task. I again drew even with him, eliciting a look of not only fear but surprise as well.

His apprehension was strangely arousing to me. The fact that the man who had beaten me to a pulp a few days ago was now stricken by fear at my appearance beside him on the freeway gave me the biggest hard-on I'd ever had in my life. I felt totally in control. The master of not only my destiny, but his as well. I cut into his lane, coming close to the side of the truck as he swerved away, almost losing control at the speed we were going. Once he regained his footing, he stared in silent horror at me, stiffening my resolve and my dick at the same time.

As he pulled ahead of me, I unzipped my khakis and eased my throbbing cock out with one hand, resting it straight up against the cool steering wheel. The wheel gave my shaft a delicious scrape as I caught up to him again. All thoughts of apologizing were gone, replaced by the sheer sensuality of stroking my cock while speeding down the freeway.

In a full-bore frenzy of flight, he floored the accelerator and the Ford shot away from me. But I was in a frenzy of my own. I slammed the Dart into overdrive and was soon pacing him again. He watched my car and the road with frantic spasms, each twitch of his head feeling like a cool hand on my engorged organ. Any gestures or exhortations would have done no good at this point, so I simply smiled at him.

He lurched towards the shoulder of the road, obviously trying to get away from me, but in my agitated state of mind, I could think of nothing but being close to him. I swept over into his lane, straddling the broken white line as the Ford moved closer and closer to the side of the road. His face was lined with terror now, and he shot me pitiful, whimpering looks that only added to my excitement. I had to make contact with him in some way. My life depended on it. The rising sun glinted off his bumper, reflecting a luscious fleshy tone like the inside of a pale hairy thigh.

Transfixed by the changing texture of the metal, I edged closer to it, my free hand dropping into my lap. I stroked furiously, my hand pumping up and down with short, panting thrusts. A drop of pre-cum seeped from my piss slit, slicking my palm enough to force a low moan from the back of my throat as I drew nearer to Billy's soft chrome. I didn't know he was that close to the guardrail.

The impact was slight but the orgasm intense. What felt like a small bump to my right front quarter panel rushed through my loins and shot straight up at my windshield, and I cried out with a gasp of relief as my load spattered the window and rear-view mirror. Billy broke through the rail and disappeared from view, having gone off the overpass onto the street below. The explosion came right after the noise of the impact, black smoke and shimmering waves of heat reflecting in my mirror.

I didn't even slow down.

—\m/—

Thanks to the holiday and early hour, no witnesses had come forward, so the police were treating the whole incident as an unfortunate accident that had involved no one else, thank God. I continue to work the same job I had before. The bandages came off a few weeks later, with little scarring. My nose, however, now has a very handsome bump that makes me look more sinister than I did before. That's what Gina says, anyway. I still see her everyday at coffee break. She has not gotten a Marketing job.

I scoured the newspaper for weeks afterwards, gleaning only a small item the day after the incident. Billy's last name was Hawthorne. He had been thirty-five years old and left an ex-wife and a daughter behind. I already knew about the last two. I should have felt guilty about leaving little Leigha without a father, but I was confident her mother would marry someone equally as red-necked as Billy and the girl would grow up more or less as fucked up as she would have had Billy been around to help raise her.

Even though I am now out at work, life goes on pretty much as it always has. Rafi still asks for my driver's license numbers when I cash my morning check, evidently considering my one lapse as some peculiar aberration, but his politeness is warier than it was before. He still buffs the floor in the morning and gives me a hearty wave when I come in. I look forward to it.

Remorse doesn't bother me much, although I will admit to having some very scary dreams at times. Most of them have to do with car accidents and would probably be very interesting to dream experts or shrinks. Not that I'm going to tell anyone about them.

I feel detached about the whole incident, as if it happened to a distant relative. I see Billy as victim as well as an instigator. And, depending on my mood I'm a killer or a hero. It's all the same to me.

I've learned a lot about obsession and what it can lead to, and I think things will be different with the guy in the green Porsche I saw this morning. His license plate reads CARL JR. I'm looking forward to meeting him.

The Telephone Line

Fantasies take you into dangerous territory, especially those with a chance of coming true. One false move, one wrong smell, one slight imperfection and the whole thing comes crashing down. Nothing—from the idea to the execution—can bear any weight again, and it can't possibly be re-constructed. Nope. Fantasies are nothing to play with.

So, when one *does* threaten to become reality, don't fuck with it. Let it flow naturally. Don't try to hurry it along or do anything differently than you have in your head the last forty or fifty times you played it. Know your lines, work your blocking, come in on cue and it'll materialize right before your eyes. That's what happened to me, anyway.

I had just gotten my first computer—back when only dial-up was available—and I soon tired of missing phone calls from friends and family because I was online having "fun," which meant trolling the few gay chat rooms available, looking for phone sex. I called Qwest, the local phone company, to arrange for a second line to be installed. A few days later, *he* showed up.

His name was Clint or Curt or Chet or something like that. I vaguely recall letters embroidered in a white oval patch on his uniform shirt. His shoulder-length hair was dirty blond and his eyes were green and reddened. Company regulations probably forbade him from smoking pot in the truck on the way to his calls, but I was certain he'd had a bong hit for breakfast.

"Wheeler?" he asked as I opened the door. He puncuated his question with a slight toss of his head to get his hair out of his eyes.

I have no idea how I answered. I was focused on not drooling. He was in his early to mid-twenties. A surfer-boy type—definitely straight and hot to death from the stubble on his face and neck to the way the frayed cuffs of his JC Penney's Levi knockoffs caught in the top of his scuffed tan workboots.

The repairman/phone guy/delivery man scenario, of course, has been a staple of gay (and straight) fantasies from the earliest days of '70's eight-millimeter film loops and probably way before then. Burly men in jeans and uniform shirts, half-sweaty from their labors, rumpled, wrinkled and ready for action they're not getting from their wives or girlfriends— what's not to jerk off over?

Most of the service guys who have come to the house haven't exactly been prime meat. I mean, some plumber's cracks you just *don't* wanna see. Clint/Chet/Curt, however, was a dream standing right on my doorstep, redolent of repair truck musk with a faint hint of a morning Lifebuoy shower. I was determined to have his dick in my mouth before the paperwork was done.

Trying to recall how much pot I had in the house, I brought him in and led him to my computer desk and the junction box where I wanted the second line installed. His jeans fit perfectly—not too tight but snug enough to accentuate the soft curve of his ass. I was glad I'd worn underwear or my sweats would have had a noticeable tent.

"Looks pretty simple," he said with the practiced assurance of a professional telephonic diagnostician. Must be something they learned at the training sessions to pacify customers. His confidence was making me hornier, if that was possible. "All I gotta do is find the phone box outside, run another line inside and bring it up though the floor. Lemme get some tools and I'll be right back."

The next fifteen minutes were torture as I rolled a joint, paced and wondered what to do when he came back in. Should I have a porn tape in the video? That was a great idea, but I had no straight porn—not even bi stuff. And gay porn might scare him off. It was too early for a beer, so I'd have to try getting him stoned.

I love straight guys, single or married. I love gay men too—when it comes to dick, I'm an equal opportunity cocksucker. Some gay men might call that self-loathing but I don't believe it. I like myself and I like being gay. However, straight guys have an enticing air of casual masculinity that many gay men just can't capture. The difference is embodied by the popular phrase, "straight-acting." Straight guys don't have to act. It's just how they are. Of course, all men have masculinity, but too often gay men tend to bury it beneath other culturally learned traits or accentuate it to cartoonish extremes. That's why they have to "act." Just like a fantasy, masculinity vanishes when you fuck with it.

Clint/Chet/Curt meanwhile had returned and was now crawling underneath my desk, drilling a hole in the floor to run the second line to the junction box. His squirming and reaching had pulled the shirt out of his jeans, exposing the small of his tanned back—dusted with a faint coat of darker blonde hair.

Trying to adjust my hard-on so it was less apparent, I resolved to scrutinize and respond to any hint of an opportunity. After all, I was a Qwest customer and he was on official company business and had to conduct himself like an employee. He could hardly punch me out if he wanted to keep his job. Besides, adverse reactions and possible physical injury go with the straight guy territory. Danger's part of the allure.

Finished with his drilling, my quarry went back under the trailer and fished the line up through the floor. As he breezed through the kitchen on his way to connect it to the junction box, I stopped him.

"You want something to drink? Water? A Coke?"

"A Coke would be great, thanks," he said, flashing a lopsided grin that stayed with me even after he'd left the room.

Grabbing a can from the fridge, I popped the top and snatched the joint I'd rolled off the counter. I lit it, trailing smoke into the office as I put the Coke down on the desk and knelt down beside him. "How's it going?"

"Almost done." As soon as he got a whiff of the pot, his head came up like a trained pointer looking for game shot from the sky. I smiled and held the spliff out to him. On automatic, his hand came up and reached out for the joint. Then he stopped himself. "Can't, man. I'm still on the clock. Sure smells good, though."

I just let him think about it. In a few moments, the junction box was back together again and he was reaching around the back of my computer. "That should do it," he said, standing back. "You wanna boot it up?"

"Yeah." I held the joint out and sat down at my desk. "Hold this for me, willya?"

This time there was no hesitation. He took a nice, long toke while Windows 95 loaded and I was soon looking at my AOL home page. He exhaled, chugged half a can of Coke and belched. "Sorry." He took another hit before he spoke. "Hey, can I use your bathroom real quick?"

Perfect. My opening. All I had to do was work up the nerve to say my line, which is where I usually choke. Either my brain or my tongue or my intestinal fortitude fails me, and I end up on the wrong side of Regret Street, just this side of Missed Opportunities. But not this time.

"Only if I can help," I said with practiced casualness. I *do* write erotica and had written that bit of dialogue countless times.

I searched his face trying to figure out which way the wind was gonna blow. I didn't have to wait long. He raised his eyebrows once, exhaled blue smoke and chuckled. *Chuckled.* "You mean, like, help me *piss*?"

"Yeah."

He took another puff and looked at me for a few seconds before he shrugged. "Okay. There's gotta be a first time for everything, right?" I didn't know if he was trying to convince me or himself, but I figured the question was rhetorical, so I didn't answer. I just led the way to the bathroom, my heart pounding.

When we walked in, my disheveled bathroom gave me a twinge of shame, but I soon got over it. A straight guy wouldn't think a glob or two of shaving cream in the sink and a few pubes on the toilet rim was much of a mess. And when he bent over and lifted the seat, he didn't recoil in horror. In fact, he just stood there, smirking at me as he hit on the joint again.

"I gotta piss," he said. "I thought you wanted to help."

Nothing—I mean absolutely *nothin*—gets me hotter than watching guys piss. I'm not really into watersports, so it's not the end product that does it. It's more the process. Pissing is the only time it's socially acceptable for guys to touch their dicks around other guys.

And touch them they do. They flop them out, shake them, pull on them and scratch them. They even sneak peeks at the other guys' dicks to see if theirs measures up, all within the furtive, nervous parameters of urinal behavior, of course. Damn those newfangled privacy shields. Give me good old fashioned trough pissing any day.

But never, before or since, have I had the opportunity to *help* a guy piss. I had meant to say *watch*, and it wasn't until Chet/Clint/Curt reminded me of my responsibility that I realized what he'd agreed to. And there he was, waiting patiently for me to reach inside his pants, fish out his dick and hold it for him while he pissed.

My hands trembled a bit as I unsnapped and unzipped his jeans, feeling the warmth of his body as I edged closer to him. He didn't pull away. It wasn't a joke. It was really going to happen. My tremors subsiding with this knowledge, I pushed the denim aside and slid my fingers down past the waistband of his white Hanes.

His pubes were lush and dense and his male scent floated up to my nose. I wanted to linger in that fragrant, wiry patch forever, but the poor guy had to pee. I took hold of his soft, warm dick with one hand and used the other to pull down the front of his underwear and ease his hairy nuts over the waistband.

As soon as I aimed his dick at the toilet bowl, he let go. A few drops became a little flow then a full, strong stream I swear I could feel between my fingers. He sighed with relief as he pissed, then he took another hit and put the joint on the edge of the sink. If I'd had a third hand to touch myself with, I would have come right then. I almost did anyway.

All too soon he stopped. Piss dribbled on my fingers. I waggled his cock in the air, drops flying everywhere, but the unsure feeling came back. Was I just supposed to put it back now? Was it all over? I didn't want to let go of it, and Chet/Clint/Curt wasn't giving me much direction now that his bladder had been emptied. I decided to take the matter into my own hands.

So to speak.

I went from waggling his dick to caressing the head of it while I brought my other hand up to his balls and stroked them. He sighed again, leaning forward and restoring my confidence. And if that motion hadn't convinced me, his rapidly stiffening cock did. I sank to my knees and took it into my mouth, pushing him back against the sink.

Size? I can't recall, and it really isn't important anyway. I remember it was cut, but that's about all. The visuals never stick with me, but the dicksmell does. Faintly pissy but mostly musky, it's an incredibly male perfume whose base is common to all guys with room for individual variation in its topnotes.

I don't know how long I sucked him, but we took turns driving. Sometimes he grabbed my head and fucked my mouth with rough thrusts. Other times I had my hands on his hairy ass, forcing his cock down my throat as far as I could take it. At last he began breathing heavy and his balls tensed.

He tried to pull me off, but I'd worked too hard to be denied a creamy dessert. I pinned his hands to the counter and used my weight to keep them down as he bucked against me a few times before he exploded. Spurts of hot, salty cum filled my mouth. He gasped as I swallowed. I didn't let him up until I was sure he'd been drained.

"God *damn*," he said. "Jesus."

I tucked his dick back in his shorts and left him to zip up. He took a few minutes to wash his hands and emerged looking hasty and sheepish. Uh-oh, I thought. Straight guilt. He didn't say anything and didn't really even look my way. He took his clipboard off the kitchen table and handed it to me.

"Um...I got another call to get to. If you'll just sign down at the bottom, so they can bill ya, I'll be on my way." Then he smirked again. Maybe handling his clipboard gave him some feeling of normalcy. "I'd let ya go for nothin', but my boss'd wonder."

But I didn't mind getting charged, and—this is the honest truth—it was $69.69. A small price to pay for a fantasy.

It can happen for you too. With a little luck, some nerve, and the right timing, your straight guy fantasy can become a masturbatory memory. Just make sure you have plenty of weed and/or beer.

And don't forget to leave the bathroom door open.

Templeton's in Love

*T*he line curled around the block like a pubic hair, I typed in my head.

Maybe not the most effective simile, but writing porn for a living leads you to make some weird comparisons. And the line *did* stretch all the way from the new faux red brick front of Carmine's Supper Club and Ristorante down to their landmark sign a block and a half away. But even landmarks change. The flowing script of the old "Carmine's" logo had been replaced with a blocky Bodoni whose straight, modern design was almost as offensive as the pretentious "Ristorante" squeezed in at the bottom.

This part of Colfax had always been the hip, trendy district, but the patchouli-fragrant head shops and musty used bookstores had been replaced by gourmet ice-cream stands and chain coffee shops with parking spots for strollers and dogs allowed on the patios. The only survivors were Sailor Jack's Tattoos—now known as BodyArt—and Carmine's.

I stepped out of line long enough to gauge the distance to the front door: about fifty or sixty people away. I hoped they wouldn't sell out. Templeton hasn't played in ten years – I *had* to be there. Seeing him without Stan would be strange, but Stan and I haven't seen each other for ten years either. I wondered if I should get two tickets and who I could ask to go with me when a familiar face emerged from the front door and began walking the line, stopping occasionally to talk to someone.

It was Carmine Jr., looking a little older than when I'd last seen him. His face brightened with recognition when he approached. "Tom!" he said, grabbing me in a bear hug. "How *are* you, buddy? How come we never see you down here anymore?"

"I'm good," I said as we separated and looked at each other. He'd filled out nicely, acquiring that stocky, barrel-chest Carmine Sr. had, little tufts of hair sticking out of the collar of his white shirt. "I moved out to the burbs. Don't get to the old neighborhood much. If I hadn't gotten your flyer, I wouldn't have known about this."

"Flyer? Wow, I didn't think the homeless guys I hired got out that far."

"Your folks still around, or are you running the place now?"

He chuckled. "They say it's mine but Mama comes down to the kitchen every day to tell me what's wrong with my red sauce and Pop's usually behind the bar buying drinks for his buddies. You know how it is." He handed me a piece of paper. "Here's a ticket voucher. Just pay when you get up to the window. I want to make sure the old crowd gets in to see Templeton."

I shook my head. "I can't believe he's playing after what—ten years? He's got to be in love again. Did you talk to him?"

"Pop did. All I know is that I had to get the piano out of storage and have it tuned. He's gonna be here for one show, tomorrow night—hey, are you still with Stan?"

I knew he'd ask. "No, not since Templeton stopped playing."

"Sorry to hear that. You guys were a good couple." He looked down the line. "I gotta finish handing these out," he said. "Look, when you get here on Saturday, hunt me down. I won't have a lot of time to talk, but I'll make sure you get a good table. If it wasn't for the old crowd coming to see Templeton, we never would have made it through some pretty lean years. We want to treat you guys right. See ya, buddy." He clapped me on the shoulder and continued his trek down the line.

The old crowd, I thought. Our crowd. Stan and I had seen a lot of the same faces every Saturday night—mostly other gay men, dykes and goth kids with bohemian aspirations, but once word spread, young straight couples started driving in from the suburbs looking for emotional diversions they couldn't find at the multiplex. Carmine always found tables for us, though—tables for dreaming of the someone Templeton sang about, tables for falling in love and tables for breaking up.

And in front of the stage sat his partner, Taylor, his bulky frame as out of place at their small table as a stuffed bear at a dollhouse tea party. He was as big and tall as Templeton was short and skinny—opposites who attracted attention. They lived in the neighborhood and Templeton was an accountant. That's all anyone really knew about them. No one knew how they met or when their birthdays were or even how Templeton had started playing at Carmine's. We didn't even know his first name.

You could spend dinner talking to them, as Stan and I had on a few occasions, and be as clueless by dessert as you were when the salads came. Taylor parried direct questions effortlessly as Templeton smiled, his skinny face full of piano-key teeth, and told another isolated anecdote unrelated to the subject at hand. They were a world unto themselves, and they never handed anyone a map.

But Gershwin was in their world—Gershwin, Fats Waller, Cole Porter, Rodgers & Hart, Dorothy Fields and Jule Styne. "Nothing past 1960," Templeton used to say, "when music became vulgar." And he sang those witty, urbane songs of love and loss directly to the man at the front table, who looked up at the stage with admiration. He played them all for Taylor. Everyone else just happened to be in the same room.

Then Stan and I started falling apart. Arguments and tantrums and nights of silent disgust for each other kept us away from Carmine's for a couple of months. When we went back for an attempted reconciliation dinner, Taylor had lost a shocking amount of weight. AIDS, cancer—who knew what he had? The rumors ran rampant. Templeton still sang to him but a shrill desperation crept into his voice, as if the melody could keep Taylor alive. And we resumed our regular Saturday night attendance, as if it could restore us as well.

But in the end, it didn't work for anybody. Taylor died, Stan and I broke up and Templeton stopped singing. Carmine tried out a few other acts, but it wasn't the same. And then the small stage was gone, replaced by a few more tables and a coffee station in the back of the room. I moved to the suburbs to hide and write.

Now, Templeton was playing. He *must* be in love again.

The box office was getting closer. Only a few more people now. We stepped around the legs of a homeless guy sleeping against the wall. His head tilted to the right, slumped on his shoulder as he snored out a foul stink of unbrushed teeth and stale wine.Homeless man sex, I thought. That'd be great for the collection of fetish stories I had in the works.

It didn't do anything for me personally, but someone would be bound to get off on it. I noted his craggy, unshaven grey jowls and the stains on the thighs of his tan work pants, forcing myself to look higher at the slight bulge of his crotch and trying to imagine his unwashed cock smell. I stepped closer, hoping no one would notice me trying to sniff a homeless guy.

"Tommy? Is that you?"

Even if I hadn't recognized Stan's voice or the way he called me Tommy, I would have known by his presence. I'd been feeling it since I stepped in line. I figured he was around somewhere. He *had* to be. I hadn't let myself look for him because I dreaded seeing him as much as I longed to. If we were supposed to see each other again, he'd have to find me. It was his responsibility. After all, he was the one who left.

"If you have to ask, I must be." I couldn't help but smile when I looked at him. He always made me smile. What would we do now? An awkward hug that reminded us of what we used to mean to each other—or even worse, a tepid handshake? What do you say to someone whose last words were "Fuck you"?

Stan solved the problem by stepping in with a combination hug and clap on the back, heavy on the reassuring clap part. I mirrored his actions, trying to ignore his smell, which I loved—a combination of aftershave and pheromones that always drove me to sniff his pillow long after he'd left our bed. He broke away first, holding me by the shoulders at arm's length.

"You look great," he said with a broad smile.

"So do you." It wasn't a lie, at least on my part. Stan used to be geek-chic, tall and skinny with a nose the size of Idaho and deep-set blue eyes. But somewhere between "Fuck you" and "Tommy, is that you?" he'd grown into his nose and put on a few pounds. None of it looked like fat, either. He'd had his teeth fixed and wore an Armani sports jacket over a gleaming white shirt, some expensive-looking jeans and loafers that looked too buttery soft to be domestic. Corporate law must have been good to him. And Connie.

"Thanks, buddy." The "buddy" sounded too foreign, too straight to be coming out of his mouth. "I can't believe Templeton's playing again after all this time. He must be in love again."

"I was thinking the same thing."

"How many, please?" The girl's face was irritated and expectant. She held a wad of tickets and a finger poised for counting. How long had I been standing in front of the window?

"Are you going?" I asked Stan. It was a reflex action.

"I wanted to, but it looks like the line's pretty long. I just got here."

I turned back to the window and reached for my wallet. "Two, please," I said.

She snapped the tickets off a roll and took my money. "*Next.*"

"Does this mean you're taking me?" he asked as we stepped away from the window. I handed him his ticket.

"I just gave you a ticket, didn't I?"

"Maybe you'd rather take your boyfriend or partner or whatever."

"Nope." I tried not to say it like I hadn't been on a date in five years.

"Great. I'm looking forward to it. Hey, how about you come over and see my place, Tommy? It'll shock the hell out of you when you see where I'm living. Or do you have to get back home to the boyfriend?"

Two "boyfriends" in two minutes, I thought. This from a guy who couldn't even *say* the word ten years ago. "Sure," I replied. "Let's go."

He took the lead as we crossed the street against the light, a weird air of expectant hesitation between us. We both wanted to talk, but how to start? True to form, I let him begin, content to admire the grey in his hair and the lines on his face. They made him look even more handsome than ever. I had always imagined they would.

"So, how have you been?" he finally asked.

"Good, good. And you?"

"Can't complain."

"How's Connie?"

"Don't know. Haven't talked to her in a long time."

"What happened?"

A half-smile crept across his face. "What you said would happen. How did you know?"

"I didn't. I mean, I thought...okay, it's what I *wanted* to happen. But at least she had the baby. You got some of what you wanted."

"Nope. She lost it, and the doctor wasn't optimistic about trying again." He fell silent for a few seconds, staring away as if another life of his was off in the distance. "We thought about adopting," he said, looking at me again, "but our lives seemed too tentative after that. After a couple of years, we got tired of making each other miserable and packed it in. She lives somewhere in Portland now."

"I'm sorry to hear that."

He grinned. "Why? Portland's nice."

"No, no—I'm sorry to hear you split up."

We paused at a curb, letting traffic go by as he squinted into the sun. "Why should you be sorry? I walked out on you—on *us*. You should be raging, but you're sorry instead."

The cars cleared and we crossed Colfax. Just like Stan to tell me how I should be reacting. I shrugged. "I don't do rage very well. Anyway, that was a long time ago."

"You're too nice, Tommy. You always have been. You know, I was the luckiest man alive, but I fucked up. I walked out on the only person who ever really loved me."

"Connie loved you."

"Not like you did. And you know what? I've never loved anyone like I did you. I can't believe I was stupid enough to throw it away. We could have had a beautiful life together, but you're probably settled down with some nice guy in the suburbs. Dogs and a mortgage and everything."

Who the hell was I walking with? Stan the Contrite? Stan the Apologetic? I wished I could think fast enough to invent a fantasy husband, but he always knew when I was lying anyway. "I do live out in the burbs, but I'm single. I haven't been on a date in, like, five years. Sad, huh?"

"Sad? I think it's a damn shame. You don't know how many times I picked up the phone to call you, Tommy."

"Why didn't you?"

"I wasn't sure if you'd hang up or not. You know I'm not good with rejection."

"Who is?" I replied before thinking.

He was silent for a few moments. "I guess I deserved that."

I hadn't meant it like that, but nothing I could have said would have convinced him otherwise. Letting him think whatever he needed to, I walked alongside him. The route was disquietingly familiar—two blocks south of Colfax and east one block on 13th to Sherman. When we turned south again, it hit me.

"You rented our old apartment," I said.

"No," he said quickly. "I rented the one across the hall. When Connie and I got divorced, I needed a place to stay, and I've always liked this neighborhood. When I was down here looking, I ran into Madeline. She told me there was a vacancy, so I took it. That's all."

Too many coincidences and too much denial, I thought. I didn't know what was going on, but it was cute rather than menacing, so I decided to let things play out—and despite the weird vibe, I was enjoying being with Stan after all this time. There was a reason I'd never fallen for anyone else.

We walked down Sherman towards Poet's Row, a series of apartment buildings named after famous poets, and stopped in front of the Robert Frost. The entry door had been refinished and some of the brickwork redone, but it was as charming as I remembered. Virginia creeper laced the eaves and framed the second and third floor windows, shadowed by huge elms that were just starting to drop leaves.

When we stepped into the entry hall, the sight of the mailboxes and the scent of mildewed carpet and wood oil took me back twenty years. We were young and in love and just coming home from a walk around Capitol Hill, fresh and energized by talking and walking. And horny. God, we were so horny then.

I had to touch him. The feeling was so instinctive and automatic that my reaction surprised even me. As he dug in his pocket for his front door key, I reached up and began massaging his shoulders. He stopped, straightened up and leaned back into me, the pressure of his body making me want to press myself into him even more. But I couldn't. I had already gone way farther than I intended.

I tried distracting myself with the distance between us those last weeks, remembering his "Fuck you, Tommy" and how I crammed our pictures into a cardboard box without even taking them out of the frames, sobbing as they crashed to the bottom of the dumpster in the alley. And how I slammed the lid down on the whole broken mess, swearing I'd never let anyone do that to me again.

"Mmmmm, that feels nice," he said. And it all disappeared into his breath and his smell and his voice and his flesh giving way beneath the flex of my fingers. He turned his head towards mine, his eyes closed and his lips parted. They looked soft and warm, exhaling a ragged passion as familiar to me as my own. All I had to do was lean forward a few inches and throw myself off the cliff again.

That's why I let go. His eyes popped open when we broke contact, and he sighed. I may have too. I can't remember. All I remember is instant regret. "I can't," I think I said.

He nodded, his lips closing around a rueful smirk. "I know. I'm sorry."

But I knew he wasn't.

"You still want to come in for a few minutes?" he asked.

"Sure." But I wasn't.

I followed him down the hall, going further back in time with each step until I got to the door of our old apartment. I felt the heft of the suitcase I left with and I swore if I'd looked at my palm, the imprint would have been there like stigmata. Stan must have noticed me staring at the door.

"It was pretty weird for a while," he said. "Now, I don't even notice it. C'mon in." The floor plan was just like our old place—same arched doorways, same radiator, same vaulted ceilings with the same ceiling fan. "Want something to drink?"

"Water would be great, thanks." Glancing around the room, I noticed a general shabbiness. The carpets were worn, the sofa fabric shiny and frayed in spots, unrefurbished second-hand furniture. Not the surroundings for a successful corporate lawyer. "So, how far is this from your office?" I asked, sitting on the sofa.

He came back from the kitchen with two bottles of water. "I don't have an office," he said as he handed me one and sat down beside me. "I'm not doing corporate law anymore."

"Did you retire or what?"

"Eh—bought some properties, sold 'em, made some money. Don't do much of anything anymore. I'm trying to live simply. Do you remember the day I left?"

"Parts of it."

"I'm sure you remember the 'fuck you' part. You don't know how sorry I am about that. But do you remember what you said right before that?"

"No." It wasn't a routine denial, either. I really didn't.

"You said I'd never be happy until I learned to live in my own skin, and you were right. Well, that's what I've spent the last five years doing—learning to live in my own skin. I'm in therapy, I came out to my sister and my folks and, believe it or not, I'm happy for the first time in my life."

"No more hiding, huh? Feels great, doesn't it?"

"It *does*," he said, "but I only have one problem."

"What's that?"

"I miss what we had." He moved so close our knees touched. I was up against the arm of the sofa and had nowhere else to go.

"You'll find it with someone else," I replied, holding my bottle of water as if that would ward him off.

He moved in even closer. "I don't want someone else. I want you." Stan took my head in both of his hands and guided it to his lips, but I already knew the way. His smell and the touch of his fingers on my cheeks rendered me helpless. Our lips met in a soft, speculative kiss that soon became eager and definite. I put my arms around him and he let go of me. I was in his grip anyway.

Dizzied by the frantic dance of our tongues, each kiss-muffled sigh cast me further and further back, into a warm, safe place I knew well but never hoped to see again—just as beautiful and narcotic as I remembered it. We waltzed dangerously close to the edge of a precipice without a rope to pull us back to reality. I had to stop the music in my head, no matter how much I liked the tune. "I can't do this," I said, pushing away from him and getting up from the sofa. My lips already felt cold and deserted. "I can't go back."

"It's not going *back*, Tommy," he said, a pleading I'd never heard before in his voice, "it's going *on*. Right from where we left off."

I didn't want to argue the point. I couldn't. "I have to get out of here," I said, heading for the door.

"Wait, Tommy, don't…"

But it was too late. I was already out in the hall. I felt something running over my hand and realized I was squeezing the water out of the bottle I'd been holding. I wiped my fingers off on my pants and dropped the bottle on Robert Frost's carpet, fighting my way to the front door through a flood of memories.

—⟋⟋⟍—

I must have taken that ticket out of my pocket a thousand times trying to decide whether or not to go. By the next afternoon, it was smudged and torn a quarter of the way through due to a hasty decision after a few vodka and tonics that were supposed to put me to sleep but didn't.

Staying home with yet another drink would have been the easiest thing to do—let it all pass me by and forget the whole damn thing. But I couldn't. If I could have forgotten it, I wouldn't have gone down there to pick up the ticket in the first place. It wasn't Templeton, it was Stan. It wasn't over between us—maybe not in the way *he* thought, but I had things to say and he needed to hear them. Or at least I needed to say them. I wasn't about to get back together with him, that was for sure. He might be in therapy, he might be sorry, he might even love me, but I'd moved on. Too bad he hadn't.

That was in my stronger moments. Other times I wondered just what I'd moved on *to*. An empty house? Meals alone by the television like my widowed dad? Not going to the symphony because I hated going places by myself? I needed to make more friends, but I didn't socialize well. I'd never acquired that skill.

I don't know if it was curiosity, fate or the unfinished business with Stan, but Saturday night found me standing outside Carmine's with my smudged, half-torn ticket in my hand watching a lot of people file in but none coming out. Hoping Carmine Jr. would make good on his promise to find me a table, I straightened my tie, brushed some lint off my jacket and went inside.

The main dining room was packed, and so were the two new overflow rooms off to either side. They had the same burgundy carpet, dark wood paneling, maps of Italy and framed pictures of Frank Sinatra on the wall. There must be an Italian Restaurant Warehouse that every Carmine's, Angelo's and Dino's in the country buys this stuff from, I thought. But the new rooms also had video screens and speakers.

"Hi Tom," Carmine Jr. said, coming around from the reservations desk. "Glad to see you. We weren't sure if you were gonna make it."

"We?"

"Follow me. Your table's this way." He zipped into the main dining room, quickly weaving his way down front between tables, waiters and customers. I almost lost him in a near collision with a family-style platter of pasta primavera, but I was able to catch up with him when he stopped for a crossing dessert cart. He motioned me closer to the stage and pointed to a small table with a huge bouquet of flowers. Stan occupied the other chair.

"Don't ask if I have another table," Carmine Jr. said. "It's here or the alley. You boys talk. I'll have Stephanie take your cocktail order. It's on me, so drink up. I'll be overcharging you for dinner." He smiled. "Enjoy."

"I'm glad you showed up," Stan said. "I would have looked pretty stupid sitting here with these flowers and no date...wait, maybe I shouldn't have called it a date." His grin was as disarming as ever, bringing to mind some of the crazy stuff I used to do to see that grin.

I had to smile. "I think this qualifies. Thanks. They're beautiful."

"And," he said, moving them between us and the rest of the room, "I got them big enough to hide everyone else, so it just seems like it's us and the stage. I hope the waitress knows we're back here."

I couldn't banter without speaking my piece first. "Look, I'm sorry about running out on you yesterday."

"I'm sorry about springing it on you like that. I should have warmed up to it first, but you know how direct I am."

"Yeah," I said. "I remember. That's why I'm going to try to be the same. I know how you feel, believe me. And if this had come right after we broke up, there would be no question about giving it another shot. But it's just too long, Stan. Too long. And I'm not sure it's what you really want."

"What do you think I want?"

"I think you want to take back ten years, Stan. You can't do that. I mean, look what you're calling me. No one ever calls me 'Tommy' anymore."

I thought I saw a tear in his eye, but it could have been a trick of the light. "But that's how I remember you."

"See? That's the problem. I'm not that guy anymore."

"I don't believe that," he said. "Do you mean to tell me the man who enjoyed romance more than anything else in the whole world is gone? What happened to him?"

"He starved to death. We can be friends, Stan. I'd really like that. I enjoyed spending time with you yesterday. Let's just be friends, okay?"

"I'm not sure I can do that," he said as the waitress appeared over the flowers.

"What can I get you gentlemen to drink?"

As we gave her our drink orders and requested two house specials for dinner, the dining room lights flickered on and off, finally settling on dim as the crowd began to buzz.

A familiar figure walked briskly from the bar and took the stage. Templeton hadn't changed much. Always small and thin, he'd gotten even thinner. His brown eyes looked hard and flinty. His moustache was still black, but his dark hair was flecked with grey and wrinkles grooved the corners of his mouth.

He closed his eyes and breathed deeply for a moment, then brought his hands to the keyboard and began to play *Come Rain or Come Shine* softly. He hummed in a barely audible voice until he'd played the verse through, then he sang out. His voice was lower, hoarser than I remembered it, but it had a gravity that wasn't there before. Finishing the opening number, he ignored the enthusiastic applause and swung into *Misty* without a break.

His voice was getting stronger, swooping and swirling sassy through *Ain't Misbehavin'* then vamping on the melody to segue into a soft, seductive version of *Mean to Me.* He was in great form, as if he hadn't been away from Carmine's for ten years. I always loved his piano skills because I seemed to hear more notes than he looked like he was playing. But as terrific as his performance was, it was different—lonelier. It needed joy.

The audience lapped it up like heavy cream. The warmth they exuded in return filled the room, but Templeton remained unaffected by it. He neither acknowledged or discouraged the attention. He let it wash over him—a wave of devotion that crashed against the stage and pooled uselessly beneath the pedals of the piano.

He continued playing for an hour, moving from song to song without a break for even a sip of the Calistoga water sweating atop the piano. Stan and I were mesmerized. Neither one of us said anything during that hour, despite the arrival of our dinners. We ate, but I don't remember a thing about the food.

The only pause in the set was before the last number. He took his fingers off the keyboard and nearly drained the Calistoga dry in a couple of swigs before leaning into the mic. "This is something I wrote many years ago," he said, "for someone who never got a chance to hear it."

He began a soft, sad intro of minor keys that bespoke major heartbreak. There were no lyrics; only a slow, desolate melody that rendered words insufficient. The middle was stronger, more hopeful, but it was only a 32-bar oasis that lingered long enough for relief before the chord progression turned somber and elegiac once again. I realized then that Templeton was *not* in love. It would have been impossible to invest that tune with that much pain, that much sorrow, if he had been in love. He was a wonderful performer, but no one was that good. Why was he performing again, then? Was it a tribute to Taylor? Some sort of closure?

Towards the end, the melody simply drifted off. Templeton played it softer and softer until it disappeared like bitter smoke over the crowd. In the silence that followed, I heard sniffling and saw many people daubing their eyes, including Stan. Without waiting for applause, Templeton left the stage and walked quickly to the bar area, disappearing behind a door in the back. He must have heard the crowd's deafening appreciation. I clapped so hard my hands hurt.

"He's not in love," Stan said as we sat back down. "There's no way. I mean, he was great, but there was no joy."

"I was thinking the same thing. You remember he used to say he couldn't perform without it. That's why he quit when Taylor got sick. So, why is he up there?"

"Mr. Tom?" The creaking, accented voice belonged to Carmine's mother, Rosa, who stood within the tubular aluminum cage of her walker. She had to be in her eighties. She was wrinkled and stooped, her black and red dotted dress draped in folds over her tiny frame. Her pulse beat through the paper-thin skin of her wrist as she held out her hand. I stood up and clasped it.

"Rosa," I said, "how are you? You look terrific."

"I look old, but it's okay. At least I don't look dead." She glanced down at our empty plates. "*Mange bella*—the special, it was good?"

"It was great."

"Grandmama Cochelli's red sauce, it don't miss. Carmine learns pretty good, but I make tonight. Good to see Mr. Templeton back, eh?"

"It certainly is. He sounded great."

She broke out in a white, dentured grin. "Beautiful. He got to have a little bit *Italiano* in him, eh? Ah, is just too sad what happened."

"I know. I still think about Taylor to this day. He was a wonderful guy."

She knitted her grey eyebrows with confusion. "Mr. Taylor, yes. He always make me laugh—but Mr. Templeton…"

"Templeton?"

"He has the cancer too."

I felt the blood drain from my face. "Oh, my god. We had no idea."

"He don't say nothing to nobody, but he hurts. I see sometime when he comes in the morning to practice for tonight. You should stop at St. Catherine's and say a novena for him before you go home. For him not to hurt so much."

I really couldn't speak.

"We will," Stan said for me. "Thanks for telling us."

"You are good people, so you should know. Nice to see you again, my friends. *Buona notte.*"

"I don't get it," I said. "He's dying, but he's playing again."

"I think you have the order wrong there," Stan replied. "He's playing *because* he's dying. He's anticipating seeing his joy again."

The lights dimmed again and Templeton emerged, taking the stage a little less adroitly than before. Or maybe it was my imagination. He sat down at the bench and began to noodle through *Come Rain or Come Shine* again. The audience fell quiet, but this silence wasn't the expectant one that had preceded his first set. It was the solemn, respectful silence that ensues after an unsettling disclosure.

Either from the wait staff or Carmine Jr., the news of Templeton's illness had spread and he definitely noticed the difference in the crowd. He continued playing with the song, running down the same sixteen bars over and over as he gazed out on the audience with a thoughtful frown.

Suddenly, he seemed to understand. His playing became more purposeful and the frown vanished, replaced by the thinnest of grins as he bent down to the mic. "Oh, I see," he said. "But you shouldn't feel sorry for me. I'm not sorry. It's the second best thing that's ever happened to me." He played harder, staring straight up as he crooned the verse loud and clear.

He could have been looking at the water-stained ceiling or he could have been looking at God, but we knew who he was looking at. My gaze went up there too for a respectful moment, but there was nothing for me in that direction. I looked at Stan, then I took his face in my hands and kissed him as hard as I could, thinking that sometimes you have to go back before you can move on.

Little Danny's Donuts

L ittle Danny Cooper may have been a criminal, but he wasn't hardcore. He stuck with the small stuff—credit card scams, real estate fraud, Internet swindles, the infrequent drug score—leaving the ugly deeds to those ugly enough to do them. Nothing big; just enough to maintain an unextravagant lifestyle without having to resort to a day job, which no Cooper had done in generations.

But as every petty thief knows, staying under the radar is as important to a successful life in crime as the hustle. Mind your own business, never call attention to yourself, don't let people see your patterns and you'll be fine. That's what made the speeding tickets so annoying to Danny.

The cops had established a speed trap the next block over from Danny's ancestral suburban home. Danny couldn't help speeding. Due to the nature of his profession, quick getaways were second nature. He'd been issued so many citations, the cops who worked the trap had memorized his driver's license number, waving cheerily whenever he remembered to creep past them.

Danny wasn't the only one. People always got pulled over there, so it was a sweet revenue spot as well. No way would the city ever abandon it. It was cramping his life and creeping him out. Who wanted the law on his doorstep? *Don't work against it,* his dad, Big Dan, would have told him. *Make it work for you.*

He knew intuitively he was halfway there. The cops had already begun looking at him as the-neighborhood-guy-who-can't-slow-down, which was a helluva lot better than thinking of him as the-career-criminal-down-the-block. If they saw him as the former, it was going to be tougher to see him as the latter. *I just need a more positive spin,* he thought. *Maybe I can do something for them.*

And that's when the idea came to him. Donuts.

One of the advantages Danny had found in staying around the house and keeping a low profile was that he became an excellent cook. All of the men he dated raved about his shrimp scampi, his paella, his salmon lasagne and his marinara sauce. But once he got them in the sack, they were never invited back for a second meal. He'd never met anyone he cared enough about to give up crime for.

He had never tried home-made donuts before but considering his culinary skills, he didn't think there'd be a problem. *It's butter, flour, sugar and eggs. How tough can it be?* So he went to work scouring the Internet for recipes.

The first batch turned out leaden and inedible. Even Bub, Danny's Great Dane garbage disposal, refused them after taking one outside and trying to bury it. Three batches later, they were getting lighter and fluffier and Bub was growing more hopeful. Danny abandoned the recipes and cooked by intuition. The next batch improved once he increased the frying temperature. He placed an order with the local Safeway store for more supplies, took a breather, then went back to his bowls.

The first few from the sixth batch were out of the deep fryer and draining on paper towels when Chad, the delivery boy, knocked on the back door. Danny put the batter bowl down on the counter to answer it.

Chad was a hipster dude about twenty-three or four with the *de rigueur* scraggly goatee, sleeve tats and sock cap, delivering groceries when he wasn't in art school classes. Hairy and fleshy—more fit-fat than chunky—he put Danny's groceries on the island in the middle of the kitchen and strode to his usual spot in front of the kitchen sink.

"What's cookin'?"

"Donuts," Danny said. "Want one?"

"Sure."

Danny brought one over on a square of paper towel, which Chad immediately crumpled and threw behind him into the sink. He bit into it and smiled, crumbs falling on Danny's clean floor. "Delicious, man," he said. "I'm not a much of a donut guy, but these are great even without frosting."

Danny stepped around the crumbs, and moved in close, cupping Chad's crotch with his hand. "Here's the only frosting they need."

Chad grinned and ground his hips into Danny's hand. "Don't know how much is down there, dude. My girlfriend stayed over last night."

"Isn't that what you said the last time?"

He popped the last of the donut in his mouth and chewed. "Probably."

Danny dropped to his knees and looked for the zipper of Chad's jeans. They sagged so low it was almost down to his knees, but Chad's pronounced bulge was exactly where it should have been. Danny ran the palm of his hand down the hard length of it as Chad sighed and swallowed the donut.

Oh yes, Danny thought. *There'll be frosting.* He grabbed Chad's belt loops, yanked his pants and boxers down to the floor and Chad's hard dick sproinged up and slapped Danny in the face. He slid one hand up and palmed Chad's balls as he took the head of his cock into his mouth.

Chad sighed again as Danny's other hand traveled up under Chad's t-shirt, making it as far as his furry belly before Chad stopped him. "No."

Danny dropped his hand into his lap, kneading his own crotch but he knew better than to take his dick out. Chad also didn't like Danny to masturbate while he was blowing him. Danny thought Chad had a lot of fucking rules, but this was hot young dick that came to your door, blew a load and went away again with no strings attached.

Danny concentrated on the crotch facing him instead, tickling Chad's hairy nutsack while he licked and sucked Chad's girthy knob. Danny took his dick in his hand and traced his tongue down to Chad's balls, gingerly taking each one into his mouth before moving further underneath. Chad groaned as Danny went vertical and began tonguing his taint.

"Oh *maaaan,*" Chad breathed, turning around and squatting slightly to give Danny access. Danny grabbed his furry ass globes and pulled them apart, rimming him gently at first then plunging his tongue deep into Chad's musky hole. Danny breathed his butt scent, giving his own hard dick a quick squeeze with one hand as he pumped Chad's spit-slick cock with the other. *He'll let me lick his ass, but I can't touch his chest. Straight guys are so weird.*

Chad moaned and bucked his cock against Danny's hand as Danny drove his tongue deeper and deeper into Chad's hole. Danny felt Chad's balls begin to tighten up but before he could cum, he spun Chad around and gorged himself on Chad's thick cock. Chad's eyes rolled up in the back of his head as he grabbed Danny's hair and fucked his face.

It wasn't long before Chad screwed his face up and started panting, his goateed chin working silently. Danny reached up and cupped his balls again as Chad groaned and spewed a heavy load of hot jizz down Danny's throat. He backed away into the counter, but Danny wasn't going to be denied his reward. He swallowed the whole thing, licking the head of Chad's dick to make sure he got the last drop.

"I guess I had some left over after all." Chad pulled up his pants and boxers, stuffing his half-hard dick back inside. "Thanks, dude."

Dude, Danny thought. *Is there a hotter word in the English language?* "Not a problem."

"Receipt's in the bag." Chad unbuckled and re-buckled his thin belt as he turned and headed for the door. "See ya next time."

Danny waved and took Chad's place at the counter, taking out his own cock and stroking it a few times as he savored the taste of Chad's load. It wasn't long before he was ready to cum. He had jerked past the point of no return, caught in that just-before-the-squirt territory when a realization suddenly struck him.

Shit, I don't want to cum on the goddamn floor. I just waxed it! Unable to stop stroking, he looked around frantically for something to shoot in and spied a measuring cup half-full of watery beaten eggs. He grabbed it with his free hand and got it to the head of his dick just before he fired off a nice, quarter-cup helping. A few more drops dribbled out, puddling and melding with the eggs as Danny sighed in relief.

A bit lightheaded, he tucked himself back into his pants and turned to the sink, intending to dump out the cummy egg mixture—but then an idea grabbed him. He smiled, grabbed his wooden spoon and poured it into the donut batter. *I've had a taste of the cops all my life*, he thought as he stirred. *Let them get a taste of me for a change.*

—ɯ—

The policemen manning the clocking van were Officer Rand and Officer McNally. Yes, they explained patiently to Danny—and countless others—those were their real names. Their sergeant thought pairing them up would be funny, especially since they looked so much alike, from the same square-jawed face and short brown hair down to their wire-rimmed glasses. They found it less than amusing, but they got along well despite or, perhaps, because of it.

That was not the case with Officers Webb and Morgan, who wrote the tickets out of the black and white parked a block away. Officer Webb was pockmarked and pot-bellied, a thirty-five year veteran of the force who felt his impending retirement gave him license to ride his younger, fitter partner. For his part, Officer Morgan was waiting anxiously for Officer Webb's retirement, hoping for a partner who was sympathetic to a more modern view of policework; someone who wasn't content to sit in a patrol car and write tickets. Maybe even someone he could come out to.

"No thank you, sir," Officer Morgan said to Danny the first day he came up to the patrol car with a thermos of coffee and a paper plate piled with six donuts wrapped in plastic. "It's very nice of you, though."

Danny smiled even wider. "I'd really appreciate your taking them—the officers in the van did. It's just a little token to show you how much the neighborhood values your presence. You've really cut down on the speeders. Me included." He tried what he thought was a self-effacing grin.

"Sure, hand 'em through." Officer Webb clapped Morgan on the shoulder. "It's not a bribe or nothin'. And if it is, it's a little one." Morgan shot him a look, indecipherable to Danny but meaningful to Webb. "What?" he challenged as he ripped the plastic off the donuts and ate one in two bites.

Smiling at Danny, Morgan uncapped the thermos and poured coffee in a styrofoam cup he took from the glovebox. "Thank you, Mr. Cooper. They look really good."

"Well, have one."

"I'd like to, but I'm kinda watching my weight."

"He's on a diet," Webb said, "a faggoty diet."

"I just don't want to turn into a lardass, that's all."

"Who you callin' a lardass?" he asked, reaching for another donut.

"Nobody, but if the pants fit...you're *lucky*."

Danny's heart fluttered, and he noticed how handsome the officer was—his close-cropped blonde hair, the dimples that appeared when he smiled, his bluish-grey eyes and noble profile that reminded Danny of a rugged Nordic fisherman he'd seen once in an issue of National Geographic. Okay, jacked off to. A *lot*.

Danny felt a stirring at the thought of it, and he pressed himself into the door of the patrol car hoping it would go away. It didn't. "I'll get the thermos tomorrow," he said, feeling the hot flush rise to his face. And elsewhere.

"Thanks again, Mr. Cooper."

"Danny."

Officer Morgan shot him a shy smile. "Danny."

"Yesh, thankshalot," Officer Webb said around the remnants of his fourth donut. He may have been a pig, but at least he wasn't rude about it.

"You're very welcome. I guess I'd better let you get back to work." Danny eased himself off the car door, catching Officer Morgan's eye as he turned to leave. *Is it my imagination or was there a little spark there?* He looked back and caught him watching. At Danny's glance, however, the cop turned away quickly and resumed arguing with his partner.

Danny delivered donuts every Monday, Wednesday and Friday—a half dozen powdered sugar and a half dozen cinnamon split between the two pairs of partners, and all laced with a generous helping of Danny's goo. He might have had second thoughts about the half-cup of cum in the batter if his Nordic fishercop had been partaking, but Officer Morgan remained true to his diet, no matter how delicious the baked goods may have been. The other officers dug in heartily, especially Officer Webb who put on a good ten pounds within the month.

That month brought an unexpected complication as well. The formerly friendly banter between Danny and the cops morphed into more salacious exchanges. Danny thought he was imagining things at first, a desperate wish for more male attention than Straight Chad would—or could—supply. One Monday, however, it became unmistakeable.

"You have such a hot ass, sir," Officer McNally said as he opened the van door for Danny. "I could eat that fuckin' ass all day, couldn't you?" he asked Officer Rand.

Rand grinned and stuck his tongue out. "Mmm-hmm. Right here, baby. Gotta lick it before you stick it." He grabbed the donuts while McNally grabbed Danny, hauled him inside and slammed the van door shut.

Only a thin crack of light came from between the drawn curtains separating the seats from the rest of the van, so Danny couldn't see much except various display panels and blinking lights. Hands clutched at his belt and zipper and off came his pants, followed closely by his boxers. His t-shirt still on, he felt his dick stiffen in the cool air of the van as he was positioned on all fours, then Rand (or McNally) went to work on his ass.

A snuffling nose rode down the cleft of his butt cheeks while strong hands kneaded them, pulling them apart as an exploring tongue traced the rim of Danny's pucker then dove in for a deeper taste. "Mmmm," said McNally (or Rand), "it ain't pussy, but it ain't bad."

"Let's see how this end is," answered his partner. Danny heard the unmistakable sound of a uniform zipper going down and then felt a hot, hard cock grazing his cheek. He sucked greedily at the mushroom head, drawing a sigh from Rand (or McNally), then took the whole length of it in his mouth. He worked it as best he could with just his mouth for a few minutes, but then he had to take one hand off the floor to reach up and cup the cop's nuts.

The other officer kept plunging his tongue in and out of Danny's asshole and licking his taint, working Danny's dick with a spit-slick palm. Danny moaned around a mouthful of hairy balls and crouched lower to the floor, opening his hole even further. He felt a cockhead prodding him and soon it was burrowing deep inside, its owner breathing heavy with lust. "Oh man, this is so fuckin' tight."

Danny kept licking and sucking, stroking the other cop's shaft until his breath came in ragged gasps. And the more he gasped, the harder Danny's ass got pumped, delicious long strokes he felt throughout his body, both men feeding off each other through Danny until their exhalations rose in unison.

Rand (or McNally) pulled out of Danny's ass at the same time McNally (or Rand) withdrew from Danny's mouth and they both jacked their dicks until they blew, waves of hot jizz raining down on Danny's back from stem to stern. When they'd milked themselves dry, Danny flipped over and began pumping his own cock as he writhed in cum on the floor of the van.

"Yeah, that's it man," someone encouraged, "blow that load."

And Danny did, spewing a geyser of cum he wished he could have captured for the next day's batch of baked goods. He was still panting from exertion when the cop at his head said, "Let's switch places and do it again!"

"I've got to take these donuts to the other officers," Danny said.

"Oh yeah," one of them said, "we still have *donuts*!"

Distracted by cinnamon and powdered sugar, they ignored Danny long enough for him to get dressed and slip out of the van, the cum on the back of his t-shirt quickly growing cold. Danny walked down the block to find the other officers standing by the door of the patrol car. Webb snatched the donuts away, put them on the roof of the car and clenched Danny in a passionate embrace, giving him a full-on mouth kiss with tongue.

"Jesus *Christ*, Bill!" Officer Morgan said, inserting himself between them. "People are watching—get hold of yourself."

Webb reached around him to grab at Danny's crotch. "This is all I want to get hold of."

"Back off, or I swear I'm gonna cuff you."

"He's mine, skank—I saw him first!"

Morgan pushed Webb away, holding him against the patrol car as he turned his head towards Danny. "I don't know what's gotten into him today. I mean, you're cute and all but he's married with three kids."

"You think I'm cute?"

Morgan blushed. "Yeah—I do. In fact, I was gonna..." Just then, Webb's flailing hands knocked Morgan's cap off, nearly blinding Danny with his brilliant blonde hair. "Listen, you'd better get out of here so's I can simmer him down."

"Gotcha. See you on Wednesday."

"Okay."

Danny walked away but turned back at the sound of Officer Morgan's voice. "Hey, your back's all wet!"

"Ummmm, I got caught in someone's sprinklers," Danny said. It wasn't really a lie.

He was concentrating so hard on the events of the morning, he almost walked past his own house. *These guys wouldn't get this way after eating any old donut. It has to be my special ingredient.* Other people might question it or wonder why, but Danny had long ago learned from Big Dan that you used the tools given to you. You seized the opportunity and made the best of things. Therefore, the only question was what to do about it. After working in the yard and taking a nap, he decided to do nothing.

If I stop, they'll wonder what's wrong and come poking their noses around here. Best to let things take their course. Maybe the effects will wear off after a while. But in the back of his mind, he knew that he'd be upping the ante, hoping to tempt his Nordic fishercop into trying one or two despite what might happen to the other officers.

In fact, he became a little obsessed with Officer Morgan, even scouring the Internet to find the National Geographic pic he'd masturbated to so often as a boy. When he found it, he was amazed at how closely the fisherman resembled the cop—even the dimples were in the right place. He had to jerk off just like he had when he was thirteen. *But it's crazy. Crazy to think things could work out between a cop and a criminal. Sooner or later, there's bound to be a collision of values. Someone's gonna get hurt, but I can't stop myself.*

Despite his misgivings, Danny went into a creative frenzy. He branched out from the ordinary everyday cinnamon and powdered sugar into maple, orange, pumpkin and chocolate-caramel, experimenting with swirls of frosting, jelly-and-jizz fillings, sprinkles and glazes. He stirred in cherry chunks, pineapple pieces and peanut butter chips, used potato flour to make spudnuts and even concocted his own sinfully rich cheese danish to tempt Officer Morgan away from his blasted diet.

Three weeks into the barrage of baked goods, a routine had developed. Danny would carry two platters of donuts and two thermoses of coffee three blocks from his house, stopping first at the van. Officers Rand and McNally would open the doors, grab the goodies, then drag Danny inside the van. Officer Morgan may have been the object of his affection, but he hadn't even asked Danny out yet. A boy had to have *some* fun while waiting for his intended.

Fuck-dazed, he'd straighten his clothes, compose himself and walk two blocks with the remainder of the breakfast delivery to his Nordic fishercop's car. Officer Morgan would be outside, leaning on the driver's side window trying to calm Officer Webb, who was securely tied with an ingenious arrangement of seat belts, shoulder harnesses and handcuffs.

Morgan would then feed Webb donuts through the window like a zookeeper tossing banana chunks to a chimp, making small talk and flirting with Danny but never taking a donut or asking him for a date no matter how hard Danny hinted. And he couldn't have asked the officer out. He'd never done anything like that. *I'd probably say something wrong and make a complete fool of myself. Totally out of the question.*

Despite Danny's experiments with bearclaws, longjohns and fritters, in the end it was a simple glazed chocolate donut that finally laid Officer Morgan low. So to speak. Perhaps it was the way the sun gleamed off the creamy white glaze or the contrast with the rich dark chocolate, but one day Morgan reached for the last donut on the plate, ready to toss it Webb's way and looked at it thoughtfully.

"This looks really, really good."

"Taste it," Danny encouraged. "You've never, ever eaten one. Don't you think it's time? C'mon. It's the last one." *Just one. He wants to ask me out, I know it. This'll take him over the edge.*

Webb whimpered in his seat. Morgan glared at him, then bit into it. Delight spread over his face. He grinned, a few crumbs falling from his full, moist lips as his blue eyes danced a cocoa jig. "Oh. My. God. This is the best donut I've ever eaten in my life. It's not greasy—it's light and chocolatey and moist and has just the right amount of glaze. Oh. My. Fucking. God. Do you want to come to my house for dinner tonight?"

Danny sighed with relief. "I thought you'd never ask."

—ᴍ—

Officer Morgan lived in a very tony neighborhood—so ritzy Danny's used Ford Escort seemed a bit shabby among the Lexus SUVs in the nearby driveways. He'd brought one of his specialties, a Key Lime Pie, but standing there on the front porch just after he'd rung the bell, it dawned on him that Officer Morgan probably already had dessert. It also dawned on him he didn't even know Officer Morgan's first name, but before he reflect on it much more, the door opened.

Even with his face shadowed from the backlighting of the entry hall, Danny's heart beat faster at his Nordic fishercop's classic features, set off beautifully by a brown cashmere sweater and jeans. Without his cap on, his mop of blonde curls looked like a shaggy field Danny wanted to run through barefoot. Officer Morgan smiled widely and stepped aside. "Right on time—c'mon in, Danny."

"Thanks. I brought dessert but if you already have something made, maybe you can have it later."

Officer Morgan took the pie, grinning as he shut the door and led the way into the living room. "Actually, I'd forgotten to mention it, but I was hoping you'd bring something for dessert. If this is half as good as your donuts, it'll be terrific."

"Yeah, well it doesn't have ..." Danny stopped, paling at what he'd almost said.

"Your special ingredient?"

"You *know* about that?"

The officer chuckled. "Well now, I'd be a piss poor policeman if I didn't wonder why your donuts drove my straight, married partner crazy with lust for you. So, I investigated. I watched you making the donuts one night." He made a jacking-off motion with his hand. "Your back was to the window, so I didn't get to see the equipment, but the technique was familiar."

Danny felt himself getting red. "Is that why you never had one until today?"

"Sort of," the officer replied, shifting nervously from foot to foot. "I mean, I really *am* watching my weight—I don't want to end up looking like Webb in five years—but I wanted to make sure what I think I'm feeling for you was true and not just because of your...um...talents in the kitchen."

"And is it?"

"You're here, aren't you?" They both looked at each other a moment, smiling.

"You know," Danny said, "I don't even know your first name—am I supposed to call you Officer Morgan all night?"

"It's Frank."

"Frank? Frank Morgan? You mean like the guy who played the wizard in *The Wizard of Oz*?"

"It was my mom's favorite movie—any wonder I turned out gay? Excuse me a minute, I've got to check on the pasta." He grabbed a remote from the glass-topped coffee table and handed it to Danny. "Find something romantic on the big screen here, and I'll holler when things are ready."

"You need some help?"

"Nope, just relax," he called over his shoulder. "It'll only take a minute."

He likes me for me. Danny smiled and turned his attention to the remote but there were so many buttons, he couldn't figure it out. The bank of equipment surrounding the huge TV was intimidating, Danny was afraid to press anything. *So many lights and switches. And that screen is at least 65 inches. This set-up must have cost a fortune.*

Danny looked around the room at the brown leather sofa and loveseat, the halogen track lighting and the framed art on the walls, none of which were prints. Nice neighborhood, good clothes, fancy paintings, big entertainment center—Danny had a feeling Frank came from money. Lots of it.

"Dinner's ready," Frank announced, leading Danny to the dining room. "I hope you're hungry. We're having a big green salad, fresh Italian bread and pasta primavera. The bread's store-bought. I'm not quite as handy in the kitchen as you are. Have a seat and I'll be right back with the salads. You can pour the wine."

Danny took a look at the wine label. He couldn't pronounce it and had no idea what kind it was, but he knew he was pouring it into Baccarat crystal. If there was one thing he knew, it was pawnables. He sat down and took a sip of his wine. Delicious. It had to be expensive. Either Frank was really putting on the dog for him or...

"Okay, salads all around," Frank said, placing one in front of Danny. "Vinegar and oil or ranch?" he asked.

"Vinegar and oil." Danny picked up one of the cut glass cruets. "So, do you live here by yourself?"

"Yep. All by my lonesome—why do you ask?"

"Okay, I'm not the kind of guy who can dance around something for long. I'm pretty straightforward, so I have to ask you ... I mean, I'm looking around and I'm seeing the neighborhood you live in, the fancy-schmancy TV, the art on the walls, and I'm wondering how you can live like this on a cop's salary."

Frank smiled, sat down and sipped his wine. "I couldn't. That's why I supplement my salary with some, shall we say, other business opportunities."

"You mean bribes?"

"You say to-may-to, I say to-mah-to. It's not blood money, and those mob boys have way more than they can spend. No one gets hurt and I benefit. What could be better than that? I just hope it's not a dealbreaker, Danny. You're a very handsome man. I like you, and I'd really like to get to know you better. I hope my trust isn't misplaced. I know a secret of yours too, you know. What are you grinning about?"

Danny raised his glass. "A toast," he said, standing up and clinking glasses with Frank. "Here's to larceny—where would we be without it?"

Cumsmoke

S tanley was amazed by his erection. It was the first one he'd had in two or three years. Maybe four. At least since Dennis left him. Not only that, but it was happening in the stall of a men's room with a mouth shoved up against the other side of a glory hole. An intense scent of cinnamon burned his nose, spicy and irritating like a thousand half-chewed Red Hots he couldn't spit out or swallow.

The mouth on the other side of the hole looked cavernous and inviting, a tunnel of wet wonder that gave Stanley thoughts he hadn't had for so long, he'd given up on their reappearance. They told him to obey the instructions printed in block letters above the glory hole: LET ME SUCK YOUR DICK!! All he had to do was stand up, turn to the left and take a step – not even a step. A half step. A quarter step. But his dick was a step ahead of him.

It drew him up and off the toilet seat, the wallet in his pants thudding against the tiled floor. He almost tripped over his baggy boxers as he turned to face the hole, the tip of his cock hitting the cold, thin metal wall between the stalls. A shock ran through his genitalia, but he didn't pull away. With one brief thought about the possible consequences of sticking his cock in a strange hole, he plunged deeply into the waiting orifice.

It felt cool at first, balm on Stanley's fiery dick, but then a warm friction engulfed him. The stranger's tongue coaxed a moan from him. He sank further into the hole, feeling his pubes scour the stall wall as he ground his hips into the unyielding surface. The mouth was working his dick now, and Stanley only pumped twice before he was ready to cum. A warm hand grazed the hair on his shaft, and he moaned again as he began to shoot.

Every nerve ending in his body seemed to be firing at once, his whole consciousness shooting out the head of his dick as he bucked against the wall. The stranger on the other side never lost contact with Stanley's cock, moving with him until the flow stopped. Stanley staggered backwards, winded, and sat back down on the toilet, a thin string of spitcum trailing from his already receding cockhead. He bent down to thank the stranger, but a sheet of notebook paper blocked his view.

NO FACES.

Stanley glanced at the stranger's scuffed Nikes and sat upright again, wondering what to do next. Gloryhole sex had never appealed to him. It was too casual, too meaningless. It seemed rude to just pull up his pants and go. *Is there a protocol here? Which one of us leaves first?* The sheet of paper disappeared and a hand came through the hole. It was smooth, yet manly. Thick veins snaked up and down the tops. No rings adorned the long fingers, but they held a note clipped to a Bic pen.

Stanley unfolded it and read the stranger's spidery script. YOU CAME PRETTY QUICK. BEEN A WHILE?

He almost laughed. YEAH, he scrawled and handed the note back. It was returned quickly.

WANNA GO AGAIN?

Stanley looked down to find his dick getting hard again. *Jesus. Nothing for four years, then twice in the same fucking day? This is too goddamn weird.* He wrote, GOTTA GO BACK TO WORK.

SAME TIME TOMORROW?

He didn't have to think about the answer. YES.

Stanley heard the sound of paper tearing, then the toilet flushed. With a rustle of clothing, the stranger was zipped up and gone. *He doesn't want to be seen, so I'll let him get a little ahead before I follow him.* He pulled his pants up, washed his hands and stepped out into the small hallway the bookstore he worked in shared with the other businesses on the second floor, but before he could get a fix on which way the stranger might have gone, Potter was on him.

"Are you feeling okay, Stanley?"

"Yeah, why?"

"You were in the men's room a long time." He paused, apparently letting the severity of the situation impress itself on Stanley before continuing. "I thought maybe you were sick or something."

"No sir, I'm fine."

Potter smiled at him but the expression dripped with condescension and insincerity. "I don't care if you *are* Margarita's nephew, I'll tell you right now I'm on to you. And I'll be watching your ass."

"Thanks for the warning." The cell phone in his pants rang. "Are we done? I need to take this call."

Potter clucked his tongue and walked away. "Five minutes, Spinoza. You're on *my* time."

Plunging his hand into his pocket, Stanley fished around for his phone. It could only be Wes. "Hello?"

"That you, Stanley?"

"Who else would be answering my cell phone?"

"You gotta stop working, Stan," Wes replied. "It's making you mean." He chewed something in Stanley's ear, a big Cheetoh from the sound of it. Extra crunchy. Stanley hated listening to him eat on the phone. "Going to group tonight?"

"Yeah, I guess." Group was the support group run by their mutual therapist, Dr. Wisencrantz.

"What do you mean, you guess? You're not cocooning or anything, are you? You don't have the urge to hibernate, do you?"

Cocooning. Hibernation. Wisenspeak for shutting off contact with people. "No, I'm not cocooning," he said. "How can I cocoon? I have a fucking job. I don't sit in front of a computer at home all day like you do and call it communicating with the outside world."

"Not in the mood for small talk, huh? Okay. I can respect that. I just wanted to make sure you were still going. We're meeting outside your building at seven and walking down there, right?"

Stanley knew he'd go. In a group of four, including the therapist, his absence would definitely be noticed. "Right. See you, Wes." He heard part of Wes's goodbye as he clicked the phone off. He hated Wes and he hated Wisencrantz and he hated the fucking court-ordered therapy.

If only he'd told Dennis he was poz before he'd barebacked him. If only Dennis hadn't sued and won, taking his savings and his house and leaving him with this shitty job at his aunt's third-rate used bookstore and a dick perpetually limp from the stress of his losses. If only. "There'll be a special place in hell for you, asshole," he remembered Dennis saying just before he left, brushing back that shock of brown hair he always had trouble keeping in place. And it *had* been hell. But after four long years, his hard-on was back.

You can bet your ass I'll be seeing this guy tomorrow. And any other time he wants.

—⁓—

Dr. Theodore Wisencrantz resembled a goateed German submarine with tiny rimless glasses—short and squat, boiler plates of flesh riveted together with acne scars. "Well," he said, looking around the office at his three patients, "unless someone has something else, that'll be it for tonight."

No one said anything.

"Next week, then," Dr. Wisencrantz said as he stood up. "In addition to your individual appointments, of course. Miss Orthonne, I'd like to see you for a moment, please. The rest of you may leave."

Stanley rose, glancing at the small, delicate woman seated next to the doctor. Her face was hidden by a Mondrian print scarf she'd felt guilty about buying at a museum gift shop. They'd heard about it three sessions ago. He was glad she hadn't returned it, but now she couldn't take it off without feeling guilty.

He turned for the door, and Wes hit him in the shin with his chair. "Sorry, Stan," he said. Tall, lanky and as awkward as a blind puppy, Wes needed extra room for everything. He followed Stanley out the door. "Ready for some Starbucks?"

"Not tonight, Wes. Sorry." Over Wes's shoulder, he saw Wisencrantz and Miss Orthonne speaking with their heads together in hushed urgency.

"Not even a double vanilla latte?"

Wes's pleading brown eyes didn't sway him. "Sorry. I've got something to do."

"That means I'll have to walk home alone."

"You could wait for Miss Orthonne."

"Fucking rich bitch heiress." Wes stopped him in front of the men's room. "I'd rather snort Drano. C'mon, you don't have anything to do."

"Yes, I do."

'Like what?"

Stanley looked around. "Like going in here, for instance."

"The bathroom? Go ahead, I'll wait."

"I can't crap on demand, Wes. Tell you what, why don't you start walking home by yourself? I'll catch up to you later."

"Sure," Wes said as he turned to walk away. "I get it. It sounds like hibernation to me, but okay. I'll go. See ya." He slunk down the hall and hit the button for the elevator. "I just hope Dr. Wisencrantz doesn't have to hear about this."

Dr. Wisencrantz is too busy boinking Miss Orthonne to give a rat's ass. Stanley pushed the bathroom door open. It was a two-stall, urinal-and-sink affair with a silver bullet-headed trash can in one corner under a cracked mirror. The room smelled like stuffy farts and fake pine disinfectant. He stepped up to the urinal and unzipped his fly.

He wagged his cock at the cool porcelain ahead. As he pissed, Stanley moved his hips and felt the weight of his cock as it bobbed in the air. *God damn. How come I haven't really looked at my dick lately?* Appreciated it? He shivered as he shook the last few drops of urine off and traced a big vein from the root to the tip with his index finger. It started stiffening.

He began to form a fist around the base of his cock, but a noise from one of the stalls startled him. Bending over slightly, he saw the far stall was occupied. Then he smelled the cinnamon again, luring him with its horny aroma. His dick bobbling before him, he stepped into the empty stall, dropped his pants and sat down. He flashed back to that morning. *It couldn't be him again. Or could it?*

One of the scuffed up Nikes from the next stall toed into view, tapping slowly. It rose and fell as if it were breathing on its own. A hand holding a piece of paper and a Bic pen popped under the wall. All three were very familiar.

REMEMBER ME? Stanley read.

YEAH. *Like I could forget.*

LET ME SUCK YOU OFF.

NO HOLE, he replied.

KNEEL DOWN.

Stanley assessed the space between the edge of the stall wall and the floor. NOT MUCH ROOM.

LOOK AGAIN.

It seemed high enough after all. *Weird. I could have sworn...ah, whatever...* He knelt down, his hips under the stall divider. Feeling sand and the edges of cold tile on his bare kneecaps, he leaned back on his hands and let the guy go to work. Flat palms over his hairy thighs led to caresses of his fat low-hangers, brushing ever closer to Stanley's asshole all while the stranger sucked his thick cock.

Stanley groaned out loud and ground his hips further under the stall, the cold metal wall edge digging into his midriff. The stranger sucked greedily, running up and down the shaft, then poking his tongue out to lick Stanley's big nuts.

He felt an incredible load building. Before it got to the point of no return, however, a different urge overtook him. He disengaged from the stranger and backed away, still on his knees, panting. The climax seeped back down to his nuts, precum trailing from his piss slit. Stanley crooked his finger under the wall. He wanted to suck the stranger. The idea thrilled him, made his skin prickle as the stranger slid his hips beneath the wall.

His cock was thinner and longer than Stanley's, surrounded by reddish gold hair. No low-hangers, either. Just a tiny, hard nutsack, shriveled around two acorns. But it was hard, and Stanley's mouth watered as he homed in on it. The stranger's dick slid inside, Stanley feeling the underside of its smooth shaft on his tongue. It felt so natural to him. So right. He brought up one hand up to tickle the stranger's scrotum.

His other hand automatically dropped down to his own tool, but he stopped himself after a couple of pumps. *I don't wanna cum yet.* Concentrating fully on the dick in his mouth, he grabbed the base with his hand and squeezed a little as he traced the stranger's circumcision scar with his tongue. Stanley bobbed his head and sucked, feeling his own nuts bounce against the tile floor, but he knew he couldn't hold it back much longer.

The stranger was almost there too, thrusting in and out as he fucked Stanley's mouth and began panting in short breaths. Stanley felt the stranger's hard nuts retreat even further under his fingers until he pulled out of Stanley's mouth and slid backwards.

The stranger's hand went to his own dick. The soles of his shoes creaked as he bounced up and down on the balls of his feet and pumped. But they weren't Nikes anymore. They were a pair of brown Oxfords... and then black loafers...then tan suede workboots...and then...hooves? *What the fuck?* Stanley blinked, and they were Nikes once again.

The stranger came first, shooting so hard that he spattered Stanley's balls. The sight and feel of surprisingly cool cum splashing on him was too much for Stanley to take. He let his own load go, watching it rocket across the floor in a straight, spurting line. His head buzzed as he sat back in exhausted pleasure, jizz dripping off his fingers onto the slickened floor. Suddenly aware of how much the wrist he leaned on hurt, he rose up and sat back down on the toilet.

Before he could unroll enough paper to clean his hand off, Stanley heard the stranger buckling his belt. He wanted to thank him, wanted to ask him how he knew he'd be here, wanted to tell him how grateful he was, maybe even tell him he was poz. But speaking would break something between them. *Anything I say would probably sound stupid anyway. And it's too late to tell him I'm poz. He might sue my ass like Dennis did.*

The stranger's stall door opened, and whoever he was, he rushed out. Stanley wasn't sure how to feel about that. All he knew was that he was tired and he had a long walk home, with the possibility of being joined near Starbucks by a waiting Wes. *I'll have to punch him.*

He bent over to pick up his pants and saw a note on the floor. BUS TERMINAL, it read. TOMORROW 2:00 PM.

Oh yeah. I'll be there.

—⁊⁊⁊—

Stanley hated Potter's smile. It was more malevolent than his frown, plus he showed his teeth. They were cracked and chipped and yellowed, home to sesame seeds from his morning bagel and the source of the coffee breath Stanley smelled from across the desk. "I don't have to tell you how good this feels, do I?"

Stanley didn't say anything.

"Late every morning, every coffee break and every lunch for the past three weeks." Potter tossed a rubberbanded stack of time cards on the desk. "And Margarita's in Europe. She can't save your ass now. Management school teaches us to ask if there's anything I can do before I fire you, not that I really give a shit. You'll just tell me to mind my own fucking business, right?"

"Mind your own fucking business."

Potter smirked again. "You just can't help some people. Pack up your stuff and get out, Spinoza. I don't even want you back here as a customer."

Stanley stood up, glad to be out of Potter's breath range. "Shows how observant you are," he said. "I took all my stuff home last week." He tried hard to think of a parting shot but none came to mind. He's not worth it, he thought as he slammed Potter's office door, hearing him chuckle behind it.

He breezed through the side entrance as he'd done numerous times in the last three weeks. He paused on the sidewalk and put on his sunglasses, squinting out the bright clear day. *11:30*, he thought, checking his watch. *I'll be a little early, but he'll be there first.*

He's always there first, no matter where it is—the bus station, the third floor men's room at Foley's downtown, the rest stop on I-70, the bathroom at Bible Park, or even this place. He took the note out of his pocket. 1285 ZUNI ST, it read. *I don't even get a name this time. Just an address.* Stanley looked up, turned and headed west.

His cock was almost fully hard, but that was nothing new. In the past three weeks, Stanley couldn't remember seeing it flaccid. Going to the bathroom without jacking off was unthinkable, never mind two or three daily sessions with the stranger. He even got a chubby eating breakfast every morning.

But I just got fired because I can't keep my dick in my pants long enough to stay at work for a whole day. How the fuck am I gonna pay the rent? Or my therapy bills? Or get my meds? That should be a problem. Dr. Wisencrantz would think so. Why don't I? How come I can't think any further ahead than the next blowjob?

As Stanley walked, the neighborhood began looking seedier. The glass and chrome gloss of the re-urbanized downtown gave way to older buildings with boarded up windows beneath layers of sleaze. Stanley's cell phone rang, but he didn't even check the number. *It's probably Wisencrantz again. Or Wes.* He didn't want to talk to either of them. He didn't want to talk to anyone.

He reached the cross street and went down a half a block until he came to an old brick building with black paint over the windows and a wire mesh screen stretched across the door. Hanging from bands of duct tape above it was a neon sign that read "1285" in pink and blue script.

As soon as he touched the wire mesh, dogs started barking behind the door, their yelps reverberating up and down the whole block. The noise continued until a panel in the door slid open and Stanley found himself staring into a pair of brown eyes. The cinnamon smell wafted out to greet him, but the eyes just looked him up and down. *I guess I have to talk first,* he thought. "Um, I'm supposed to meet someone here."

"You're expected."

A buzzer sounded somewhere, and the door opened. It led into a small anteroom with a counter, a window and another door beside them. Perched behind the window was a small dark man. "You've also been paid for." He pushed a starched towel and a key on a leather thong through a slot at the bottom of the window. "Locker 49."

The buzzer went off again, and the other door opened. Stanley grabbed the towel and the key and went through but stopped at the darkness in front of him. He couldn't see a thing, and he saw even less when the door closed behind him. He began to panic, the fear growing so real he started to lose his boner, which hadn't happened in almost a month. In a moment, however, warm red light started to penetrate the dark, and he saw a room at the end of the hall.

His boner re-solidified, urging him forward. The cell phone in his pocket began to vibrate again, startling him. He ignored it and marched ahead, coming to a dimly lit room with a bank of small lockers, a couple of benches and a folding chair with a worn leather seat. Locker 49 was on the end, next to another hallway. When he opened it, he saw a note.

STRIP. KEEP YOUR TOWEL BUT DON'T COVER UP YOUR DICK. PUT THE KEY AROUND YOUR WRIST OR ANKLE. FOLLOW THE HALLWAY DOWN TO THE END, TURN RIGHT, WALK ABOUT FIVE FEET AND YOU'LL BE IN A LARGE ROOM. I'LL FIND YOU.

He unbuckled his pants, but the cell phone went off again before he could get them off his hips. *Fucking Wisencrantz.* He snapped the phone off and throwing it in the back of the locker. The boxers next, then his socks and then he was totally naked, his fat dick bobbing as he locked the locker, put the key around his wrist and headed down the dark hallway with his towel around his shoulders.

There were rooms on either side of him, some with their doors closed and others open. The open ones all had beds with men either alone and jacking off or fucking in pairs. A few of them motioned him inside or made a grab for his cock from the door, but Stanley stayed on course.

The room was almost pitch black except for the dark red lights hanging above, but Stanley could tell it was large. Concentrating hard, he could see the faint outlines of benches against the walls and the men on them. He couldn't tell how many guys there were, but they clustered together in small naked groups of parts—asses, knees, feet, dicks, arms and chests, forming cells that moaned softly as they pulsated. Stragglers orbited the benches like horny electrons, joining or departing the groups or just watching. A few of them grabbed at Stanley, but he turned away.

Then, a very persistent hand cupped his balls and tickled the sides of his scrotum. He knew that touch well. His stranger. "Mmmmm," Stanley breathed. He reached for the stranger's crotch, but he had already pulled away and was settling down on his knees. Stanley felt his cock slide into the stranger's mouth as he ran his hands up and down Stanley's hairy thighs.

A strange hand ran itself though his chest hair, another caressed the curve of his ass, then two massaged his shoulders while yet another brushed his buttcrack. Fingers fondled his balls while the stranger worked his dick. Rough bearded cheeks from nowhere and everywhere nuzzled his neck and brushed their lips against his ear. Stanley's own hands touched at will, grazing nipples and cocks and holes and patches of hairy skin. The stranger stopped sucking and grabbed Stanley's dick, leading him like a pull-toy over to one of the benches. The cluster followed in a tangle of disembodied hands.

The stranger got on all fours beneath one of the dark red light bulbs, and Stanley knew what he was supposed to do. *Oh my God, he wants me to fuck him.* "I'm..." he started to say, but the thought died on his lips. Strong arms raised him up on the bench, and he stood facing the stranger's spread pucker. From out of nowhere, a hand gooey with gel greased up Stanley's dick while another greased the waiting hole.

The hand lubing Stanley guided his cock to the stranger's ass, using it like a paintbrush to daub precum and lube down his asscrack until the head finally reached the hole. Stanley breathed and sank himself in, feeling the tight warmth wrapping his dick as he went deep, drawing a sigh from the stranger.

"Yeah," someone growled deeply. "Fuck that ass."

Stanley with shallow thrusts, but soon the hands were helping, pushing him into the stranger and pulling him out again faster and faster. Stanley tried to stop himself, but there were too many hands and it had been too long and it felt too good, too fucking great to say no.

He was just finding a rhythm when he heard voices. He assumed they were coming from the men around him, but he wasn't sure. He couldn't really see their faces, except for one that looked terribly familiar— especially that shock of brown hair falling across his forehead. *Dennis? What the hell?* He tried to focus on the face, but the harder he tried, the more it eluded him.

The voices built in intensity, chanting indecipherably in a rhythm that married itself to his thrusts in and out of the stranger. Stanley wished he could understand where they were coming from or what they were saying. Latin? No, English. He could almost figure it out, but not quite.

He surrendered to the touch and the smell and the chant, arching his back and raising his head high in the air. The red light bulb above seemed to grow brighter as the hands took control and the voices grew plainer.

SEND, they said.

They pumped Stanley's cock in and out of the stranger again and again until his load started building.

SEND HIM

His nuts churned as they slammed into the stranger's ass and he felt the sharp edge of a climax start to ripple up.

SEND HIM THERE

His breath short, he started to gasp and felt himself about ready to shoot.

SEND HIM THERE

He thrust deeply on his own and exploded inside the stranger's ass, feeling his cum spurt.

SEND HIM THERE *NOW*

Warmth flooded him, as if he was standing over a fire. The scent of cinnamon became heady and overpowering. He looked down at his arm but couldn't see it. He blinked as the second shot of cum spent itself, and Stanley realized he couldn't see his chest either. A shadow? A trick of the light? Or was it a trick of the dark? When he tried to pinch his own nipples, he felt nothing grabbing nothing. He screamed but couldn't hear his voice. His legs were gone too—his hands, his neck, his dick all disincorporated into a thin wisp of cumsmoke that rose through the air towards the hooded red light bulb overhead and vanished from sight.

You Know You Want To

E verything you know about angels is wrong. This whole "winged messenger from God" bit is a crock. We're *not* messengers, the wings are artistic expression, and there *is* no God—or rather God is a huge pool of energy that ebbs and flows as life-forces are added or subtracted. But the Jesus-died-for-your-sins-heaven-and-hell crap so many of you believe in is just that—crap.

Angels, like ghosts, are merely larger, stronger life-forces who, for some strange reason, survive the corporeal body that sheltered them in life. Don't ask me why or how because I couldn't tell you. Death doesn't come with a manual. There is no friendly spirit guide to explain how it all works to you when you die. It just unfolds.

So call me an angel or a devil or a ghost or whatever fits your favorite concept of the afterlife. Doesn't matter. All I can tell you is that I had to get back to Nick. Something compelled me. I couldn't even say *how* I got back to him or how I knew he needed me, but he was on the brink of a big mistake and I had to keep him from doing something he'd end up regretting. That's what exes are for, right?

I'm not sure you could call him my ex, though. I mean, we were perfectly happy together, content with our fund-raisers and Pride parties and being movers and shakers in the local queer community until I fell off a curb and got hit by a bus. And no, he *didn't* push me. At least I don't think so. I guess you could say he survived me, but that makes me sound like lung cancer.

The first time I actually saw Roger, the new boyfriend, he was sitting outside at a sandwich shop on the 16th Street Mall waiting for Nick to keep a lunch date. He held his Reuben in one hand, taking large, meaty bites as he probed the corners of his mouth with his tongue for stray smears of Russian dressing and dipped french-fry bouquets into a paper cup of ketchup with the other.

Nick was running late as usual, for some reason. He always had a reason. Sometimes they were better than other times, but he always had one. I used to tell him he'd be late to his own funeral. He was for mine. Roger was almost finished with his lunch by the time Nick arrived, apologetically offering a pitcher of beer he'd gotten from the bar.

Nick pulled out a chair and sat on its edge, gesticulating his inability to prevent whatever had caused his tardiness. Roger, however, kept a stern countenance, staring directly ahead. Nick made a few more tentative stabs at begging forgiveness then shrugged his shoulders and left, looking back at Roger once.

I knew exactly what the deal was. He was going back to work. Nick was the grants manager for the local AIDS non-profit and really loved the job. He had probably missed a deadline or forgotten a meeting or something and spaced out lunch. Things like that happened all the time with Nick. Sure, it was annoying the first couple of times, but he was such a great guy that you learned to look past that.

Roger wasn't at that stage yet. In fact, he seemed ready to kill. A disproportionate wave of negativity rolled off him like an angry tide. He drained his water glass, refilled it with beer and sat there drinking and sulking. I was about ready to pop into his head—just for a second, you know—to plant a little chill-out suggestion, when this dude in black jeans, biker boots and a tight black t-shirt sat down at the table opposite him.

Out of either natural inclination or spite for Nick, Roger immediately went into hunt mode—fixing his target with a steady gaze, smiling and grasping the pitcher of beer getting ready to join him. Before he could make his move, I made mine.

Head-hopping is easy enough. Most of the time they don't even know you're there. The tough part is planting thoughts, trying to convince the head you're in that the idea you're giving it is original. Otherwise they think they're delusional, and that won't get you far at all. It's always smart to stay unnoticed in the background, working in small, steady steps.

...tap that ass, Roger was thinking. *That'd show the motherfucker he can't stand me up. Goddamn...HEY, WHO'S IN HERE WITH ME!?*

I froze—well, that's impossible since I have no body. Rather, I tried to make my presence as small as I could. Exiting would draw more attention than staying put. I hadn't expected him to be so sensitive or aware, and that meant trouble for Nick—trouble because this was a cold, calculating head that had no difficulty making tough decisions or carrying them out. It was a dry, prickly, unwholesome place to be.

Hey, I asked you a fuckin' question *– who are you and what the hell are you doin' in my head?*

Roger certainly liked to get to the point. No use trying to hide. *I'm Michael, Nick's late partner.*

I sensed no shock, no disbelief—only contempt and the odd feeling that I was the one being probed instead of him. Roger's was easily the most challenging head I'd ever been in. *Listen buddy,* he replied, *I don't know what you think you're doing, but you're dead—D-E-A-D. Why don't you go lie down and leave me the fuck alone?*

You're not good for Nick, I said. *You have to stop seeing him.*

He almost laughed out loud. *Yeah, right...*

I don't want to have to force you.

Roger poured himself a beer and took a long sip. *You can't force me to do* shit. *I give Nick something he couldn't get with you—a little edge. He needs someone to tell him what to do, how to act, who to be. For the money you left him, I'm happy to step up to the plate.*

I'd forgotten about the money.

There's not much you're gonna be able to do about it anyway—and I wouldn't plan on playin' around with Nick's head if I were you. If he starts hearing his dead boyfriend's voice, he'll think he's going off the deep end. And who do you think he'll come running to? Me. So you see, you're pretty much screwed before you start.

You're a real shit, aren't you?

He shrugged and took a long sip of beer. *I've learned to live with it. Now why don't you go back to wherever the fuck you came from and let me drink my beer in peace?*

I hated to leave it like that. I wanted to smack him down, show him he couldn't get the last word in. I wanted a big, blue bolt of lightning to hit him and reduce him to a pile of smug, smoking ash—but as I said, there is no God, and lethal atmospheric pyrotechnics aren't exactly up my alley. In the end, I wound up slinking away mortified but determined to bring Roger to his knees one way or the other, for Nick's sake as well as my own.

—⚋—

I did exactly what I would have done during life. I watched and waited, knowing that one of the keys to winning is picking the time and place of the battle, and I'd have to choose carefully with Roger. I also popped into his head now and then, not saying or doing anything but letting him know I was there. I wasn't sure if it was unnerving or annoying him but either way, he knew I hadn't left Nick to him without a fight.

What did I see as I watched and waited? I saw Roger move in with Nick, sharing the condo on the lake as well as the apartment in the city. Nick, of course, paid all the bills. Roger sat home all day, ostensibly studying for his realtor's license but mostly watching satellite TV and smoking dope purchased with money Nick had given him or he'd taken from Nick's wallet.

But the drugs, the indolence and the dishonesty was nothing compared to the sheer volume of men Roger went through—a constant parade of tricks culled from Craigslist, reaped online or trolled for in bathrooms. Roger was insatiable. He was also a consummate liar, able to use his winning grin and wounded puppy-dog eyes to make even the most bald-faced untruth sound palatable.

Worse, Nick seemed to trust him implicitly, which galled me. One of the sticking points in our relationship was Nick's jealousy. I believed in monogamy as firmly as he did and thought I showed that at every opportunity, but whenever I worked late or did something the slightest bit out of routine, I'd get questioned and cold-shouldered until he was satisfied I hadn't been fooling around. It was insulting to see how easily he accepted the lamest excuses from Roger. And he was about to get another one.

A well-dressed guy at the end of the bar was eyeing Roger. I didn't see the attraction, personally. My taste ran to pretty boys like Nick, not trash like Roger with his visible tattoos, longish dark hair and scruffy beard. In his mid-thirties, he was way too old to be that unkempt. He might not be bad if he cleaned up, but that look appeals to some guys. It was sure appealing to the one in the business suit at the end of the bar. He was practically licking his lips.

Roger worked his bad-boy 'tude, staring up at the big screen TV on the wall opposite the bar, drinking with a sullen, unsmiling smolder. He glanced at the suit every once in a while, leaving the man's half-grin unreturned as he turned his attention back to the TV. After ten minutes of this dance, Roger caught his eye and held his gaze for a good ten seconds before getting off the barstool and heading towards the bathroom.

The suit, a clean-cut guy in his late forties or early fifties with salt and pepper hair and a firm, trim frame, smiled to himself and followed Roger. By the time he entered the men's room, Roger was already positioned at the trough urinal, a thin stream of piss trickling out of his half-hard dick.

The suit sidled up beside him, nodding as he eased his fully erect cock out of his slacks. Roger watched him stroke it as he shook the last drops from his own, tugging on it a few times for good measure. He put his hands behind his head and let his dick bobble stiffly in the air. The suit reached over with one hand and gave Roger's cock a squeeze.

"Suck it, dude," Roger said.

The suit nodded and sank to his knees in front of the urinal, taking Roger's dick in his mouth. He cupped Roger's balls with one hand while he stroked his own cock. Roger put his hands on either side of the suit's head, steadying it as he started to fuck the man's mouth. "Mmmm, yeah."

Maybe I could break up this little party—frustrate him and get under his skin—but if I was going to do anything, now was the time. I crept into Roger's head as quietly as I could, unprepared for the intensity of feeling that waited for me. I felt drowned in the silken waves of pleasure pulsing through his brain, the glorious friction of skin on skin and the bitter, illicit scent of the urinal disinfectant. I could even feel the gel from the suit's hair on the palms of Roger's hands.

You like that, don't you? Roger cooed to me. *Don't pretend you're not here, and don't tell me you can't feel that even if you don't have a dick. You've been skulking around my head for weeks now and why? For this. Admit it.*

His orgasm was building up as he fucked the suit's mouth harder and harder, ramming his dick into it again and again. He began to breathe faster, thrusting his hips with panting exertion as his whole body tensed.

This is wrong, I managed to reply, nearly swooning.

His body took over before another thought could assert itself, flooding his head with sensation that pushed him over the edge and he came— *we* came—with a shuddering cry and a death-grip on the suit's head. He bucked and struggled to avoid the explosion of cum in his mouth, but we held on to his hair and forced him into the edge of the urinal until we were spent.

Roger then grabbed the suit's jaws with vicious pressure. "Swallow it. Don't spit it out or I'll kick your fuckin' ass all the way out to the bar." The man's throat moved and his Adam's apple bobbed, and Roger forced his mouth open to make sure he'd swallowed the load. "Nice," he said, releasing the suit.

He instantly jumped to his feet, rubbing his head. "What the fuck's wrong with you, man?"

Roger shrugged, his attitude intact. "I just don't like to waste it, that's all." He threw his head back and laughed as the suit exited, not even washing his hands. Overcome by shame, guilt and a host of other emotions, I got the hell out of Roger's head as well.

"Come back any time, Michael," he shouted, his laugh reverberating around the metal and tile of the suddenly cold men's room. "Any fuckin' time!"

—◊◊◊—

"A job interview? Really?" Nick said, sarcastic instead of supportive. "Is that why you're an hour late for dinner?"

His estimate was conservative. The sex hadn't taken long, but with three drinks during trolling time in the bar, he was more like two hours late for dinner. Either way, it was nice to see Nick suspicious for a change.

For his part, Roger rocked the innocent, betrayed look. His face was all confusion and indignation and, even more convincingly, he was able to carry it through with his voice. "I thought you'd be happy for me," he not-quite-whined.

"Which bar was your interview in?" Nick asked. "You smell like a brewery."

"I was a little nervous, so I stopped at the Wrangler before I went."

"I'm sure the interviewer was impressed by the stench."

Roger's mask of hurt indignation never dropped. "Why are you being so mean? Did you have a bad day at work?" Nick didn't pull away when Roger put his arm around his shoulder. "That Johnson grant you were looking for didn't come through, did it? Or are you just hearing voices in your head?"

He said the last as a joke, but I knew he was fishing. At least he was taking me a little seriously.

Nick sighed. "No. The Johnson grant didn't come through." He put his head down on Roger's arm with a weary smile. "You always know what's wrong with me, don't you? I shouldn't bring work problems home, but $350,000 is a lot of money to let slip through your fingers. We could have done so much with that."

"You didn't let it slip through your fingers. I'm sure you did all you could. It's not your fault."

Nick raised his head off Roger's arm and faced him. "I'm glad you have such faith in me. I'll try to remember that when mine is running low. Sorry to take it out on you—forgive me?"

"Sure." Roger leaned in for a kiss, Nick snaking his hand around Roger's back to pull him close.

And that's when I made my mistake. I can't say why I chose that particular moment to pop into Roger's head—I'm not even sure it was a conscious decision. Maybe Roger even dragged me in, though that would be giving him far more credit than he deserved. Despite my care, despite my making a point of not entering Roger's head when he and Nick made love, I found myself inhabiting Roger just as his lips met Nick's.

Here, Michael, he said. *I'll even let you drive.*

And he was gone—well, not totally gone. I could still feel his presence, as if he was sitting in a corner watching, but Roger wasn't my focus. Nick was. For the first time in five years, I was kissing the man I loved. I raised Roger's arms and cradled Nick's face in his hands, feeling the comfort of his stubble on Roger's fingers as we engaged in earnest.

His kiss—his humanity—was wonderful and warm after five years of the disembodied existence I've been used to. I don't know if you can call what seized me passion because I'm not sure energy can actually feel anything, but I filled Roger's being with something. I clutched at Nick and pressed Roger's lips into his as if I could seal us together forever.

Our tongues began an old, familiar dance whose steps were second nature to us both by now, falling into their alternating rhythm of passionate exploration and languid rest so easily, so naturally, that it was a few moments before Nick opened his eyes wide and broke the kiss off with the sudden shock of realization. His eyes narrowed for a second.

Roger took over in a flash. "What's wrong?"

"Nothing." But there was hesitation in Nick's voice. "It's just that for a minute, it felt like ... *you* felt like..."

"Like what?"

He looked like he was going to explain at first, but then realized any explanation for what really happened would sound crazier than just putting the whole thing down to a bad day, distractions or a simple "never mind." He settled for the latter and Roger knew better than to press the issue.

See Michael? Roger said. *He's not as strong as I am. If you get inside his head, you'll drive him batshit. And neither of us wants that, do we?*

I left without responding, not knowing what I wanted.

—⟨⟩—

As I said, everything you know about us is wrong—including the assumptions that we are always right and that we know what we're doing.

Neither of these is necessarily true, at least in my case. I had no idea what I was doing. Roger was ahead of me at each turn, making me unsure of my own motivations.

What was it to the universe that my former lover was going out with a thieving, cheating, substance-addicted sponge? People have been making that same mistake for centuries, and the world has continued to revolve. What was there about this situation that was so urgent?

Nick, of course. A sweet, innocent guy who didn't deserve to be taken advantage of, and it was my job to make sure that didn't happen. Maybe Nick needed to be chumped. Instead of saving him, I was stunting his experiential growth. Unless that was an excuse for inaction because I was afraid of Roger.

And I *was* afraid of Roger. His confidence and surety of purpose were terrifying. Even more terrifying was the fact that, deep down, I wanted to be like him. I wanted some of his confidence, his surety and, yes, his success with men. I was never too keen in that area when alive. I still don't know how I managed to snag Nick, but part of the reason I was so committed to him was that I didn't want to lose him and have to start all over again.

You'd think since I was dead and part of the "angel" set, my human deficiencies would no longer matter, but some scars run deep enough to show up in the afterlife as well. Your inadequacies follow you even in death, which should be reason enough to try resolving them while you're alive.

Roger's constant hunt for cock fascinated me, despite the fact that each new conquest underscored my reason for being there in the first place—to save Nick. I rationalized it by telling myself I was gathering information and material for one, swift killing blow of some sort, but I was awed by his complexity of technique and the balls-out nerve that put him in some bad situations. Like the Craigslist ad that read:

Rape Me!!!

GL, 32 y/o, DD free gym rat looking for someone to break in and rape me. Must be between 30-50, stealthy and able to scale a privacy fence. Attack dog will be locked up. No fats, fems, pussies or safewords.

If you can give it, I can take it. BB preferred. Burglar mask optional.

Don't do this, I said to him.

Hello Michael I figured this'd get you riled. Nick's working late tonight and I'm by myself—well, except for you, that is. Why shouldn't I do it?

Because it's wrong.

Look, Jiminy Cricket, I'm not in the market for a conscience.

Doesn't it bother you to cheat on Nick and lie to him?

He laughed, finished typing his reply to the ad and clicked on 'send.' *Does it look like it bothers me?*

Okay, think about yourself—this looks dangerous.

What do you care? You don't have to come. But you will.

He was right. I stayed in his head, quiet and still, during the drive to the McMansiony part of town, all smooth concrete and trimmed greenbelt landscaped to within an inch of its life. The neighborhood was so fussy, the trees were afraid to drop their leaves in autumn.

Roger parked a couple of blocks away and walked in the quiet moonlight, trying to avoid the pools of light from the lampposts that studded the sidewalk. At last, he saw the address given him in the detailed e-mail his 'victim' had sent in reply.

The street light around back's supposed to be burnt out, so there's a dark spot against the privacy fence. I have to climb over, go through the back yard and enter through the unlocked sliding glass door.

Oh, I said, *are you talking to me?*

No, I'm talking to myself. You just happen to be in the same room.

Roger slipped around the side of the house to the back, finding the strip of yard along the fence quite dark indeed. He jumped up, grabbed the top of the fence and hauled himself over, landing awkwardly on the other side. The backyard was as antiseptic as the rest of the grounds, all the trees and flowers potted and perfect, not one piece of dyed gravel out of place.

Dogs barked somewhere in the distance, and the breeze blew a mild chill that stirred the shrubbery. Miller moths beat around a dim patio light that shone down on a gas grill and the sliding glass door. Roger approached, looking around the yard before peering inside and putting his fingers on the latch tentatively.

Scared? I asked.

Cautious.

He drew the latch back, eased the door open far enough to slip inside, then shut it. He stood with his back to the door, staring into the room. As his eyes adjusted to the darkness, Roger saw he was in the kitchen. Cutlery and pots and pans hung from a rack over the island in the center of the room, on which sat a lone, unwashed plate with the remnants of a t-bone steak and half a baked potato.

Following the e-mail instructions, Roger crept through the kitchen and down the hall, flooded with a faint bluish-green beam from the small nightlight plugged into an outlet next to an open door at the far end.

Goal in sight, he said. *This is giving me such a fucking hard-on.* He paused outside the door, massaging his stiff cock through his jeans as he surveyed the bedroom. Another nightlight cast a pale green glow inside, illuminating a naked, tanned figure sleeping on his stomach atop the rumpled white sheets. His breathing was slow and steady. The sole of his right foot was flat against his left thigh, forming a dark triangle between his legs and asscrack.

Roger slinked to the edge of the bed, his hand still rubbing his dick, then he sank his knees level with the bed and pushed himself on top of the figure, slipping a stiff arm under the man's throat. "Don't fuckin' move," he breathed into his ear, "don't talk, don't scream and don't fight me or I'll choke the livin' shit out of you—nod if you're with me so far."

The man nodded.

"Good. Now, I'm gonna let you go. I don't want anything comin' outta your mouth except a few grunts. My hands are gonna be close to your balls at all times, so if you want 'em to stay where they are, you'll play it my way. Got me?"

He nodded again. His eyes were open and full of terror. Was this even the right house? I wondered. I popped out of Roger's head and into his, encountering an overpowering mix of fear and lust so palpable I could feel its sludgy weight all around me. Definitely the right house.

Where did you go? Roger asked when I came back to him. *I wouldn't want you to miss any of this. It's what you came for, right?*

I felt dirtier and more ashamed than I ever had while alive. *Yes.*

Then take half of me over—I know you can do it. If you can get into my head, you can get into the rest of me. We'll both do this. C'mon. You know you want to.

And I did it. I imagined myself fog and simply misted myself throughout his body, feeling the cool air on our skin, the wrinkled bedsheets under our knees and the nervous anticipation of the body beneath us. We nibbled the back of the man's neck, running our tongue down the tangy salt of his sweat-soaked back until we reached his furry ass. Roger brought our hands up and spread the man's legs apart, lingering on his taint and playing with his nuts. He buried our nose deep into his crack, nuzzling the musky hair until we reached his hole. Our tongue darted out, grazing the silken, wrinkled pucker then lapping at it in earnest, tasting it in long, broad strokes and rubbing our nose deep into its spit-slicked center. We probed his asshole with one hand while Roger used the other to undo his belt and get the front of his jeans open, easing out his hard, dripping cock. Roger spat into that hand, wetting his dick even more before he finally lowered it into the crevice of the man's ass, sliding it up and down with shallow grunts before he finally slipped it in. The man gasped and whimpered, but Roger slapped his ass sharply.

"Not one fuckin' word." Roger's voice was hoarse. "Or I'll rip your fuckin' balls off—I swear I will." Roger buried his cock all the way in the man's tight hole, grabbing onto either side of his ass and thrusting long and slow. The man squirmed beneath us, burying his face in his pillow until Roger reached down, took hold of the man's hair and dragged his head backwards. "Take it like a man."

It was a cruel, harsh fuck—no tenderness or passion, only coercion and control. I've heard of mercy fucks, but this was a merciless one. Roger kept driving his dick home, harder and harder with each thrust, and at some point in the heedless, robotic slavery to pleasure, something clicked for me.

I found I liked it. No, I *loved* it.

I knew you would, he said. *Nick doesn't matter anymore, does he? All that matters is this. Am I right?*

I didn't need to answer. He knew.

Then Roger's thrusts increased in intensity and I began to feel the load building up in his balls. His breathing became ragged and short, coming in gasps as he rammed the man viciously.

"Don't come in my ass," the man managed to say.

Roger pulled back on his hair so hard, he screamed. "I'll...come... anywhere...I fuckin'...*want*....to!" He barely got the last word out before he came in convulsive jerks, his dick all the way inside. He held the man's ass tight against his body until he had spurted his last.

Still breathing heavily, Roger pulled his dick out of the guy's ass and again forced a stiff arm under his throat. "Didn't I tell you to shut the fuck up?" he wheezed in his ear. "You just said five more words than you should have, and I ought to kick the holy shit right outta you." He tightened up on the choke hold and held on as the man bucked furiously for a second.

Roger suddenly let go, scrambling off the side of the bed as he zipped up his jeans with a deft, fluid motion. By the time the man was sitting up recovering, Roger was tucked and ready for anything. "You wanna fight, motherfucker, let's do it—I'm just givin' you what you asked for."

Long seconds ticked by before a grin split the man's face. "Ain't that the truth. You throw a mean fuck, dude. My ass is gonna be sore for a week." He laid back down and covered himself with the sheet, snuggling into the pillow. "Make sure the sliding glass door's closed on your way out."

Roger laughed, but as he turned to leave he saw the man's Rolex on the dresser near the door. He snatched it up on his way out, sliding it onto his wrist. The man didn't even notice. I was so stunned I couldn't say anything until we were well into the kitchen.

Stealing? Really? That's about as low as you can get.

Roger shrugged as he opened the sliding glass door and stepped out into the night's breeze. *Call it the cost of doing business on Craigslist. Besides, I don't care what you think anymore. You're as bad as I am now.*

Right then I couldn't think of anyone I hated more than Roger. Except myself.

—⁂—

I wasn't the best angel. I knew I had a problem and hanging around in Roger's head wasn't going to solve it. The situation was only going to get worse now that I had a taste of Roger's experience. I could see myself sliding into his addiction, and that would serve no one well; least of all Nick, who I was supposed to be rescuing, after all.

But how could I turn my thoughts to my original purpose when recalling last night's experience set my senses reeling again? I'd never felt so powerful or masterful before. That feeling was tough to forget and even tougher to forego, and if I stayed with Roger, I knew I'd be feeling it again. For my own sake, I had to leave—but I couldn't leave until I'd helped Nick.

I even debated getting into Nick's head again but Roger was also right about that. He wouldn't be able to stand that strain. It had taken five long years for Nick to move on to someone else, even someone as spurious as Roger. If I got into his head, I might do more damage than good even if I convinced him to ditch the loser. He might become dependent on me and never want me to leave. That wouldn't be healthy, either.

No matter how hard I wished, no resolution magically appeared—just complicating factors. Nick's late night at work was the harbinger of a business trip to rescue another grant situation, leaving Roger and I free to indulge ourselves. I couldn't let that happen. Action had to be taken as soon as possible, whatever that might be.

Nothing presented itself during the trip to the airport. I just listened to small talk between Nick and Roger as Nick checked his bags and they went to an airport lounge for a drink before Nick's flight.

Grinning over his gin and tonic, Roger said to Nick, "I got you something."

"What?"

"Oh, just a little going-away gift."

Nick beamed. "When could you have done that? I just told you last night—you haven't had a chance to shop for anything."

"Actually, I got this a few days ago. No real occasion. I know work's been stressing you out lately, and ... well, I thought now would be as good a time to give it you as any. But you have to close your eyes. I didn't have time to wrap it or anything this morning."

"You shouldn't have," Nick said, closing his eyes, "but I'm glad you did."

Once Nick's eyes were closed, Roger reached into the pocket of his jeans and pulled out the Rolex he'd taken from the trick's dresser the night before. I was stunned. The more I thought about it, the angrier I became. It was a slap not only at Nick, but to me as well. He knew where he got it from, and what's more, he knew that I knew. That smug, motherfucking asshole.

And that's when it hit me. I had no idea if it would work, but I took the memory of where that Rolex came from and about fifteen or twenty of Roger's encounters I'd been privy to, fixed those images firmly in my mind, summoned up all of my anger and frustration and hatred, focused it all in a narrow beam, and threw it with everything I had at the face of the watch.

"Okay," Roger said. "Open your eyes."

"It's beautiful." Nick looked at the watch hanging off Roger's fingers, then he slipped his off his wrist and took the new one. "I'll think of you whenever I check the time."

"I was going to get it engraved, but... "

Nick smiled, leaned over and kissed Roger. "It's wonderful like it is. I don't know what I've done to deserve you."

Then he put it on. The smile dropped from his face. He seemed to turn inward for a moment. I didn't know exactly what was happening to him, but with each split second that passed more and more anger and distrust built up in those eyes. I knew the look well, and this was fiercer than any of the ones I'd gotten. The desire to get into his head overwhelmed me, and I tried to enter but couldn't get through. I couldn't get into Roger's, either. Moreover, the airport lounge was growing dimmer. Whatever I did, I had depleted my energy to an extent I didn't know was possible.

Nick, however, was on fire. His face turned from doting love to white-hot rage. "You fucking *liar*," he hissed. "This watch came from a trick, didn't it?"

"What? No, I-I…bought it."

"With what? The few measly dollars you get peddling pot out of my apartment won't buy a Rolex. Tell the truth for once in your life, bitch. How many others? You can't even count them, can you? You can't even fucking *count* them."

"I--"

Before Roger could finish his excuse, Nick threw his drink in Roger's face, the lime clinging to his collar. "Keep this for your next trick," he said, tossing the watch back at Roger. He picked up his briefcase and swung it at Roger, connecting with the side of his head. "We're done. Pack your shit up and get out. If you're there when I get home from this trip, I'm calling the cops."

He strode out of the lounge. I wanted to follow him, to cheer for him, to raise his hand in victory, but the whole scene was starting to swim before me. I felt Roger searching around frantically for me, but he couldn't find me anymore—which was a shame. I would have gloated, I would have laughed in his face, and I would have rejoiced in the power of love, even in the afterlife.

But that was impossible. I don't know if I'd used up all my energy or simply accomplished what I'd intended and needed to go back. The lounge got darker and more indistinct, and Roger's shrill cries to Nick grew fainter until I couldn't hear them anymore, and I felt myself tugged away from that reality. I was going into nothingness or another level or the next step or something. I had no clue. We fly as blindly in death as we do in life. Not a comforting thought, I know, but there you have it. Nick was finally on his own.

And so was I.

Yuri: A Pride Memoir

I'll call him Yuri. He was short and stocky, with short brown hair and watery aquamarine eyes. In his early thirties, Yuri had only been out for a few furtive years in his native country. He was staying in Denver on a tourist visa with some people he'd met online. It would be his first Pride parade.

My friend Arthur had found Yuri in a chat room and asked him out to the Wrangler, a local leather-and-Levis bar, for a drink the Friday of Pride weekend. I went along to provide moral support for Arthur and an excuse to leave if necessary.

Their eyes met, and it was magic. It was bliss. It was heaven. It was a quick drink and then total abandonment. They hopped in a cab before my ice could melt, leaving me at the north end of the bar to be pawed by a drunken bear with a shaved head who leered at me, fell asleep, then woke up and leered at me again. I wasn't sure if he was tired, drunk, or narcoleptic.

When Arthur and Yuri arrived at my Pride party the next day, they looked as if they hadn't seen much daylight. Their eyes may have been dull, but they only looked at each other anyway. Yuri sat on Arthur's lap or with his back between Arthur's legs as they stretched out on the lawn beneath the shade of the box elder in the backyard, eating from the same plate. They were at the charged particle stage of the relationship, where constant physical contact had to be maintained or they'd be thrown off into the dating vortex once more.

We hated them. No. We envied them. We didn't hate them until after the third pitcher of margaritas, when we started taking bets on whether the relationship would last hours or days. And even then, we *still* envied them—because they were long gone by that time, off to Arthur's apartment where Yuri was spending Pride weekend, leaving us to speculate on their future until well past midnight.

We reconvened at eight the next morning at Arthur's love nest, where he answered the intercom in the foyer of his condo building on the first ring and buzzed us in, bounding down the hall to greet us.

"This one's a keeper!" he said, pointing back at his apartment and leaping around us with the glassy-eyed glaze of too much love and too little sleep. That clarified the situation. We'd all had experience with Arthur's keepers before, kept for somewhere between a week and a month before being thrown out like overripe bananas.

Once inside, we smiled, nodded, and made nice with the doomed Yuri, treating him with goodhearted generosity, secure in our assumption that he probably wouldn't last past Wednesday. It was, after all, Pride weekend—as Yuri continually reminded us. His enthusiasm was as refreshing as it was irritating. Charming in a goofy way, he wore a snug NYPD logo T-shirt, matching ball cap, black leather shorts, and boots.

"I have uniform fetish." We smiled and nodded some more. "When do we leave?"

"In a few minutes," Arthur replied, his hands on Yuri's shoulders. "Don't worry, we won't miss anything. We just have to go two blocks."

We downed our mimosas, made last minute bathroom trips, and moved in the general direction of the door. Yuri prodded and swept us along, his camera already out of the bag. He snapped pictures of Arthur locking the door behind us, and then he was gone, covering the two blocks by the time we had congregated on the sidewalk. We heard him calling Arthur's name, and Arthur was soon running off, too. As we got closer, we saw Yuri, posing with his arms around a group of Denver cops, his grin as toothy as a sturgeon's. Arthur manned the camera while Yuri shouted out the angles he wanted.

"From *here*! Now *here*! Try one from *this* side now."

The shoot might have gone on forever if we hadn't heard the motorcycles. The crowd buzzed and necks arched as parade watchers tried to see down the street. Yuri leapt away from the policemen with quick thanks, grabbed Arthur's arm, and disappeared into the crowd. We followed more slowly, taking time to say hello to people we knew as we worked our way towards the Colfax Avenue parade route.

Motorcycles roared as we approached the curb, and there was Yuri, giving a "thumbs up" to the camera, posing on the knee of a butch leather dyke on a Harley. Then Arthur and Yuri scurried to the sidelines, where Arthur lit a cigarette. Yuri frowned at him when he wasn't looking, pretending to check the camera.

A disco thump preceded the arrival of the twink bar float, but Yuri saw it coming first. "Look," he shouted, "they are *dancing*." And then he broke into the most arrhythmic cluster of moves a non-neuropath could possibly make, whipping his baseball cap in the air and grabbing Arthur from behind. Yuri ground his crotch deeper into Arthur's ass with each block the float progressed, until it was finally within leaping distance. He then tossed Arthur aside like Godzilla discarding a busload of tourists and advanced on the dancing twinks with his finger on the camera's shutter trigger.

They must have seen him coming. Just as he moved within focusing range, they began pelting him and the rest of the crowd with a mix of condoms and rainbow refrigerator magnets. Yuri seized upon the trinkets as if they were manna from Heaven, lowering his camera and stuffing the tiny pockets of his leather shorts. It didn't take long until they were full.

Throughout the morning, Yuri collected kitschy favors and free passes from every float and car that passed, hauling Arthur around by the waistband of his cargo shorts. He crammed Arthur's pockets so full of loot that his misshapen thighs bulged—picture Pan in flip-flops and a Cher T-shirt. And when Yuri wasn't picking up treasure, he was taking pictures of banners and political candidates stumping for votes.

"Look, look," he said excitedly, pointing at a tanned woman with graying brown hair, sixtyish but marching enthusiastically in a PFLAG T-shirt, her face polished with a thin sheen of sweat. The placard she carried read "I LOVE MY GAY SON!!!!" Yuri snapped a picture.

"I *love* my gay son!" he said. "Can you fucking believe it?"

—⁓⁓—

I could believe it, but apparently he couldn't. Ugly American that I am, it had taken me that long to understand that he was documenting a sentiment that he didn't see expressed regularly at home, as if to prove to himself that a place existed where you could be proud of who you were.

Yuri's enthusiasm took on a more poignant note for me after that. I saw him with admiration instead of annoyance, watching a man in the throes of becoming, of stepping out from behind whatever walls trapped him so that he could gaze at the vistas they had obstructed. I had scanned those same horizons long ago, but they were too familiar to move me anymore. Their magic had turned to monotony. Watching Yuri discover them gave them a vitality they hadn't had in years for me.

For a moment, I was nineteen and going to my first Pride parade—innocent, vulnerable, and staggered by the complexity of my newfound community. My stomach became queasy with possibilities, the way it had then, and standing right there on the corner of Colfax and Emerson in Denver, on a bright, hot morning in late June, with thousands of my fellow queers surrounding me, a tear welled up in the corner of my eye—just the way it had that day, so many years ago.

Three hundred and seventy two pictures later, it was over. The last banner had flown and the last float had dropped its loot. Yuri stood holstering his camera amidst the parade detritus. Stray condoms dropped out of his overstuffed pockets every time he moved. Plastic bracelets were stacked like vertebrae up his arms. The Mardi Gras beads garnishing his head and shoulders clacked as he and Arthur jogged toward us.

"Did you see the parade?" he shouted. "It was so *beautiful!*"

"Of course they saw it," Arthur said, beaming at Yuri.

"What now?" Yuri shifted his weight from one foot to the other like a five-year-old who needs to pee.

"I thought we'd all go back to my place for another round of mimosas, then head down to the festival," Arthur said. "Is that okay with everybody?"

We all nodded and murmured our agreement as Yuri's brown eyes widened.

"More? You mean there is *more*?"

"Of course. There's a whole festival with food and music and stuff."

"Just for being gay?" Yuri asked.

Arthur grinned with smitten indulgence. "I guess you could say that."

Back at Arthur's place, Yuri downloaded photos onto his laptop. He shouted and pointed at the images, reliving the last forty-five minutes as heartily as he'd spent them. He catalogued and sorted the pictures, and when he was finished, he fidgeted in Arthur's computer desk chair while we talked and drank.

Finally he sighed, went into the kitchen, and came back with a bottle of water. "When is festival?"

"Oh, it goes on all day," Arthur said. "We don't want to get there too early—it'll be easier to move around once the parade crowd thins out."

Yuri sipped and frowned as if he was swallowing more than water, a look Arthur must have noticed. "But we could start walking down there," Arthur hedged, looking at everyone else for agreement. "C'mon, drink up and let's hit the road. Anyone need the bathroom?" Even when he was in love, he was still in total control.

The reek of funnel cakes, deep-fryer grease, and warm beer hit us as we were crossing Broadway in front of a verdant drag queen—stick-thin and outfitted in green tights, green tutu *avec* spangles, bobbing antennae, magic wand, and green platform boots. Yuri grabbed her around the waist and posed with her in the middle of the intersection while Arthur snapped his brains out.

They hit the festival like a tornado gutting a trailer park, cutting a random swath of mirth and exhilaration. We were swept along breathlessly, lurching from one destination to the next until we couldn't do it anymore. We wanted some time to talk with friends, have a quiet beer, or at least sit down. We made plans to meet them by the fountain in two hours to go to lunch.

They showed up two hours and forty-three minutes later, staggering under the weight of at least ten plastic sacks full of T-shirts, brochures, flyers, and handouts. Well, Arthur was staggering anyway. Yuri looked as if he were ready to run a marathon.

"*Three* memory cards!" he shouted as he ran toward us. "Three memory cards *full*!" Clearly a personal best.

His energy was no longer infectious. It verged on annoying, but we were all showing signs of Pride wear and tear—especially Arthur, who had a good ten years on Yuri.

"Are we ready for lunch?" Arthur asked wearily, dragging his bags on the ground.

Lunch threatened to be more of the same. Yuri snapped various views of us at the table, demanding smiles and poses until the waitress politely forced him to sit down and look at the menu. He wasn't even going to drink the Jagermeister shot we ordered for him until we convinced him that it was a Pride ritual. The next three shots were *his* idea.

The alcohol kept him in his chair long enough to scroll through his pictures until the food came, passing the camera around to share a few choice shots. Once he had eaten, he sank fast—into drunken gratitude.

"I say thank you to all my new American friends," he slurred as he put his arm around Arthur. "And I especially like to thank my daddy, Arthur."

Arthur choked so hard, it appeared that the Heimlich might be in order. His face reddened and his eyes bulged until he swallowed the word *daddy*. And the sour look on his face said he didn't much like the taste of it. Yuri was too busy hugging us to notice. A photo of them at that moment would have proven more prophetic than any taken that weekend. They broke up in less than a week.

Arthur soldiers on, in search of yet another keeper. Yuri moved to Canada and got married to a sugar beet farmer named Dale in Saskatchewan a month later, but that doesn't matter. I only include it because the stories I like best have endings. That weekend is all that matters. Both Arthur and Yuri will have that to savor whenever their lives get too bland.

Because Yuri's life *will* become bland. If he stays in the gay community, no matter where he is, leather dykes on motorcycles and green sequined drag queens will become as commonplace as putting on his shoes or brushing his teeth. And even though all the fanfare is *not* just for being gay—even though it's about history and civil rights and struggle and oppression and celebrating the escape from our collective closet— he'll find that freedom breeds complacency, even though it shouldn't. And when that happens, I hope he finds a way to fill his eyes with wonder once again.

We should all be so lucky.

A Thirst for Talent

I knew from the moment I sensed the prey that Seth and I would end up fighting over it. We often fought over the choicest morsels, but then we were the oldest and strongest of our kind left—except for the Old Man, who hadn't walked in centuries. We couldn't even feel him any more. But I felt Seth's desperation. Neither of us had fed in a long time.

Unlike our blood-sucking cousins, our kind's needs are different. They cannot be fulfilled by just anyone walking the street. Our prey is rarified. I suppose that is why we must compete to feed. Only the strongest and smartest survive—Seth is a formidable opponent indeed, especially when desperate.

I knew he was already in New Orleans before I stepped off the plane, but there was no hurry. I caught a cab to the bed and breakfast I always stay at in the Marigny, dropping my bags in my room and heading out into the courtyard. I sat down and closed my eyes, letting the hot afternoon sun steam the grimy stench of the city into me until sweat rolled off my brow and soaked my back. When sufficiently acclimated, I napped, showered, changed and headed into the Quarter as the twilight dawned.

New Orleans is one of those places, along with Memphis, London and New York City, where I can always find a snack to tide me over until someone worth feeding off comes along. The quality we seek is in abundance here, but I could never move back to the Quarter—too many memories, too many close calls, too many who still bear grudges. I might be able to alter my appearance a bit and change my name, but my presence is far too well-known for more than a brief visit. I don't fear competition, but I embrace anonymity.

On Friday and Saturday nights, the tourists on Bourbon Street are layered as thick as powdered sugar on a beignet. They weave about in sloppy, drunken patterns. These days they wear t-shirts, cargo shorts and flip-flops. They laugh too loudly so as not to feel the ghosts of the city shuddering past them. I love those spirits. I've known many. But I follow my nose and my instincts rather than the tourists.

And they lead me to a small doorway off Royal and Tolouse. It's painted black, and has no sign outside, but I know its the Club Du Monde. And I know Seth will be inside, waiting for the object of our search. When I open the door, a cold blast of air conditioning shocks me. I sigh, remembering when the city was not chilled for tourism, and remind myself that change is neither good nor bad. It is simply change.

A jazz quartet is on the small stage, the saxophone player riffing a sweet, slow twilight song as the bass and drums structure the beat and the guitarist drops in a patented Wes Montgomery run now and then. They are adequate. Nothing like what will be on stage later, but appetizers nonetheless. However, I'm not looking for *hors d'oeuvres*.

There are others of our kind here—lessers--but they know Seth and I have first claim on the real prize. They will settle for the quartet because those are the meals they are used to. Seth, of course, is sitting alone at the front table, but he is not wearing the usually unshaven, sallow, snaggletoothed visage I'm used to seeing. He is the woman this time— what is her name? Laura? Laurene? No matter. He's probably changed it again.

His eyes, however, are the same deep green and I know the scalp beneath that long, blonde hair still bears the scars of our last encounter. He is wearing a crisp, light blue strapless summer dress that shows off his ample cleavage. I have to smile. He thinks a female guise will give him an advantage, but such artifice only expends energy.

He drained his drink as I slid into the empty chair at the table. "Hello, Seth."

Munching an ice cube, he grinned. "Warner—how lovely to see you again. Please call me Laura."

"I'll try. I might forget. What are you drinking?"

"Amaretto on the rocks."

I signaled the waiter for another round as the band left the stage to a smattering of polite applause. "You look marvelous. All healed?"

"Ah yes—that was a nasty blow. You certainly won our jazz man. Did you enjoy him?"

"I did. I fed from him for five years until his gifts dissipated. After that, there was no reason to hold on to him."

Seth clucked his tongue. "Even the most talented eventually run dry." He tossed his hair and smiled as the waiter brought our drinks. "However, five years is a long time. I imagine that has sustained you for...what, ten years or more?"

"Twelve years. I don't waste my energy on frivolities like useless shape-shifting."

"Useless? This shape will win the quarry, I guarantee."

"If you say so," I said with the barest of shrugs. "But take care not to overestimate the power of your breasts." I sipped the too-sweet drink and grimaced. "For argument's sake, let's say you *are* the victor this time— would you share the prize? Properly nurtured, his gifts could last us both decades. We could be sustained for several lifetimes after that."

Seth shook his head. "Dear Warner. I appreciate the sentiment, but you know that's not my way."

"I suppose not." I sighed. "Your way is all death and destruction. No remorse for the talent you've denied the world time and time again? Let me see if I can remember all the names. Billie Holiday, Janis Joplin, Hank Williams....You could have sipped them for years instead of sucking them dry."

"A lecture, Warner? How tedious. We don't all have your sense of fair play. I refuse to share my meals with others." He shifted and I again saw his true face for a moment. "Nurturing your prey....I'm a vampire, not a wet nurse."

"Being a vampire doesn't erase conscience. That's your choice."

Seth raised his head high and sniffed, a look of rapture in his eyes. "Conscience? How can you even think of such a concept when you smell something like this? Our quarry is in the building, if you hadn't noticed."

I had. The scent was overpowering—a splendid *melange* of murk and musk that conjured visions of a vast, limitless sea of talent; heady with the rich, briny funk of Delta blues, all swampwater moonshine and bitter greens drowned in bacon grease. But that was just the topnote. I also smelled undercurrents of the lush, heavy cream of 70's soul, sweaty cocaine-fueled disco, hip-hop's pungent relentlessness and the bitter, regretful smoke of late-night jazz.

As I drank in the amazingly complex influences that comprised the aroma of his singular talent, I vowed that Seth would not win this prize. No matter what the cost. I would fight as I had never fought before.

Seth, I knew, was making the same vow. "You must go. He should not see us together."

I left both him and that horrid drink and got a good seat at the bar, ordering a very dry martini as I waited for the first show to begin. Looking around the shabby dive, I formulated a plan. His massive talent rested on the twin supports of ego and ambition, both of which I could also smell. Clubs like this would not hold him for long.

With my industry contacts, I could give him a career he'd only dreamed of and as his manager, I'd be closer to him than anyone. He'd be vulnerable to me in so many ways and I would, indeed, nurture him. Even if Seth got to him first, the greedy bastard couldn't take all his talent as quickly as he'd done with others. He'd explode like an over-engorged tick. He'd have to take this one slowly whether he liked it or not. And time would not work to his advantage here.

"Laaaaydies and gennnlemen," a disembodied voice slurred into a microphone somewhere, "the Club DoooMonde is proud to present, from Lafayette, Louuuusiannna, the sennsaaaational Missssstah *Wade Dixon!*" For a sparse crowd the applause was enthusiastic. The others of our kind were gone, leaving the main course for us.

As the booming voice faded, Wade strolled out on stage. He was somewhere in his early twenties—short, dressed in a plain white t-shirt and jeans with a pair of expensive-looking yet well-scuffed snakeskin cowboy boots. His dirty blonde hair fell in a careless wave over his forehead, nearly obscuring a pair of dark brown eyes, and he wore a delightful three-day scruff of beard. He carried a stool and an acoustic cherrywood Gibson with a pick-worn scratch plate around which was printed THIS MACHINE KILLS.

He plopped the stool down in front of the center stage mic, perched and grinned. "I hope y'all like blues out there." His sweet, slow drawl drew the ear as he hoisted the guitar up on his lap, "'cause that's what the next hour or so's gonna be about. If that don't suit ya, come back for the 8 o'clock show when my rock and roll band'll be with me."

He struck up a standard 8-bar blues run with a 12-bar break before it became Sonny Boy Williamson's "Bring It On Home." His phrasing was derivative, drawing on the original as well as Van Morrison's take. The boy had clearly taken cues from the classics and the master interpreters but was not yet confident enough to put his own stamp on the material. No matter. That would come in time.

His playing was not astonishing. But his potential...I heard what I wanted, what he could be one day. Seth would never understand that a vampire could not just feed *on* an artist's talent. Such a trait required nurturing first; to savor when the potential is finally reached. Otherwise, it doesn't nourish you the way it should. It's the difference between eating a green apple and a ripe one.

There was something else Seth didn't understand about Wade Dixon, at least not yet, and that was how little Seth's disguise would impress, let alone arouse, Wade. I had suspected as much from the rumors my connections told, but seeing him in person confirmed it. The advantage was mine.

I listened to Wade run through a virtual catalog of bluesmen, from Robert Johnson to Charley Patton to Big Bill Broonzy, but I did not stay for his whole set. I'd gotten the information I'd come for. And the next show with his band—far less talented than he, else I would have felt them—would consist of Lynryd Skynyrd and Springsteen covers for the tourists. My eyes watered from the smoke in the club, and the martinis had given me a headache. I longed for the quiet of Washington Park near Elysian Fields.

"Giving up so soon?" Seth whispered inside my head as he watched me from across the room, a grin on his painted lips. I shook my head. Yet another energy-expending talent that he insisted on using constantly. I grinned back at him and walked out of the club.

—ɯ—

I heard the high whine of the mouth harp long before I saw the player. I was at the corner of Frenchman and Dauphin next to Washington Park, but he was inside the park close to a stand of bougainvilla. Street musicians rarely stray far from the Quarter. I thought perhaps this one had decided to work the Marigny arts district, which had less competition. The music lured me, but I was also hungry. Smelling Wade's talent had unleashed a horrific appetite in me and it needed to be sated, if only by a busker's snack.

When I entered the park, however, I knew it was a trap. I saw no one around the musician, but I felt the presence of at least two other men nearby. It was almost dark and passers-by were few. No one would see what would happen. I smiled. Let them set upon me however they wished. I would have my snack regardless.

Sitting cross-legged on the grass, the bearded musician vamped a brighter, more sprightly tune as I approached. His aroma wafted toward me, quickening my steps. I put my hand in my pocket as if to dole out some change and felt the other men stirring. They were about ten or fifteen yards away, but my meal would take only seconds. I'd be finished and ready to deal with them long before they arrived.

A battered, bright yellow slouch hat lay before him, already containing some bills and change. As I tossed my offerings in, I caught his eye. That was all I needed. He rose at my silent command and I stepped close to him, hearing the clink of the spilled change as my foot upset the hat.

I grabbed his face with both hands and drew him to me, his beard rough on my palms. It smelled of soap and cleanliness, so he wasn't homeless. And up close, he looked all of twenty-one or two—just a suburban kid out to relieve a tourist of a few dollars. I looked deeply into his blue eyes and brushed my lips against his. They parted easily, and I pressed into him.

His breath was stale at first, then sweet as I drank in his essence, the taste sharp and acrid, a hallmark of the marginally talented. Like drinking swill instead of fifty-year-old scotch. I could have consumed all he had and still been hungry, but I took only a few breaths worth. I wanted to leave him at least able to play his instrument.

As I finished, I felt two men coming up behind me. I did not hurry. Their hatred and scorn were palpable even though my back was turned to them, but I expected no less. They were young and far too foolish to feel anything else.

"Jesus *Christ*, Ryan—are you letting this faggot *kiss* you?"

Rough hands grabbed my arms and wrenched them behind my back, spinning me around to face a man wielding a knife. I could have told them Ryan wouldn't answer for a while. He was still entranced. I hadn't released him, but it would wear off in time. He wouldn't remember a thing.

"Empty your pockets, faggot."

I chuckled. "That's going to be hard to do with my hands behind my back."

"Stick the cocksucker, Shaun," the one holding me hissed.

"You boys haven't done this a lot, have you?" I asked. "The idea is to keep your identities secret. I know two of your names already."

"*Stick* 'im!"

"Oh yes," I said. "By all means, *stick* me."

The boy with the knife lunged forward and drove it into my stomach. The look of shock on his face when I didn't crumple to the ground was priceless. Even better was his astonishment when he withdrew the weapon and I began to laugh. He stabbed me again with the same result. I laughed again and broke the hold behind my back, twisting my assailant's arm as I forced him to his knees in front of me. I snapped his wrist and he screamed, his companion dropping the knife and turning to run.

Before he could get away, I grabbed his shoulder and pulled him close, putting my arm around his neck in a choke hold. I didn't smell any talent, which was a shame. I would have drained that one dry. I tightened the hold, relishing his struggle as he clawed at my arm and gasped for breath.

"Don't play games you cannot win, Shaun," I said into his ear. "I'm going to let you go in a moment, but you mustn't let revenge cross your mind. That would be counterproductive. Help your friends instead. Ryan will be fine in an hour or so, but…well, that other boy will need a trip to the emergency room. Count yourself lucky I didn't kill you. Are we understood? Stop struggling and nod your head."

He did as he was told and when he was calm, I let him go. He fell on the ground and stared up at me. I felt his unblinking glare on my back as I turned and walked away.

"Who *are* you?"

"Ask me no questions," I said over my shoulder, "and I'll tell you no lies."

"What makes you think I need a manager?" Wade asked, barefoot and shirtless as he scratched the patch of thick blonde hair between his navel and the top of his jeans. We were standing on his balcony overlooking Dauphin, the early afternoon smell of the Quarter drifting up to us. Birds were singing, but I couldn't say what kind. I don't know much about birds.

I shrugged. "What makes you think you don't?"

He didn't reply.

"You're an extremely talented man, Wade. Anyone can see that, but you need shaping. You have to hone your abilities to become what I know you want to be."

"What's that?" His sly, toothy half-grin made me giddy.

"The best."

His brown eyes read me up and down, strangely inexpressive. For a moment I thought he was going to ask me to leave, but then he chuckled and leaned close to me, throwing his arm over my shoulder as he walked me inside. His very air thrilled me. "Well, now if you'd said you were gonna make me a star, I'd have said you were a lyin' motherfucker. But the best? That's somethin' else."

"Of course it is. And it's well within your grasp."

"For how much?"

"Nothing at first. If you like what I do for you in the next two months, we can make an arrangement. It won't be painful to you. I won't bleed you dry." I had to grin. "But there's always a price to pay, Wade. You know that."

"Beware of men who talk about prices," Seth said from a doorway leading to what I assume was a bedroom. "They always get raised in the end." He still wore the same dress from the night before, obviously having spent the night. I could feel his hunger. An odd silence hung in the air on his entrance. I had the distinct impression that whatever happened last night had not yielded the result Seth had expected.

"Sorry," Wade said, remaining at my side. "Did we wake you up? Warner, this is Laura. I met her at the gig last night. She had a little too much to drink and, well, kinda passed out."

I nodded. Seth nodded back. "Pleased to make your acquaintance," he said.

It had to be a ruse. Seth could out-drink any mortal. Yet he hadn't fed last night—that much was certain. What was he playing at? "Likewise. But you must forgive us. We have business to discuss."

Wade scratched his left nipple. "Warner is my new manager."

Seth smiled. "Really? Well, you mustn't let me interrupt you. I'll just get a cab home."

"I could drive you," he said.

"No, no—a cab will be fine. They're easy enough to find in the Quarter." He sauntered up to Wade and reached for his hand, clasping it with both of his. "Wonderful to meet you Wade. You're a very talented man, and I enjoyed the show last night. Thank you for rescuing me and putting me up for the evening. We'll talk again soon, I promise." He faced me and smiled.

"Dear Warner," he said inside my head, "did you think I was going to pounce on him like a mouse? This one is different—thus, the hunt must also be different. I am not desperate enough to be foolish. For now, I am satisfied to drink from his aura, but rest assured he will be mine in the end."

What he said aloud was: "It was lovely to meet you, Mr. Warner." He turned and walked out the door, the clicking of his high heels echoing down the staircase. We both stared after him a moment, apparently lost in our own thoughts.

"Weird girl," Wade finally said. "She sat at the front table all night long looking like she wanted to eat me up. We barely got finished with the last set before she came bouncin' up on stage and followed us to the dressing room. I was hopin' she'd go for our drummer, Dave, but no—she goes straight for me." He stopped to light a cigarette he shook out of the pack on the coffee table. "Now, I don't do the groupie thing," he said, exhaling. "Never have. I don't wanna end up with herpes or warts or some shit like that, but she's sweet and she won't take no for an answer, so we end up havin' breakfast at the Clover Grill and pretty soon we're back here talkin' on the couch. She's askin' all kinds of questions about me, and all of a sudden, she's sound asleep. I carried her into the bedroom, tucked her in and slept out here."

"That doesn't sound so weird."

He gave me a grin that could break hearts. "I guess not, but she was so intense. I can't describe it, man—it's like she wanted to gobble me up."

"Did you get her phone number?"

"That was the other weird thing." He stubbed his cigarette out. "These days, people are always on their phones—talkin' or takin' pictures or checkin' e-mail or what not. I think it's stupid, but I got one too. I don't even think she *had* a phone. Or a *purse*. Now, that's kinda strange, right? But I think she'll find me again even without a phone."

"Not in the next two weeks she won't," I said. "You'll be in St. Louis."

"St. Louis?"

"That's right. Then Los Angeles for a bit. Perhaps New York."

"Wait, wait—I've got a gig *here* for at least two weeks. I can't just up and go to St. Louis."

"You mean at the Club DuMonde? I know the owner, Gene Jaquet, quite well. If he won't let you out of your contract as a favor to me, he'll do it for money. Either way, I'll make it work."

"What about the band?"

"What *about* them?"

"I can't just leave 'em. That wouldn't be right."

Principles in prey were such an aggravation. "I'm not managing the band," I said with a firm sigh. "I'm managing *you*. You're the only one I'm concerned with. They will be left behind at some point—why drag it out? If you're too nice to do it, leave it to me. Part of a manager's job is delivering bad news."

"Lemme think a minute," he said as he flopped down on the sofa, interlocked his hands behind his head and propped his bare feet up on the coffee table. I didn't see what there was to think about, but a forced decision is easier to renege on, so I let him consider his options in silence. After a minute or two, however, my curiosity was getting the better of me.

It wouldn't hurt to pop into his head for a second, I thought. Just to see which way he was leaning and give him a bit of a push in the right direction if need be. His furrowed brow and flatlined mouth indicated difficulty making a choice, and I expected him to be envisioning an angry confrontation at the very least, perhaps considering means of avoiding potential violence. To my astonishment, that was not the scene playing in Wade's mind.

His thoughts were of a more pornographic nature. The vision he conjured was of me on the sofa, him kneeling between my spread legs. My pants were down about my ankles and his head bobbed up and down on my prick. His fantasies were more generous as to its length and girth than reality deserved, but I took it as a compliment. And just as I had fathomed that scenario, his thoughts switched our places, me with my head between his legs, cupping his balls while I gobbled his cock.

My knees grew a bit shaky as I withdrew from his head, and I sat down on the sofa next to him. He shifted slightly, keeping his eyes closed. I looked down at his crotch, watching the bulge in his jeans expand until the length of his shaft was clearly outlined. My own prick grew in response, my hunger increasing as my defenses lowered.

Seth was right. His aura was strong, exuding enough of his essence to tantalize me. I leaned a bit closer and tried to take in as much of it as I could. It rose in my senses, fragrant and masculine as my cock hardened and my will softened. I drank it in deeply, feeling it nourish each cell it touched. Instinctively, I reached out for him but stopped myself.

Now is not the time.

His eyes popped open. "I'll do it," he said with abrupt conviction. He shifted the hard dick in his jeans and stood up, turning his back to me.

I could see the flush creep up the back of his neck. "Just let me tell 'em. They shouldn't hear it from anyone but me."

"That's fine. Don't let them talk you out of it, though."

"Nope. Not a chance. But now that I don't have a payin' gig anymore, what am I supposed to do for money? I lead a pretty hand-to-mouth kinda life, y'know."

"Let me worry about that. My pockets are deep, and you'll be earning your own way soon enough."

He turned to me, his brown eyes shining with a curious mix of glee, avarice and ambition. "Y'know, I think I been waitin' all my life for somebody like you."

I smiled. "The feeling is mutual."

—ᴍ—

Stacks sat back in his tattered leather swivel chair, pushing a few sliders up and some others down on the console as Wade switched guitars. "I don't got to ask where you found this one," Stacks said. "I smelled him too, but I knew you and Seth'd be on him like stink on shit." He flipped the studio intercom switch and leaned forward. "Okay, Wade boy—try it again, only use that open tuned National."

We'd been friends since 1925, when he wasn't Stacks Jackson but Robert Johnson and he hadn't sold his soul to the devil that night near Dockery Plantation in exchange for the blues. I'd taken it. But I'd given it back to him and so much more with it. What happened after that was a shame.

"Yes sir," Stacks said, smiling though his chipped, nicotine-stained teeth as he lit another cigarette. "He's powerful talented, that's for sure. Reminds me of myself back in the day. You gonna take him all the way, ain'tcha?"

"I'd like to try. That's why I brought him to you. But to teach, not to feed."

Stacks wheezed out a laugh. "Sheee-it. I'm done feedin.' Ain't got long left on this earth, and I'm glad of it. 'sides, I ain't fool enough to step between you and Seth. He comin' for your boy there, y'know. I can feel him."

"So can I. That's why we need to hurry."

"I can't teach him no faster'n he can learn. But he's quick—don't take him no studyin' at all to pick somethin' up. He just goes ahead and does it." He stubbed the half-smoked cigarette out in the full ashtray with rough, callused hands. "You stayin' here? All I got's a spare room upstairs and a sofa. Like this here studio—nothin' fancy but you're welcome to 'er."

"If it's no trouble. Wade needs to eat and breathe this stuff, and he can't do that in a hotel."

"No trouble. I owe you my life. Ain't your fault what I done with it." His eyes were yellow with age-old regret. "Anyway, old Seth be sniffin' around, but he ain't found us yet. We'll do what we can."

"I'd appreciate that, old friend."

He put a hand on my shoulder and grinned. "Your 'preciation gonna get you in trouble some day." He went back on the intercom. "You wanna lay one down, Wade boy? Go on over and getcha a beer from that cooler in the corner and we'll try a little 'Dust My Broom' once you wet your whistle. This time lean in close to the mic and don't be poppin' your p's. Nasty habit."

"Yes sir, Mr. Jackson."

"That's Stacks, son. Mister Jackson's my daddy and he been dead almost sixty year now. C'mon, let's lay this down."

Stacks tucked a wad of mashed potatoes and gravy into his cheek. "You got to walk out on stage like you *own* that motherfucker 'cause you *do*. You got to feel it *here*," he said, tapping Wade's chest. "If'n you don't, it ain't comin' out nowhere else." He resumed eating. "You readin' me?"

Wade grinned back and saluted him with a chicken leg. "Like a book, my brother. Like a book."

If either one of them were exhausted by two and a half weeks of sixteen hour days in the studio—playing, tuning, writing, talking—

neither showed it. Stacks worked like a man half his age, and Wade rode a palpable adrenaline high most of the time. He only slept a few hours a night, spending most of his time staring out the window of our small room as he listened to the day's work on headphones.

We were yet again having dinner at Stacks' favorite all-you-can-eat buffet restaurant. He claimed to enjoy the variety, but the food all looked the same to me—salty, greasy, slathered in sauce or gravy and pawed over by a particularly obese segment of society. But I could hardly refuse my old friend, and I always managed to find something to eat.

Unlike our famous cousins, we can savor the same repasts we used to as mortals. We don't *have* to eat—however, many of us do. Not only does it mark a fuller, more enjoyable life, but it allows us to blend in and gain the confidence of our victims. Disappearing Dracula-style while the guests in your castle are left to their own mealtime devices is a bit off-putting, if not altogether rude. The problem is that food doesn't really nourish us. We could eat three times a day and still starve without feeding.

I picked at my pasta salad, feeling unaccountably distracted as I took in the bright lights, bland music and clashing of cutlery from nearby tables. Stacks and Wade debated some obscure tuning question I only half understood, but I didn't mind being left out of the conversation. Anything that helped Wade was fine with me.

That's when I saw Seth sitting across the room. He was at a table by himself and as himself. None of that Laura sham. Now he wore a dark green workshirt, jeans and workboots with a Cardinals baseball cap turned backwards on his head. But his "regular guy" look couldn't hide his ugliness—his long face and sharp nose, his oddly spaced teeth, his sallow complexion and mean muddy brown eyes. He smirked as he put his fork down and blew smoke towards the ceiling fan. "I knew I'd find you here," he said inside my head.

I looked at Stacks, but he was still engrossed in his discussion with Wade and showed no sign of feeling Seth's presence. Either Seth had learned how to hide himself from others or Stacks' powers were failing.

Seth answered my question. "He doesn't know I'm here—and if you're depending on him to help protect your protégé, your faith is sorely misplaced. He has nothing left. He'll be dead soon, by his own choice as much as anything. But I'll help him along as much as I can. You may count on it.

"There is, however, a solution…give Wade up to me. I promise the safety of your old friend. Perhaps even give him the gift of a second chance. He'd like that, wouldn't he? It's a shame you never made a study of our kind—what we can do if we apply ourselves. You don't even know how to kill one of us, do you? You were always too busy playing with the prey to bother about such things. But you won't give this one up. Not even for your friend."

I would not be baited. I kept my mind blank.

"I thought as much." Seth stubbed his cigarette out, pushed his chair away from the table and turned to leave. "At least I've made the offer. I'll see you when you least expect it, Warner. Or I'll see your friend."

And I knew he would.

—〰—

"Ain't afraid," Stacks said, staring off in the distance as we rocked back and forth in the old caneback rockers on his front porch. "Been ready to go for a while now. He can't do nothin' to me I wouldn't welcome, and dyin' for a cause…well, that's just about the best way a man can go."

"Cause? What cause?"

He stopped rocking and took a long swig of sweet tea from the glass on the windowsill. "Wade. That boy's got the biggest gift I ever seen. You got to win this over Seth. He won't treat the boy right. But you'll see to it the world gets to hear him, and I can die knowin' I helped pass on what I learned from my betters."

"There *is* no better than you, my friend."

Stacks wheezed out a chuckle. "You hush, now. They's lots better'n me—him for one. I just been lucky."

"Forget lucky. You need to be careful."

He shrugged and squinted, looking down the street. "Here comes your boy with our libations. I hope he got somethin' a little finer than that horse piss he bought last time. Micro-brew, my ass."

The Jack Daniels in the bag Wade brought back was more than acceptable to Stacks, and we poured healthy slugs in our sweet tea, sipping and talking as the sun went down. Wade didn't bother with the tea, preferring to drink his straight. Thus, his conversation quickly passed from reasonably coherent to a maudlin muddle.

"All I ever wanted to do's play guitar," he said from his seat below us on the porch steps, "and I'm lucky—*damn* lucky—to meet up witchoo guys. We're gonna go places, boys—and I mean *go* places." He lifted another shot into the air and knocked it back, his torso weaving.

Stacks smiled and got up from his rocker, tossing a half inch of watery tea and Jack out of his tumbler onto the grass near the porch. "I think the only place this one better go is to bed. We got a long day tomorrow and he gonna be sufferin' enough as it is. You need some help with him?"

"I think I can handle it." I shook his shoulder, and he swiveled his head slowly towards me. "Let's pack it in, Wade. Time for bed."

He nodded and almost stood up. I grabbed his hand and put him on his feet, helping him shuffle his way inside.

Stacks followed. "See you boys in the mornin'."

"Remember what I said about being careful."

He waved me away as Wade stumbled on a throw rug and fell on me to keep himself upright. His smell was so enticing, I could barely restrain myself. I could feel his emanation feeding me; making me stronger. I turned my head away, but the temptation was still there. It took an eternity to reach our room, and we fell heavily onto his bed—him face up with me on top of him.

His eyes were closed, and I thought he must have passed out. I slid my hand out from underneath his back, intending to retreat to the safety of my own corner cot. Maybe I'll just take his boots off, I thought, so Stacks' sheets don't get ruined. I pulled off his well-shined snakeskin cowboy boots, inhaling the delicious, faintly leathery aroma of his socks and feet as I took them in my hands and swung his legs into bed.

I should have stopped there, but I couldn't let go. I sat on the edge of his bed and ran my hands slowly up his jeans-clad shins, past his bony knees to his firm, warm thighs. My prick grew hard at once, and his crotch began to bulge as well. He emitted a soft moan and arched his back slightly. I kneaded his stiffening cock, exulting in the rush as his dick lengthened at my touch. Untucking his t-shirt, I ran my fingertips over his treasure trail and worked my hands up the warmth of his hairy chest, flicking his nipples when I reached my destination.

He jerked awake and sat up quickly, his brown eyes wide. He grabbed my shoulders roughly, and my heart sank. I had been betrayed by my worst instincts, but there was no turning back or undoing what I had done. Before I could speak, however, he pulled me close and put his lips to mine.

His essence exploded into me with so much force I had no chance to savor it or experience it as anything else but a flood, like a deluge after months of drought. It washed over me instead of seeping into me. Nourishing, yes, but without pleasure. And then it simply became too much. It crushed me against its wave, taking me under, rendering me helpless and short of breath. I had to break the kiss or drown.

The look on Wade's face was devastating for both of us—shame, regret and rejection flashed through his eyes and leaked from his parted lips like the steam of his essence. I knew that I had erred. I should have embraced him and begun the kiss anew, my own discomfort be damned. But in that moment of hesitation; that fleeting second upon which everything hinges, he bolted from the room.

"Wade!" I shouted. "Wait!" Hot on his sock-clad heels, I followed him through the house and out the front door. He quickly sprinted away from me, running silently through the neighborhood. I could have easily overtaken him but I hung back, allowing him time to exhaust himself. He did so as he reached a small park tucked away between blocks, falling on the grass near a bench.

He was in tears when I approached him, sitting up and hugging his knees as he sobbed. I slowed to give him some additional privacy, but he sensed my presence and looked up, standing as if to start another sprint. Before he could escape, I rushed to him and took him in my arms. He put his head on my shoulder and started to cry again, choking out indecipherable words.

I held him for a long time, listening to the sound of sirens in the distance as I tried to calm him. He quieted in a while, his emotions subsiding, and I felt him try to pull away, but I held on to him. He did not resist. "Stay close to me," I said into his ear. "I must share some private thoughts, and I would rather do so with you in my arms." I expected to feel reticence, but he clutched me tighter instead.

"Never feel shame or disgust at who you are," I said. "You will be far happier if you acknowledge it and move on to the great accomplishments you have before you. I accepted it when I was a young man and have not thought much about it since. Let me also say that the attraction you feel is entirely mutual, Wade. I have wanted to kiss you for some time."

I let him raise his head from my shoulder. "Then why did you--"

"Break away from you? You were drunk, Wade. You must have realized by now that I am an honorable man in both my business dealings and my personal affairs. To take advantage of you in that condition would have been scurrilous at best; a violation of your trust. Were I to lose your trust, that loss would be inestimable. Do you understand?"

He wiped his eyes and gave me that half-grin of his. "Yeah, I get it. Warner, I gotta tell ya, I think you're...well, I never met anyone like you before."

Smiling, I put my arm around his shoulders and began to walk us back to the house. "Thank you. I feel the same way. And this changes nothing between us...professionally. In the years to come, we will make a formidable team and I would be loathe to see anything prevent that. I hope you agree."

"Absolutely. If it wasn't for you, I'd still be at the Club DuMonde wondering how I wanted to get where I want to be. I owe you so much already."

"Let us speak no more of it. This adventure is just beginning—who can say what will happen."

Seeing he was able to walk on his own, I withdrew my arm and we ambled side by side for a few blocks. "So when did you find out you were...you know?" he asked.

"When I was a young man."

"Did your folks kick you out when you told them or what?"

Careful, I thought. You must not be too candid. "I was at university. My first love was a linguistics instructor, but he was too bold. There was a scandal. He was discharged and I was disinherited. I have been on my own since then." For four hundred years.

"My dad purt'near broke my arm when he caught me and my cousin Joe messin' around out in the hay field. Told me he'd chop off my pecker and stuff it down my throat if he ever saw me doin' somethin' like that again."

"Charming."

"But I'll tell ya somethin,'" Wade said. "I like girls too."

"I have sought female companionship at times myself. We're lucky to be living in an age where making a choice between the two is not always necessary. If we..." The flashing red and blue lights ahead stopped me from saying anything else. They looked as if they were right in front of Stacks' house. Wade saw them too.

"What the..."

We ran the last few blocks, my worst fears confirmed as we reached the house. It was blocked off with yellow police tape, with an ambulance parked out at the curb and uniformed policemen crawling in and out the front door, crowding the front porch. Neighbors and passers-by were gathering across the street. Wade took off and began questioning every officer in earshot.

I had no need for the details, but when they carried the body out of the house, Wade beckoned me over. The EMTs laid the gurney down on the bumper of the ambulance and pulled back the sheet. Stacks' face was puckered and wrinkled, as if the life had been sucked right out of him. His mouth was twisted and his eyes bulged, but the terror was not confined to his face. His limbs were contorted and his back arched, as if in eternal pain. He had not died a quiet death.

That's him," I said. "Stacks Jackson." They nodded, covered him up again and drove off.

"What the fuck *happened* to him?" Wade asked.

When I looked up, I saw Seth standing on the fringes of the crowd, grinning at me. I did not hear him in my head, but what was there to say? He had kept his promise in spades, adding pain and a horrible death in the bargain. My relationship with Seth changed at that moment. We were no longer engaged in a mere competition over prey. I vowed then that he would die, just as terribly as Stacks.

Even if I perished as well.

—ᴡᴡ—

Hymns are not my favorite type of music, I'll confess. The lyrics are almost uniformly puerile and the tunes are insipid. There is, however, something to be said for the fervency of the performance, especially live Baptist gospel. The sweaty, exuberant perfume of talent rose from the choir—a heavenly offering of "Abide With Me" and "Amazing Grace." Stacks though would have enjoyed it immensely.

It was hot in the church and the sermons had been long. The mourners stuffed in the pews fanned themselves restlessly, knowing more was in store at the graveside. I wondered if they would have been so eager to bury him in hallowed ground had they known what he really was. Then again, as I looked around I realized that many *did* know—for there were many of us in attendance.

Considering what we subsist on, I suppose it's not surprising that the music business is rife with our kind acting as producers, managers, agents, A&R men or just *entrepreneurs* like myself. And we would, of course, turn out in droves for Stacks, who was well-loved.

But I also believe many had gathered at Stacks' funeral to personally witness the next episode in the drama playing out between Seth, Wade and myself—our kind was there. Seth was there. He sat in the back, once again masked as Laura, which meant he intended to approach Wade in some fashion, either here or at the graveside. Let him come. I had no intention of stopping Seth's game. Indeed, I had to *see* his next move in order to counter it.

The prayers concluded, we rose respectfully and filed out of the church into waiting limousines and private cars. Stacks had no family left, and as I was the executor of his will and both Wade and I were there the night he died, we were accorded *de facto* main mourner privileges and were in the first car. Wade looked a beautiful wreck. His eyes were soft and vulnerable and he was unshaven, his blonde stubble melding with lines of grief to etch a sad masculinity into his boyish face.

Wade had not said much since Stacks' death, bearing it with a blank stoicism that was as attractive as it was frustrating. I could have peeked into his head to see how he was handling the affair, but such matters should remain private no matter how curious their shielding may make others.

If Seth wanted to gain an unfair advantage by poking around and seeing which of Wade's thoughts might be useful, he was certainly free to do so. In my experience, such subterfuge only results in knowledge ripe for misinterpretation and, thus, will backfire when all is said and done. The disconnect between thought and action is rarely taken into account.

"Is he happier, d'ya think?" Wade asked. "Y'know, like the preacher said?"

I sighed. "Perhaps there are things the living should not know lest it affect the way their lives are led. The solution may be less satisfying than the mystery itself."

He nodded then went back to looking out the window. Even though I was not in his mind, I could hear it whirring, and it wasn't being driven by grief alone. He was creating. He was writing—either music or lyrics—applying the lessons Stacks taught him about making art with what life hands you. The old man would have been proud.

The trip to the graveyard was mercifully short and the graveside service brief. Most of the church attendees showed, but more of Stacks' fans were waiting in the cemetery. The gravesite was so festooned with wreaths that finding a place to stand was difficult. After the service, I found myself pressing the flesh, working my contacts and setting up Wade's next move. And everyone, it seemed, wanted a piece of Wade.

The only person who was currently getting that piece, however, was Seth. Wearing a tasteful black sheath and pearls, he was speaking earnestly and quietly to Wade in the shade of a large tree. I had no idea what he was saying, but I knew he was laying his own groundwork. By the time I worked my way over to them, I had two potential bookings of professional studio time Wade could choose from. I'd surprise him with that.

"Ah, there you are," I said as I approached them, "and I see you've found your friend from New Orleans. What a surprise—Shirley, isn't it?"

Seth smiled sweetly. "Laura, Mr. Warner."

"Just Warner. It's my first name. I doubt you'd be able to pronounce my last. What are you doing in St. Louis?"

"It turns out she was a big fan of Stacks'," Wade said, a grin splitting his face. "She came just for the funeral. Wasn't that sweet?"

"I simply had to pay my respects," Seth said. "His music meant so much to me, but seeing you both here is an incredible coincidence."

"Isn't it?" If my voice betrayed any annoyance, no one seemed to notice.

"We were just going to grab some lunch," Wade said. "You wanna come?"

I smiled and sighed. I'd been doing that a lot lately. "Thank you for the offer, but there are still some people here I should speak with. You two go ahead—and when you're done, why don't you bring Laura back to the house, Wade? You can show her the studio." I wasn't about to be cowed by Seth's presence.

"I'd *love* that," Seth cooed. He crooked an arm and offered it to Wade. "But let's stop by my hotel first and let me change. My car's just over there. Shall we?"

Wade took Seth's arm and grinned at me. "We'll be home in a while— got some good news for ya, too. We'll talk later."

"I have news for you as well. Have fun at lunch."

I was not surprised that, after our ill-fated kiss, Wade had swung toward the distaff side. He was so uncertain of his proclivities—thus his need to brag about "liking girls." Besides, what could I do? Any attempt to interfere with their budding affair would only drive Wade away from me. So Seth would feed from Wade in the interim. *C'est la vie.* There was more than enough to go around. Let Seth have his moment. Let him drown in Wade's essence. The game was not finished, was not won yet.

—⚘—

As I suspected, Wade's good news was that he had some song ideas—his first original work. He also wanted to pick out a few of Stacks' guitars to keep. A blues museum in Mississippi had also requested them, but I saw no harm in letting Wade have what he wanted and giving the museum the rest.

The next month saw us living at Stacks' place while I had his possessions packed, sold or otherwise apportioned out and settled the details of his will as Wade worked on songs. He spent mornings on the sun-soaked front porch, playing snatches of melodies again and again, adding or changing notes. Sometimes he wrote in a battered spiral bound notebook, scribbling down lyrics he'd been mumbling in a maddeningly indistinct tone.

At first, he went down to the studio unobserved—usually when I was out on an errand. When I came back and settled down in the booth to listen, he'd stop and either go back to the front porch or sit there quietly humming until I left. After a few weeks, however, he grew more confident of his material and let me help him in the booth, even asking my opinion occasionally.

Nights were spent with Seth in his Laura guise. Seth would pick him up around dinnertime and Wade would not return until later. Wade never stayed with Seth the entire night. I have no idea why he declined or if Seth even offered, but Wade was always home by two or three in the morning, back at his post on the front porch once the sun came up.

As a result, Seth looked very well-fed at month's end. However, he was tired and irritable, quite the opposite of what I would have expected. He seemed increasingly nervous, casting his eyes about furtively when he came to pick Wade up, and he scrutinized me during our chance encounters. Once I felt him inside my head. Silent, waiting for something. It was most curious and a bit disconcerting.

I had been competing with Seth for centuries and can honestly say that nothing he did surprised me. Even Stacks' murder, as reprehensible as it was, was wholly in line with Seth's behavior. He said he would do it, and he did. If nothing else, he was a man of his word. He would pay for that, make no mistake, but that particular bill had not yet come due. His next move, however, shocked and puzzled me beyond measure.

Wade was in the studio and I was behind the controls in the booth. He played a tune he'd been fiddling with for days, but now he picked it confidently, adding a snatch of lyric:

When I play this dead man's guitar
Whose music will it turn out to be?
Should the change feel this strange to my fingers?
Do I even know this key?
My head swims with all his ideas
And places that I've never seen.
If I become a star
Playin' this dead man's guitar
Will it be him or will it be me?

"Did you want to put that down?" I asked.

"Not yet. Hang on a sec."

He bent over the Gibson and began strumming lightly, mumbling as he worked out the next verse or a break or something. I felt a disturbance in the booth and suddenly Seth was sitting next to me, in his own body. The effect was just as disquieting as I'm sure he intended it to be. He smiled at me and winked.

"Afternoon, Warner."

"Good afternoon, Seth," I replied, returning his smile thinly. "Another energy-draining party trick, I see. Quite amusing."

He shrugged. "I have energy to burn, thanks to Wade. He has nourished me well these past few weeks and seems to have suffered no ill effects."

"In sharp contrast to yourself."

"Whatever do you mean?"

"I mean—to use the vernacular—you look like shit, Seth. Your face is drawn, the skin sags beneath your tired, red eyes, your complexion is even more sallow than usual, and...well, I needn't go on."

He was quiet a moment, listening to Wade strum with his back towards us. "You're right, of course. That's part of why I'm here. Have you felt anything *odd* lately?"

"No. Why?"

"I suppose you wouldn't be as attuned to it as I. After all, you were not made by the Old Man."

"The Old Man hasn't walked in centuries." Some of our kind considered him a myth.

Seth shook his head. "You're wrong, Warner. He's risen. He's walking toward us. Toward *Wade*. I've dreamed of him. And he covets what we have. Don't scoff. Wade is the rarest of meals, a prodigy born only every few centuries. All our kith and kind feels his essence. To think it wouldn't have woken the Old Man is foolishness. And what is the first thing anyone wants after a long nap?" Seth stared at Wade. "A good breakfast."

I felt a chill. "Don't be daft."

"I've a proposition--"

"I'll strike no bargain with *you*."

"Because of what I did to your friend? Loyalty...a trait that will be the undoing of us all. Put that aside for a moment. Punish me later, provided we survive the trials ahead of us. First, we must share Wade."

"Share? I did not think you understood the concept."

"The situation has changed dramatically. To fend off the Old Man, we will both have to be well-nourished. That is one reason Wade will be coming to you tonight."

"*One* reason?"

Seth frowned. "He has...confessed to me—to Laura, rather—his attraction for you. I don't understand it, myself," he said with a disdainful sniff. "Oh, I suppose you're handsome enough. How old were you when you were made? Nearly forty?"

"Twenty-five." Wade's natural instincts are winning out. But I wondered if the Old Man really walked or was Seth bargaining from a losing position.

"You have not aged much since. Your profile is not as noble as mine, but..." He waved a gloved hand in the air. "There is no accounting for taste. Besides, he insists on taking me from behind every single night. It's unsettling."

"Poor Seth," I said, grinning. He started to say something, but I held up my hand to stay him, listening to Wade pluck, strum and mumble. "There is more to your proposition, I assume."

"I will also teach you some defensive strategies—words of binding and the like—I hope you are a quick study. I will be unable to shield such activities from the Old Man for long. And you must swear to use them only against him. Despite your grievance with me.."

"'Scuse me," came Wade's voice from the studio. "Warner, is there somebody else up there in the booth?"

I flipped the intercom switch. "Yes, Wade. One of the producers I was telling you about dropped by to see how the demos were coming along."

Wade put the guitar in its stand and stood up from the stool. "Um...I don't wanna be fussin', but this is a closed session. No visitors, okay?"

"Of course, Wade. I apologize. Give me a minute, then we can get back to work." There was an audible click as I flicked the switch off again. "You'll have to go now—by the door this time."

"Are we agreed?"

"Give me a day to think about it. I'll let you know."

His face darkened. "No more than one day. Don't doubt the danger. To us, to your precious Wade." He vanished. I looked to see if Wade had seen, but he was bent over getting a drink from the cooler.

The Old Man walks and Seth bargains. Even after four hundred years, life can yield surprises.

By six that afternoon, "Dead Man's Guitar" was a finished demo, joining "Front Porch Blues," "On the Horizon," "Spark," and "Jesus Doesn't Even Know You're Dead" as Wade's first completed songs. The first two had gone slowly but the last three were all done in a day each. His confidence in his own abilities was growing, and he was becoming more assured with every session in the studio.

"I think that's gonna be the title track," he said as put the Gibson down and got up from his stool. "And I even know what I want the cover to look like—a picture of Stacks' National down here in its stand. Over there by the chipped acoustic tile. Yeah…kinda like that Yoko Ono album cover with John Lennon's broken, bloody glasses. Think you can make that happen?"

"Not a problem," I said, leaving the intercom open as I finished up some paperwork. "I'll set the shoot up before we leave."

"When do we have to leave?"

"In a few weeks, probably. The realtor is bringing some people by to look at the house tomorrow. I'll try to minimize the time they're down here so you won't have to stop working for long."

"I'd 'preciate that. I think I'm done for today, though. How 'bout we order a pizza and kill the rest of that beer in the fridge?"

I feigned surprise. "You're not seeing Laura tonight?"

"Nope," he said, using that wicked half-grin on me. "I thought I'd stay home and see what kinda trouble we can get in around here."

"I could do with a bit of trouble." I matched the salaciousness in his voice.

"No doubt. So could I."

"Are you sure we have enough beer?"

He chuckled. "I don't plan on gettin' that drunk."

"Good."

Wade exited the studio and bounded up the few steps to the booth. "Let's hear the playback," he said as he walked in. I queued it up and hit the button, Wade's crystalline picking filling the room. I expected him to take a seat beside me, but he stood behind my chair, put his hands on my shoulders and began to rub them. He leaned over to nuzzle my neck, and as we listened to "Dead Man's Guitar" for the thousandth time that day, his lips brushed my skin and I breathed in his nectar.

My thirst rose and my prick stiffened, and I couldn't decide which appetite needed to be sated more. Wade spun my chair around to face him, then he closed in for the kiss. The smell of him was everywhere, making me dizzy. He put his mouth on mine and unlike before, I did not flinch or back way. This time, however, there was no suffocation—only the bliss of his essence filling me evenly and steadily.

His taste was warm and sweet with a slight pungency, like the bayou air after cleansing rain. I felt myself rising to gain more leverage, the kiss becoming serious and passionate. My hands went to his face, caressing the stubbly roughness of his cheeks as I pressed myself into him. Wade snaked his arms around my waist and drew me close. We could have kissed for an eternity. I was lost in him.

"Jesus," he breathed into my ear as he held on to me. "I've wanted to do that ever since that first day you came to my apartment."

"Was it as you thought it would be?"

His grin as all the answer I needed. "But," he said as he stepped away from me, "we better get that pizza ordered. We're gonna need some strength. You make the call, and I'll grab a shower." He headed for the door. "Get anything you want on it, just no green peppers. Can't stand 'em. Breadsticks, too—don't forget the breadsticks." I watched his ass as he left.

My cock deflating, I savored his lingering aftertaste as I reached for the telephone and ordered our meal. I finished up my paperwork, but my mind was elsewhere. I considered Seth's proposition, trying not to feel jealous that he'd had Wade to himself as long as he had. I castigated myself at such an unproductive emotion at first, but I had to let it wash over me so I could rid myself of it. It was only natural. To not feel it would have been less than human.

Well, you know what I mean.

As far as what Seth told me, I hadn't felt the Old Man walking and I considered myself fairly sensitive to such matters. However, there was something to what he said about being better attuned since he had been made by him. Such a bond would indeed enable Seth to feel his presence more keenly that would the rest of us. Seth's sharing of prey also alarmed me—a first to my knowledge. He wouldn't be taking that measure without a good reason. Seth never did *anything* without a good reason.

I collected my things and went upstairs to wait for the delivery boy. I heard the shower running through the bathroom door as I passed, leaving the papers on the desk in the living room. At length, our meal arrived but Wade was still in the shower. I paid the boy, took the pizza into the kitchen, got plates and napkins from the cupboard and sat down at the table. Wade finally emerged from the bathroom, appearing in the doorway clad in only a pair of thin boxer shorts.

I'd seen Wade in his underwear often, but this was the first time he was so accessible—so *mine*—that it seemed as if I'd never before examined his flat, hairy stomach, the patch of fur across his chest, his strong, naturally muscled arms and his fuzzy, well-formed thighs and calves. The light from the living room window silhouetted his tantalizing genitalia through the threadbare fabric of his cotton boxers. I knew I was staring but couldn't help myself.

"Too formal for pizza?" he asked.

I grinned. "I think it's just about right."

He slid around the back of my chair and leaned into it, his meaty cock grazing my shoulder through his boxers. As I looked down to admire the bulge, it began growing and tenting the fabric out further until finally the bare head poked through the fly. I took it between my fingers and guided it to my lips, sucking gently as he grew to full hardness in my mouth. He arched his back slightly and ran his fingers through my hair, murmuring curses of endearment.

Even his prick leaked the sweetness of his essence. I lapped hungrily, searching inside his boxers with one hand and cupping his balls as he fell back against the wall with a moan. I rose, stroking his slicked cock as our lips met and I once again began to drink my fill. His hand clutched the crotch of my slacks, grasping my stiffness and drawing a sigh from me. It had been a long time since another man had touched me there.

He broke away, smirking as he ducked away from me, grabbed my waistband and led me into the living room. "The pizza can wait," he said, throwing me down on the sofa as his prick bobbed in the air. He knelt on the floor and began unbuttoning my shirt, kissing my chest as he freed it. Unbuckling my belt, he unsnapped my pants, eased down the zipper and pressed his nose into my crotch. "God, I love that smell," he breathed. My hips rose as he tugged down my pants and shorts, my dick slapping my belly as it came free. I threw my head back in ecstasy as he took me into his mouth, caressing my balls with his hands.

I grabbed his head and brought him to me for another kiss, our lips never parting as his boxers and my clothes came off. I landed on top of him as we rolled off the sofa onto the floor. I kissed and bit his tiny nipples until he writhed beneath me, then I sucked his cock until he was within a hair's-breadth of shooting, but I would not let him come. So he always took Seth from behind? We were going to change all that.

I flipped him over and beheld his marvelously fuzzy ass, running my tongue down his crack until I reached his deliciously wrinkled pucker. I traced it with my tongue and teased it with my lips, inhaling his musk mixed with soap from his shower, gently sucking and nibbling his hole as he grunted low, guttual joy. I even found his essence there, which only increased my ardor. Then I wet my index finger and pushed inside.

"Easy," he groaned. "I've only done this once before."

"We can stop if--"

"No." He, raised his ass higher. "I want you to fuck me."

My prick was aching for him, but I worked him with my fingers until he sighed with satisfaction. I positioned my cock at his hole then slowly pushed in. He let out a small cry and I stopped, allowing him to relax for a bit before I continued. When I was fully inside him, he threw his head back. "Yeah," he moaned, "that's it, dude. Fuck me."

His ass was hot and tight, slick with spit and sweat as I slid in and out with ease, but I was not satisfied. I wanted to see his face. I withdrew and turned him on his back, kissing him long and slow before I went back to fucking him. "Do it, man," he breathed as he stroked his own hard cock. "Fuck your boy." Dripping with sticky sweat, I pumped in and out until my balls began to tighten up and I whimpered with helpless lust. "Fuck yeah," Wade said. "You got it, dude—come in my ass."

I exploded into him, shuddering as I spurted. Wade closed his eyes and frigged himself faster and faster until he also came a long, ropy shot that nearly went up to his chin. Instinctively, my tongue went to his chest and belly. Even his come tasted of essence. When I had finished feasting on it, I fell on top of him, kissing him even though we were both out of breath. "Jesus," he said. "That was incredible, man."

I nodded, laughing.

"Okay, *now* I'm hungry for pizza," he said after a long sigh.

—ᴍ—

I stood naked on the beach of a vast ocean, staring at the light of the full moon reflected off the waves. In the improbable manner of dreams, a figure stood atop the water, waving to me as it came closer. I smiled, thinking it a friend or acquaintance, but as it drew nearer to me, my smile vanished.

Its face was a grotesque white with sunken cheeks, sparse hair flying in all directions. Dressed in tatters, its sleeve flapped about its elbow with every wave. Its thin, red lips parted to show teeth stained yellow, some broken, some pointed and some missing. Dark and disgusting matter drooled from the corner of its mouth. Its eyes were black and deep— no white or iris to be seen. They were malignantly vacant, even more shocking set against the unnatural whiteness of the face. The creature called my name as it neared the beach.

Before I could flee, it was on me. Foul, mouldy breath assaulted me, but maddeningly, there was an essence in it. I couldn't help but breathe it in no matter how repulsive I found it to be. And I felt nourished. It gripped my shoulder with clammy, chill hands as it held me fast.

"So," it said in a deep voice, "you and Seth seek to overthrow me. That will not happen. I will have your prize no matter how well you prepare yourselves. All you shall be left is the black ruin of the grave, if I am kind enough to kill you. In your own words, 'do not play games you cannot win.'"

Laughing, it pushed me backwards into the water. I staggered and fell, swallowed up and sucked under by the sea. Instead of a mouthful of brine, I swallowed the foulness of his essence instead, but it pulled me further down. I closed my eyes against the water's salty sting but all I could see was the Old Man's loathsome face. I sank until I awoke.

I was lying next to Wade, my pillow wet with nightmare sweat, a first for me since my mortal days. His steady, calm breath soothed me, decelerating my rapid heartbeat. I breathed in his sweet essence and felt refreshed. Still, I could not get the Old Man's visage out of my mind. It leered at me from every corner of the room when I closed my eyes. I drew back the covers and sat on the edge of the bed.

This could not be one of Seth's parlor tricks. The Old Man had mocked me personally, bringing back what I had said to the boy who assaulted me in New Orleans. Seth could not have known that. As difficult as it was to admit, Seth was right. The Old Man *was* walking, bent on our destruction. And even more difficult, I had no choice but to accept his proposition. I was not foolish enough to think I could fight him on my own. I *needed* Seth, damn him. Very well. I would work with him for now. And kill him later. If we survived.

"Warner? Are you okay?" Wade's sleepy voice brought me back from my thoughts.

"Fine. Indigestion, perhaps. It will pass." I laid back down and drew the covers over us. Wade snuggled into my chest, his essence rising up to my nostrils as I drank it in.

"I could get used to this," he said.

"Used to what?"

"Sleeping with someone. Not fuckin' or anything, but just sleeping."

"You've never slept in the same bed with anyone?"

"Nope."

"I'm honoured to be the first."

He chuckled. "This feels right."

My heart swelled, beating so fast I thought it might burst. "Yes. It does." I scooted us down, burrowing under the covers as I held on to him. "You'd better get some sleep. Good night, Wade."

"'Night, Warner."

In four hundred years, I have been companion, friend and beast to many men and women. I have badgered and nutured prey, lectured it, held its hand, drunk with it, gotten it to the show on time and applauded after it performed, but until that moment, I had never fallen in love with it. I had gone out of my way to avoid such sordid entanglements, but with a smile and a confession, this one had captured my heart.

And, while that brought new thrills to my ancient soul, it rekindled that oldest of emotions. Fear.

—∞—

The next two months bordered on the most surreal I'd had for years, an observation which struck me on a plane from one gig to another, a snoring Wade slumped on one of my shoulders whilst Seth gripped the other, whispering into my ear a centuries-old Etruscan incantation for repelling evil that he expected me to repeat flawlessly after having heard it only once.

Seth traveled with us as Laura, much to Wade's surprise. He had temporarily dropped Laura after we began sleeping together, but I knew he'd want a change eventually. As long as he came back to our bed—and he *always* did—I had no problem with letting him have his way with Seth whenever he liked. Wade hinted at a *menage a trois* once, but our refusal was so adamant, he never brought up the subject again.

Consequently, Seth became less an enemy and more a..., I hesitate to use the term comrade. Perhaps ally. I tried to become comfortable with this new role, but I could not allow myself to trust him completely. His smile always carried a hint of disingenuousness that alerted me to study anything he said carefully, analyzing it for potential untruths or misdirections. His frantic, hurried lessons in spells, magic words of binding and other defensive strategies did not add to his credibility, either. I did, however, learn many useful tactics at his hand.

Both of us dreamed of the Old Man regularly. Seth more than I, but his tether to the Old Man was shorter than my own. For my part, the bastard seemed to be taunting us. He had to know full well where we were. Wade's tour schedule was plastered all over the internet, but he never showed himself at the gigs. Only in dreams.

But what dreams they were. I do not know what nighttime realms Seth dwelt in, but mine were dark and horrifying—full of vivid splashes of blood, sharp teeth rending tender places to shreds and puckered corpses sucked dry of life and essence, leaving shriveled husks behind. The danger and sense of dread increased daily.

As did Wade's fame. We polished the demos done at Stacks' house in various studios whose owners were friends of mine. The CD dropped in late October. The video of "Jesus Doesn't Even Know You're Dead" went into heavy rotation on a couple of country outlets, leading to a "Saturday Night Live" spot where Wade premiered "Dead Man's Guitar," which ascended the country charts quickly and began rising on the pop ones as well.

Wade coped admirably with the brutal tour schedule, always obliging and friendly to fans and supporters, ready to break out his guitar and sing in airport lounges or sign autographs during meals. He was even writing on the road in whatever spare time we could cadge away for ourselves. He thrived on the activity, which only sharpened his essence. And I fed daily, becoming as strong as I had ever felt in my life. Let the Old Man come. I'd be ready for him.

"When he comes," Seth had said, "he will come quickly. There will be no warning and no chance for mistakes. We must be on our guard at all times, each ready to come to the other's defense, for he will try to defeat us singly. Even he would not chance to fight us simultaneously."

I did not entirely believe that claim.

A promoter friend of mine had gotten Wade a weekend gig at the Beacon Theatre in New York City. We had been scheduled for that time off before the next leg of the tour, but this was an important venue with some well-placed people to be in attendence and my friend had called in some favors to win us the slot. We could hardly refuse.

And I could hardly refuse Wade his chance to stay at the Chelsea Hotel, host to Leonard Cohen, Bob Dylan, Jack Kerouac, Janis Joplin and Sid Vicious among other icons, especially when he read it was soon to be closed for remodeling.

I was no stranger to the Chelsea, having already encountered many of the ghosts Wade so eagerly sought there—some while they were still alive—but I was not enthusiastic about once again negotiating its threadbare carpets, antiquated plumbing and stifling rooms. I warned him that historic hotels often have less than luxurious living conditions, but he would not be swayed. No matter that the knob fell off in his hand when he opened the door, he was—as he confessed—"jacked."

"This is so fuckin' *cool*," he said, looking around the tiny room and pointing at two mismatched chairs around a marred table under the window. "I mean, Bob fuckin' Dylan could have been writing right *there*."

His zeal did not spread to Seth, who yawned and stretched, his cleavage on display to whatever spirits happened to be looking. "I'm going to my room for a lie down," he said.

Wade made a grab for him as he left. "Don't get too comfy. I'll be in to see you after a little nap myself."

"Make it a couple of hours." The door beside ours slammed shut.

"I'll unpack later," I said, putting my suitcase into the doorless closet. "There are a couple of people I should see, and I want to check out the theatre."

"When will you be back?"

"Not for a while, I think." I grinned. "Don't worry. You'll have enough time for Laura." He smirked at me. "And I doubt you'll take a nap. If I know you, five seconds after I'm gone, you'll be sitting in that window with your guitar, strumming and looking down five floors to 23rd Street."

"You're probably right about that." He walked over to the window, looked down then over to the left. "Hey, I can even see the pigeon shit on the sign."

"This is New York—the whole city's coated with it."

Wade chuckled, then crossed over to me and took me in his arms. "You don't mind about Laura now and then, right?"

The musky scent of his essence always overwhelmed me, but now it made me hard as well. "Wade, we've been over this."

"I know, I know. I just…"

I stopped him by brushing my lips against his. They parted, his tongue searching for mine as we kissed in the open doorway. Nothing new for the Chelsea, I'm sure. My hand went to his crotch, kneading and tracing his fattening prick. "You'll need to save that for Laura," I said with a smile. "And I have things to do. I'll see you in a few hours."

I took my leave, truly regretting Seth's presence. The waiting for whatever encounter was to take place was becoming interminable, and I found myself wishing something—anything—would happen, so we could get it over with and move on to who would be the eventual winner of Wade's heart. I was sure it would be me, but Seth was probably as sure it was him. Who knew what promises were made when I was not with Wade?

Putting the affair out of mind so that I could do business, I saw a promoter to finalize details of a new East and Southeast leg of Wade's eternal tour as well as took a meeting with a representative for a digital radio station who wanted Wade to be a guest DJ. I knew he'd love the latter. Wade liked to talk about music almost as much as he loved playing it. Then, I stopped at the Beacon, where my contact showed me around the theatre.

By the time I got back to the Chelsea, night had already fallen. As I approached the hotel, I saw the lights were off in our room but on in Seth's. They must not yet have finished with their tryst. I stopped on the sidewalk beneath our windows.

At length, I saw a bare-chested Wade cross the room and draw the curtain. At that moment, I despised Seth more than when he had murdered my old friend. But I had long ago abandoned impulsiveness, and so I could only stand there on the sidewalk, looking up at the draped window.

My foot brushed a grate in the sidewalk, which gave beneath the toe of my shoe. I stepped back as pebbles and small chunks of concrete from around the edge fell and clattered below with a deep echo. Exploring its surface with a light tap of my shoe, the whole grate—approximately six feet square—pitched and shuddered.

Damn dangerous, I thought. They should have this blocked off. I cast my eyes around for orange warning cones or something to place near the precarious grate but could find nothing. I decided to speak with the hotel manager about it. As I bounded up the steps and entered the revolving door, Seth burst into my head.

"Warner, come quick! It's--"

A curtain of silence descended, shocking me even more than the voice inside my head. I ran past the desk and up the stairs, taking them two or three at a time. The abhorrent vision of that foul white beast with his mouth pressed to Wade's, I have no memory of thinking anything else. All the spells and incantations and words of binding vanished, supplanted by blind anger and fear.

I barely noted that the door was partially open, and I had no idea what I would see when I entered. I thought briefly of a *tableaux*—perhaps two muscled Greek warriors engaged in hand to hand combat, the prize recoiling in horror in a corner. Instead, I saw Seth on the bed, his head bent at an unnatural angle with a figure covering him, its mouth pressed to his. The figure had no shirt and wore Wade's boots, but it looked up at me as I entered and I saw the disgusting white visage that had haunted my dreams.

It returned to sucking at Seth's mouth, and Seth's limbs shriveled into emaciated appendages then disappeared altogether. His trunk shrank and then finally his head, until all was subsumed beneath the victor and nothing remained of Seth except a spot of smouldering shadow on the sheets.

"This one was easy," the Old Man said. "I made him. I knew his weaknesses and his flaws. Exploiting them was the most natural way to get rid of him. I appealed to his vanity and his hunger."

"What have you done with Wade?"

He laughed. "Don't you know *yet*?" His leering countenance changed to Wade's handsome boyishness. He gave me that heartbreaking half-grin one last time before it flickered and faded back to its previous hideousness. "There *is* no Wade, you fool. There is only my deception. My beautiful lie."

I shook my head dumbly, disbelieving him even though I knew in my heart what he said was the truth. That's why his pool of essence seemed inexhaustible. It was the body from which we all came. "I...I..."

His mirth echoed throughout the room. "Have all your clever ripostes been reduced to mere stutters? How flattering that I inspire such fear in you. Allow me to answer the question you appear unable to ask, and that is 'Why?'"

"Yes. Why?"

"I knew you'd find your tongue," he said, smiling. "As to why... well, you and Seth were becoming far too powerful. You felt too many ripples, became too well-known. It was only a matter of time before you both felt you could challenge my supremacy. Oh, *you* might not have had the idea—there is a streak of decency in you I find repellent but fascinating. Exploiting that enabled me to deceive you. But such an act was not unworthy of Seth's hubris. He would have lured you into cooperating eventually. See how easily he enlisted you against me this time? I am merely culling the herd of the most powerful opponents to serve as a warning for the rest."

"But why would either of us want to overthrow you?"

"You really don't know?" He chuckled again. "Seth was correct regarding your lack of curiosity about our kind. Let me be plain, then. My powers give me access to a never-ending, self-sustaining body of essence. You have tasted of it and have sensed a part of its vastness."

"That first night…the first time we…"

"Yes. I should have killed you then, but I must confess I was having fun. I have not needed to hunt for some centuries now, and I had forgotten how enjoyable the experience is. But the endgame is at hand. I weary of explanations and am ready to finish this."

An invisible force grabbed both sides of my head and drew me slowly, inexorably, to his vile mouth. I smelled mould and brine, as if being dragged into a beachside grave. I struggled to recall even the simplest tactic Seth had taught me, but fear and horror crowded out all else. I reached his arms, embraced by his chill grasp, and then his cracked lips were on mine.

To my surprise, I felt an onrush of essence similar to that I had experienced the first time but just as I began to feel drowned, it rushed back like a tidal force, sucking out all I had been given. Then, the tide came back in once again and rushed out. At last I understood. He was gathering strength and momentum for a final draining. I struggled him off the bed and we fell onto the floor, but the impact would not loose his hold. I had to find a way to break his kiss.

Once more, essence blew in until I felt I could hold no more, then drew back with a monumental force. My time was short. Unconsciousness crept up on me. I felt weaker and more limp with every wave. I got us to our feet again, and we staggered around the room in a deadly clinch. Then a sudden thought seized me. I dug down, summoning reserves I did not know I had, and ran us towards the fifth floor window. If the fall did not break his hold, I would be lost.

We crashed through the glass, still locked together as we hurtled towards the sidewalk below. As we fell, I began to lose consciousness once more. But I was not so drained that I did not feel something. A force, like an invisible hand—Seth's hand, my imagination told me—guided our fall. It pushed this way and that, as if aiming us towards a precise spot below. And then it was gone.

My shoulder and right side crashed into the sidewalk, on the very lip of the loose grating under the window. The collision with the cement broke his grasp on me. And then *he* was gone. Screaming in frustration, he had fallen through the grating and into the hole, chunks of concrete and sharp sections of broken metal chasing him into the depths below. One of Seth's words of binding came into my head and I hurled it as well as a few other accompanying incantations.

I was free, but not for long. I had to escape while I could. I struggled to my feet, ignoring the gasps from the startled onlookers who had just witnessed two men plummet five stories and watched one get up. A few souls shouted encouragement and whipped out their cell phones to call the emergency services, but I had no need of such support. I needed a place to hide and think, so I ran. I ran as fast as I could from the crowd, from the hotel, from whatever had happened to the Old Man, not knowing how long the word of binding would hold. I could not feel him in my mind, but my strength was severely depleted.

I do not know how long I ran, but the cool night air recharged me somewhat, and the physical exertion brought some clarity back to my thoughts. I reached the far western edge of Central Park and took refuge on a bench in the night shadows of the trees, keeping watch up and down the path as well as in my head.

I was both heartsick and heartbroken. My narrow escape meant nothing to me alongside the knowledge that Wade—*my* Wade—had never existed, and any fantasies I had entertained about making him one of us, spending the rest of eternity together, were foolish schoolgirl dreams. Who was I to believe I deserved love? I felt gulled. Cheated. And I had lost both my best friend and my worst enemy in the bargain.

The role of worst enemy, however, had been recast, the new player far more deadly and devious than Seth had ever been. But I could not ignore the enormity of my losses. The Old Man would find me a force with which to be reckoned in future. I would have that which he most feared to lose. I would be master of that vast, unending sea, consigning him to eternal torment on its shore.

His power was great and I would have to learn much to vanquish him. But it could be done. I had to seek out the knowledge; make it my life's work, for without that work my life might end. Until that knowledge was mine, I would have to be very, very careful.

Very, very careful indeed.

About the Author

Editor of *Tented: Gay Erotic Tales from Under the Big Top* (a Lambda Literary Award finalist) as well as *Riding the Rails* and *The Dirty Diner* (both Bold Strokes Books), Jerry L. Wheeler lives, works, and writes in Denver CO. He and William Holden co-founded *Out in Print: Queer Book Reviews* (www.outinprint.net), so reading for the blog takes up much of his time. What's left is misspent in fleeting encounters with men best described as trashy. Some on work release programs. Despite this predilection, he still manages time for writing, including book reviews, short stories, essays and a novel-in-progress called *The Dead Book.* Please feel free to contact him at either *Out in Print* or his website, www.jerrywheeleronline.com. Furry men with tats and shady backgrounds please step to the front of the line.

"Waafrneeaasuu!!" originally appeared in *Bears in the Wild: Hot and Hairy Fiction*, edited by R. Jackson (Bear Bones Books, 2010)

"Changing Planes" originally appeared in *In Plain View: Hot Public Gay Erotica*, edited by Shane Allison (Bold Strokes Books, 2011)

"Love, Sex & Death on the Daily Commute" originally appeared in *Law of Desire: Tales of Gay Male Lust and Obsession*, edited by Greg Wharton and Ian Phillips (Alyson Books, 2004)

"The Telephone Line" originally appeared in *I Like It Like That: True Stories of Gay Male Desire*, edited by Richard Labonte and Lawrence Schimel (Arsenal Pulp Press, 2009)

"Templeton's in Love" originally appeared in *I Do! An Anthology in Support of Marriage Equality*, edited by Kris Jacen (MLR Press, 2009) and was reprinted in *Best Gay Romance 2010*, edited by Richard Labonte (Cleis Press, 2009)

"Cumsmoke" originally appeared online at Velvet Mafia.

"You Know You Want To" originally appeared in *Wings: Subversive Gay Angel Erotica*, edited by Todd Gregory (Bold Strokes Books, 2011)

"Yuri: A Pride Memoir" originally appeared in *Focus on the Fabulous: Colorado GLBT Voices*, edited by Matt Kaily (Johnson Books, 2007)